Twisted Crimes

ALSO BY MICHAEL HAMBLING

THE SOPHIE ALLEN BOOKS
Book 1: Dark Crimes
Book 2: Deadly Crimes
Book 3: Secret Crimes
Book 4: Buried Crimes
Book 5: Twisted Crimes
Book 6: Evil Crimes
Book 7: Shadow Crimes
Book 8: Silent Crimes
Book 9: Ruthless Crimes
Book 10: Brutal Crimes
Book 11: Hidden Crimes
Book 12: Vicious Crimes

Michael Hambling

TWISTED CRIMES

Detective Sophie Allen Book 5

JOFFE BOOKS

Revised edition 2024
Joffe Books, London
www.joffebooks.com

First published in Great Britain in 2017

Cover art by Nick Castle

ISBN: 978-1-83526-892-6

To Margaret and our three sons, Stephen, Malcolm and David.
I'd also like to acknowledge the support of
my two daughters-in-law, Kate and Katherine.

PROLOGUE

It was a fine, mild afternoon in late April and the spring flowers were putting on a display worthy of midsummer. Poole Crematorium is a lovely place, its flower beds and swathes of grass set off beautifully against the backdrop of pine trees. The scent of evergreens hung in the air, perfectly complementing the faint sound of humming insects. Sylvia and Edward Armitage waited patiently outside the crematorium building, having arrived rather too early for the funeral of Georgie Palmer, an ex-badminton club colleague of Sylvia's. The roads had been surprisingly quiet on the drive down from Blandford Forum, hence their early arrival. They studied the afternoon schedule, pinned to the wall of the entrance, noting that there was an hour's gap between the previous service and the one they planned to attend. They'd already walked around the flower beds and the shrubbery. Now, with only fifteen minutes to go, they were back at the entrance waiting for someone else to arrive. Anyone else, to be honest. The problem was, they knew none of Georgie's family or friends. Sylvia would be the sole representative of the Blandford Belles Badminton Group and she'd never met any acquaintance of Georgie's other than fellow club members and few of those now remembered the retired librarian who had left the group a decade earlier when she'd moved to Poole. Sylvia had only visited Georgie two or three times during that decade, and it had come as a complete shock to hear of her death from an unexpected heart attack.

The elderly duo looked up as a small funeral cortege appeared, slowly making its way towards them. The hearse drew level with the doors, the three shiny black limousines following it stopped and disgorged their mourners onto the tarmac area and suddenly Edward and Sylvia found themselves surrounded by a cluster of about two dozen people moving towards the entrance. They followed the group inside. The coffin, an ornate box almost hidden under a mass of brightly coloured flowers, was brought in, held up on the shoulders of six dark-clad men who deposited it on the bier, bowed and moved to a row of empty seats in the second row. It was only when they sat down, in a row behind most of the other mourners that the two pensioners began to feel uneasy. Sylvia realised that only four members of the congregation were women, and they didn't look like the kind of family or friends that she'd ever imagined the retired librarian to have. They were all dressed in black, true enough, but they looked more like models, with stiletto-heeled shoes, tailored dresses and expensive-looking leather jackets. The men made her feel even more uneasy, they spoke in growling voices and seemed tense. The three sitting immediately in front of her and Edward appeared to be arguing in semi-whispered tones. She turned to her husband.

'Are we in the right place, Ted?' she whispered. 'These don't look anything like the people I'd expect at Georgie's funeral.'

Ted looked at his watch. 'It's still only ten to three, and the list said her funeral was at three. I wonder what's going on?'

They watched with some bemusement as a stocky man from the front row stood up and took the few steps to the front. 'So. We're here for the committal. Five minutes and it'll all be over.' He turned to face the coffin. 'Dad, we're gonna miss you, you old letch.' He turned back to face the small congregation and spotted the Armitage couple. 'Who the hell are you?' he demanded.

Every head in the congregation swivelled around to look at the elderly pair. The three men in front of them seemed particularly menacing. Sylvia couldn't help but notice the fine scar that ran from eye to chin on the face of the middle one.

Edward stuttered an apology. 'So sorry. We seem to have come to the wrong service.' He took Sylvia's hand and quietly led her out of the chapel, back into the bright sunshine outside.

'I'm feeling quite queasy, Ted. Who were those people?' Sylvia's voice was quivering.

Her husband shook his head. 'Don't know. Look, that's more like our lot.' He pointed towards a group of elderly people making their way along the drive towards them, several of them using walking sticks. A hearse appeared in the distance, turning in from the road outside.

'Thank goodness,' Sylvia said, feeling calmer. 'Normal people at last.'

They didn't see the man who'd slipped out of the crematorium building behind them. He was obscured by shrubs but had found a gap through which his telephoto lens pointed at the Armitage couple.

CHAPTER 1: MISSING

Monday, Week 1

Sharon Giroux was starting to feel worried. She was standing in the front porch of her parents' bungalow in Blandford having rung the doorbell three times, and still there was no response. The bell was most certainly working. The sounds of the electronic chimes had carried clearly through the door, but no movement could be seen through the thick, patterned glass. She pressed her nose to the door and tried the bell one last time. Nothing. Sighing, she opened the zip on her shoulder bag and felt down through its assorted contents to the smaller inner compartment, extracting the keys kept inside. Nothing serious could have happened to her parents, surely? Admittedly she hadn't seen them for two weeks, having returned from holiday with her own family only the previous day. They hadn't answered her phone call, made immediately after she and Pierre had put their two young children to bed, and that was strange. Her parents rarely went out on a Sunday evening, not with one of their favourite historical dramas being broadcast mid-evening. There had been no time to check on them earlier in the day, not with her own return to work and its incessant pressures. A GP's working life is one continuous logjam of problems that require immediate action, especially after a fortnight's absence.

Sharon turned the key in the lock and opened the door. 'Mum? Dad?' she called. There was no answer, no sound of movement. The air seemed slightly stale as if no window had been opened for days. Impossible, surely. She'd phoned her younger brother the previous evening after their parents' lack of response, and he'd said that the elderly couple had been fine earlier that weekend. But then, he would say that, wouldn't he? Sharon realised with some certainty that her brother had been lying. He hadn't called in to see them. He probably hadn't even bothered to phone. Absolutely bloody typical of the lazy, irresponsible toerag. Well they certainly weren't anywhere inside the small dwelling. It had taken Sharon only a few moments to glance in all of the rooms. They were all neat and tidy, as expected. She peered out of the kitchen window with its view over the garden, her father's pride and joy. Birds scattered as a neighbour's cat sashayed down the path from the shrubs at the far end. No sign of her parents though. She turned back to the hallway and then her heart lurched. That pile of post gathered on the mat behind the door wasn't just from a day or two. It looked more like a week's accumulation. Most of it was junk mail, as she would have expected, but there was a lot of it.

She pulled her phone out of her bag and called her brother, tucking her long hair behind her ear as she waited for him to answer.

'Rod? You lying toad. You said you'd called in to see Mum and Dad at the weekend, but you didn't, did you?'

There was a pause before he answered. 'Well, I was kind of busy. Things were happening, you know?'

'I bet you didn't even phone them. When did you speak to them last? Tell me.'

'I'm not answerable to you. Why do you still think you can tell me what to do even now, you stuck-up cow? Bossing me about, bossing everyone about, as if you run everything.'

‘Shut up, Rod. They’re not here. It looks as though they haven’t been here for days. So where are they? Can you tell me that?’

There was a short pause. ‘Why worry about it? They’ll be off somewhere, probably enjoying themselves. Maybe getting away from you and your obsession with controlling everything and everybody. Maybe they’re as sick of you as I am.’

‘Oh, bugger off. You’re worse than useless. They’ve left no note, there were no messages from them on our phone at home, nothing. That’s not like them. I’m worried and I need to find out where they are. I’ll have a quick chat with the neighbours. I could say that I could do with your help but you’re so crap at anything you’re asked to do that you’re better off staying away. If I don’t get a satisfactory answer from anyone around here then I’m going to the police. Okay?’ She hung up and took a deep breath to dissipate the intense anger that she felt. She took another, more careful tour of the bungalow before heading towards the neighbouring property. Worry was making her feel slightly nauseous.

* * *

‘And there’s nothing out of place? Nothing obvious missing? It’s just the car that’s gone?’ PC George Warrander was working his way through a mental checklist. The dark-haired, well-dressed woman sitting opposite him in the lounge of her parents’ bungalow shook her head. She looked under strain but was probably wrong to be worried, he thought. It was likely that her parents would turn up safe and sound sometime soon, but meanwhile he needed to err on the side of caution, not only because he was a young, inexperienced copper but also because she was one of the GPs in the practice he used. He knew that she was intelligent, thorough and unlikely to be a fantasist. ‘The house is secure,’ he said. ‘I checked, and there are no signs of any forced entry. And you say that no one in the immediate family knows where they are?’

Sharon shook her head. 'There's only me and my brother, Rod. I've been away on holiday for two weeks, only getting back yesterday evening. My brother lives locally and he was meant to keep an eye on them but I don't think he bothered, despite what he said to me. It's that pile of mail inside the front door. It looks as if it's a week's worth, maybe even longer. The thing is, officer, our holiday was in Cornwall and my parents knew that. It would have been easy to contact me. Mum often calls me on my mobile and if there was a problem of some kind she'd have let me know. The same if they made a sudden decision to go away for a few days. She'd have called or sent me a text.'

'Some elderly people don't know how to text, or feel reticent about it.'

'Not Mum. Dad maybe, but Mum often texts me. Look, this is so unlike them. I'm really worried.'

'What about their passports? Do you know where they're kept?'

'I hadn't thought of that. It's so rare for them to go abroad, you see. They'll be in a drawer in the bedroom. I'll go and check.' Sharon left the room for a few minutes, time that allowed the young constable to marshal his thoughts. When she came back, she looked puzzled. 'They're not there. Mum keeps them in a plastic wallet in the top drawer, but it's missing. I just don't understand it. She'd have let me know if they were going abroad. And the suitcase set they'd have used is still there, tucked under the bed where it's always kept.'

'What was the mobile signal like where you were? Is it possible that she tried to contact you but couldn't get through?'

'It was a bit weak at times, but she'd have left a message for me if she couldn't get through. I know she would.'

'Depends on the phone company and the contract, as far as I know.' Warrander came to a decision. 'Right, Dr Giroux. I can see you're genuinely concerned, so I'll report it as missing persons. I'll also ask for it to be made a high priority. That means someone more senior than me will take over. Do you want to remain here or go back home?'

'I'll stay here for a while. My husband is at home and can look after our children. How long is this likely to take?'

He removed his uniform cap and ran his fingers through his spiky hair. 'I can't be sure, but the quicker we get the ball rolling the better. I'll have a quick chat with the immediate neighbours then wait with you until the team arrive. Maybe then I'll call on your brother.'

Sharon grimaced. 'Good luck to you. I have to tell you that we don't get on. This is so typical of him, not checking up on them when he'd agreed to. He makes my blood boil. It's got to the stage where I can hardly stand being in the same room as him.'

Warrander nodded but said nothing. It wasn't for him to find out more about the obvious fragility of this particular brother-sister relationship. Better to leave that to someone senior or the detectives, if they were called in.

* * *

The young PC quickly understood the source of the antagonism between the two siblings. Whereas Sharon was everything he expected of a professionally qualified woman in a responsible job, her brother was the opposite in almost every way. Untidy, offhand and smelling of drink. His small flat was grubby and appeared to be badly maintained. It smelled of stale food, the aroma probably generated by the stack of empty pizza cartons and curry containers littering the surfaces of the tiny kitchen area. Rod sprawled across a threadbare couch, a cigarette dangling from his lips. He hadn't offered the police officer tea, coffee or anything else to drink. Not that Warrander would have accepted. He'd already noticed that every cup and mug that he could see was chipped or badly stained or both.

'She's too uptight. Paranoid even. Give her half a chance and she'll get herself worked up about next to nothing. And when it comes to the old couple, she goes off her rocker.

They'll be fine. They'll have gone off for the weekend and forgotten to tell anyone, old codgers that they are.'

'So when did you last see them, sir?' Warrander asked. He saw a flicker cross Armitage's face.

'Sometime last week. Can't remember exactly. I called round.'

'What did you talk about?'

'Oh, the usual stuff. Were they okay, was I okay? And Mum lent me some cash. I needed a bit to tide me over.'

'And this was after your sister went on holiday?'

'Yeah. I didn't see much of Dad. He spends most of his time in the garden. It's his hobby. Can't see the point, meself. Waste of bloody time.' He laughed.

'So was it the first week of your sister being away or the second? Try to remember.'

Rod looked blank for a moment. 'Probably the first week. Mebbe near the start?'

Probably a day deliberately chosen if he was cadging money from his parents, Warrander speculated. It would maximise the time between the cash being borrowed and his sister returning, with him hoping that his mother wouldn't mention it to her, or possibly even to his father. That had probably been the truth of it. But at least Rod had been honest enough to tell him about the loan. He could have kept quiet about it and who would have known?

'Did you phone? Did you speak to them last week?'

There was a telling pause. 'Don't think I did. Too busy, wasn't I?'

Warrander nodded. 'What do you do, Mr Armitage?'

'General stuff. I help out my mates when they need an extra hand. You know, a bit of labouring, some painting and decorating for my Uncle Pete. He's got a decorating business. I never got any qualifications, see. Waste of time, I think.' Rod looked across at the young constable.

'I'm not judging you, Mr Armitage. I'm just trying to build a picture that might help us to trace your parents. As you say, they're probably fine. But we can't afford to take any chances, can we?'

Rod shook his head, then took another swig from the beer can that sat on the table in front of him. 'So what happens now?' he asked.

'I've already reported it to my boss as a potential missing persons case. It'll be up to her as to what happens next. She'll probably already be at your parents' house talking to your sister. I expect you'll be needed again so don't hide away, will you?'

'Why would I do that?' Rod looked mystified.

'I was only joking, Mr Armitage. Is there anything else you think I should know about? Anything out of the ordinary that you can remember?'

Rod shrugged. 'No, nothing.'

'I'll be getting back to the bungalow then. You'll hear from us as soon as we find out anything. Okay? Call us if you remember anything that might be important. Are you likely to be out most daytimes?'

'Yeah, I'm working for my uncle at the moment.'

Warrander made his way out of the tiny apartment and into the outside world. It was pleasant to be in the fresh air, even with its slight misty drizzle, after the stale, slightly foetid atmosphere in the flat. Who would have thought that the neat and efficient Dr Giroux would have a brother who appeared to be such a total waster?

* * *

Warrander had a few minutes to chat to his sergeant, Rose Simons, before he went off duty.

'She's a bit up herself, isn't she?' Rose said.

'I didn't think so. She's a GP remember, boss, and has two young children. That's a lot for anyone to cope with.'

'Hmm, you might have a point. I reckon the brother's probably right, though. The chances are that they're off somewhere, gallivanting around the country or gone to London to see a show and decided to stay over. Why anyone would stay in a backwater like this when they could be off enjoying themselves beats me. I'd be off like a shot if I wasn't tied to this sad excuse for a job and to my snotty-nosed kid. I pray every weekend that my lottery ticket comes up. Never happens though.'

He chose not to answer. Whatever he said, he'd be walking into a potential minefield. Sergeant Rose Simons could sometimes be a cynic of the first order, and he thought it wise to refrain from comment when she was in a mood like this. Better to remain silent.

'So where do we go from here, boss?'

'A couple of detectives from the illustrious Missing Persons Department will turn up tomorrow morning. They'll look at our reports, drink some tea, visit those two peculiar offspring, drink some more tea, go to the pub, then piss off back to headquarters. More importantly they'll take this case off our hands completely. With a bit of luck the parents will turn up before things get too heavy. Then I can go back to thinking about my long overdue lottery win.' She winked at him.

George Warrander was not much impressed with his boss's attitude, but he knew better than to mention it. She was a good copper underneath the bravado. Or was it just that nothing very challenging ever happened in this sleepy little town?

CHAPTER 2: BAD MOON RISING

Tuesday, Week 1

Sharon Giroux had been reassured by the attitude of the young PC — what was his name? Warrander? She had been less impressed by his superior, the world-weary sergeant. And as for the duo of detectives interviewing her this morning, well, they didn't appear to be taking her concerns seriously at all.

'We deal with missing persons cases a lot,' stated the overweight detective sergeant, Stu Blackman, nibbling at his third biscuit. They were meeting in her office at the medical centre during a late morning lull, after her pre-noon surgery sessions had finished and before she started her house calls. 'I can reassure you that there's nothing to worry about. Everything points to them having gone away somewhere, what with the passports not being in the house.'

'But they never take the car when they plan to fly anywhere, not that they've been abroad for ages. Mum hates flying and Dad hates airport car parks. The few times they've done it, they've gone to the airport by train or bus or even taxi.'

'Maybe they booked the car onto the shuttle. They've gone to France on the train using the tunnel. That would have solved your mum's flying worries, wouldn't it?' This was the junior detective, Phil McLuskie, older, thinner and seemingly more alert than his boss. Why was he still only a detective constable? Sharon mused. His skin had a slightly yellow sheen to it, probably jaundiced, she thought. Heavy drinker, maybe? She was glad she'd slipped into the jacket of her dark business suit just before she'd greeted the two men. The eyes of the older detective were all over her.

'Look, why do I keep having to convince you people? You're coming up with guesswork all the time. These are my parents. I know them. I know what they do and what they don't do. And I can absolutely assure you that they wouldn't do any of the things you've suggested without letting me know. They would have phoned me or sent a text message. And there's the other thing. When they have gone abroad, they've taken their passports and medical cards but they leave that pink plastic wallet behind. It's too big, too awkward. So why is it missing?'

McLuskie shrugged. 'Maybe they were in a hurry.'

'There you go again. Everything I bring up that doesn't fit with the way they do things, you just shrug and say, well it could be this reason or that reason, because other people *may* have done things that way. But these aren't other people. They are my parents and I know the way they do things. And nothing fits.' She paused. 'Are you treating their house as a potential crime scene? Have you arranged for fingerprinting?'

Blackman pursed his lips. 'I have to be convinced a crime's been committed before we arrange for that, and we're not there yet. There's no sign of a forced entry of any kind. Your parents had a safety chain at the front door. How could anyone have got in against their will? And anyway, what would be the motive? They weren't wealthy, were they? You've said that yourself.'

Sharon shook her head. 'This is mad. Something has happened to my parents, I can assure you of that, and I'm deeply worried.'

'Your brother isn't,' Blackman said.

'He's clueless, as you should have worked out by now. He wouldn't recognise a problem if it was staring him in the face. I told the uniformed lot I spoke to last night, you can ignore anything he says. It'll all be unreliable and made up on the spur of the moment.'

'Are you implying he might know more than he's letting on?'

She was aware that he was watching her carefully. 'Christ, no. I can't stand the little toerag, but even he wouldn't harm them in any way. He's not that bad.'

'At least you don't think he is,' added McCluskie.

'Oh God, this is getting ridiculous. Is this the best you can do? Treat me as if I'm some kind of irrational obsessive worrying over nothing, then when you do start thinking that I might have a point, you home in on the easiest target imaginable? I don't believe it.' She held her head in her hands. 'Rod is too stupid to have done something and left no clue, trust me. He's totally inept when it comes to using his brain. In fact I sometimes wonder whether he actually has one. He doesn't even drive. Last time he tried, he crashed the learner car into a parked van, a telegraph pole and a wall. The instructor refused to take him out again.' She paused to gather breath. 'And why would he do anything to them? They're not insured for any massive sum.'

'What about the house? Would he inherit half of that?' Blackman asked.

'Yes he would, but I told you. He might annoy me to bits, but he's not that evil, for pity's sake.' She shook her head in frustration and looked at the clock on the wall. 'Look, I have to start my house calls in a few minutes and I need to go to the loo first. Please take me seriously. Think over what I've said, and do something.'

They left and she sank back into her chair, wanting to scream.

* * *

'You're looking miserable, Rod. Too much of the old wacky baccy and booze last night?'

Rod Armitage stopped in his task of sanding down the old window frame and looked across at his temporary employer and uncle, Pete Armitage, a local painter and decorator. Should he tell Pete what he really thought of his job? He hated any form of systematic work with a vengeance but had always tried to hide this fact from Pete, who'd proved to be a reliable source of work when he, Rod, had ever needed some extra cash. The additional money was useful, particularly since he'd managed to rupture relations with most of the other local builders and decorators through no real fault of his own. It was just unrealistic for them to expect him to start work at such god-awful times in the morning and he'd let them know his opinion in no uncertain terms. Pete had been the only one who'd been adaptable enough to allow him some flexibility, permitting him to start an hour or two after everyone else. He even let Rod finish work early if he needed to, although even he'd been a bit grumpy about it recently. Why couldn't bosses be more flexible? That's all he wanted, a bit of adaptability. He despised rigidity. Take life as it comes, that was his motto. Even Pete had never understood his point of view when it had been offered. 'Can't run a business like that, Rod,' he'd said. 'When people hire me they want the work done quickly and at prearranged times. I can't just turn up to start a job when I feel like it. My reputation would go down the pan right away and the business would fold. Good quality work, on time, quick and efficient, that's the way I keep my head above water. It's a cut-throat business nowadays with all the overheads being so high.'

Rod finally responded to Pete's overture. 'It's that bloody sister of mine. She's been having a go again. She's only gone and got the police in because Mum and Dad weren't at home when she got back from holiday. Stupid cow. They've obviously gone away for a few days but she can't stand the fact that they did it without telling her. She says it's all my fault for not keeping an eye on them. She bossed me around as a kid and is still trying to do it now.'

Pete frowned and rubbed his nose, his dark eyes glaring at Rod. 'You shouldn't talk about Sharon like that. She's as much my niece as you are my nephew, and I think a lot of her. We're all working class folk and she's done brilliantly to get herself where she is. She's never let me and my family down in anything. You ought to be proud of her instead of running her down. If she's worried about your parents, then maybe you should show a bit more concern. Ted's my brother, for God's sake. I had no idea that he and Sylvia had gone missing.'

Pete asked more questions about the missing couple but Rod had become even surlier. Suddenly he put down his sander, turned tail and stalked off. Pete was left scratching his head in bewilderment. His nephew was fast becoming totally unemployable. He'd only agreed to take him on as a favour to his sister-in-law, who was worried that her son's life was disintegrating into a shambolic mess of drink and drugs. His standard of work was, at best, mediocre and his attitude was often surly and uncooperative, as it had been this morning. Well, if Rod didn't return before the morning was out, that would be his job over. He'd walked out once too often, leaving Pete in the lurch. He looked at his watch. Maybe he should give Sharon a call to get the facts. It wasn't like Ted and Sylvia to wander off without telling anyone.

* * *

Back at the local police station the two detectives investigating the disappearance of the Armitage couple were checking flight records and ferry bookings. So far nothing had shown up but it was early days, and they'd only examined details for fairly local points of departure: the airports at Bournemouth, Southampton and Bristol, and the ferry terminal at Poole. Even so, Phil McCluskie, the older of the two, was mildly surprised. He was midway through checking recent departures from the larger airport at Gatwick and still nothing had shown up, nor had there been any car park bookings made in the couple's name. He would have expected something by now if they had gone abroad. If nothing showed up at Gatwick, then that really only left London's main airport at Heathrow, and the daughter had assured them that her father would never fly from there, having had luggage vanish on a trip some decades earlier, never to be seen again. It tended to point to his original feeling, that they'd gone for a short break within the UK.

His boss, the wheezing Detective Sergeant Stu Blackman, thought otherwise. 'Abroad,' he'd stated, as if it was a concrete fact. 'Or an internal flight. The passports are missing. It'll be one or the other. Trust me.'

McCluskie sighed. Trust in the judgement of this overweight joke of a DS who temporarily headed up the unit? Who was he kidding? Christ, he needed a drink. He imagined the warming bite of whisky trickling down the back of his throat. He'd have to do something soon, maybe see a doctor. He'd noticed the way Sharon Giroux had looked at him when they'd spoken to her earlier at her surgery. She'd probably spotted the signs and had already written him off as a waste of space. No wonder she'd seemed angry. Two detectives assigned to the case, one with a drink problem and the other as mentally sharp as a pigeon. He turned back to the job in hand, completing the Gatwick check. Nothing.

* * *

Sharon Giroux opened her front door, entered, dropped her keys onto the nearby shelf and her bag on the hall floor. 'Hi,' she called. 'I'm home.' She sniffed the air and the welcoming smell of her husband's chicken casserole.

'In the kitchen,' he replied. 'Cup of tea ready for you, my sweet.'

She walked through and hugged the tall, dark-haired man wearing a crimson apron. 'Pierre, you're the perfect man to come home to after one hell of a day.' She kissed him on the lips. 'I love you madly. The children?'

He waved a spoon in the direction of the doorway to his left. 'In the study, doing their homework. At least that's what they claimed to be doing when I checked last.' He set the spoon down and poured out two mugs of tea. 'Any news?'

Sharon shook her head. 'Nothing. Two detectives came to interview me this morning and when they went away I felt more despondent than before. To say I was unimpressed by them would be an understatement. Let's hope they're more thorough and open-minded than they appeared to be.' She sighed and sipped her tea. 'Uncle Pete called me this afternoon. Rod had told him about Mum and Dad, and he was worried. He agrees with me. It's just not the kind of thing they do, disappearing like that without telling anyone. With me not around, one of them would have told him, that's what he says. He saw them the day after we went on holiday, apparently. He called round with some paint that Dad had asked him for. They never mentioned the possibility of going away to him. In fact, the exact opposite. Dad told him how much he wanted to get done in the garden before the weather gets too warm. All his bedding plants were ready to go out, he said. I think I might go round again tomorrow afternoon to check on that, to see if he'd transplanted them. He wouldn't have gone away and left them, not Dad. You know how keen he always is to have the best flower display in their street.'

Pierre frowned and shook his head. 'I took a walk around there this afternoon. There are no summer flowers out in the front garden yet, just the spring ones.' He put his arm around his wife. 'This is a puzzle. You are right to be worried, *ma chérie*.'

* * *

George Warrander, the uniformed officer who had first called on Sharon the previous evening, slid his mobile phone back into his pocket. He'd just called the missing persons unit and was disappointed that the inquiry seemed no further forward than when he'd first logged the disappearance with the official channels. He walked across to Rose Simons who had just appeared in the station foyer, ready to go out in response to a reported pub brawl.

'There's still no information about that missing couple, Sarge. The tecs haven't found anything yet.'

Rose turned to face him. 'Will you just give it a rest? I told you to leave it to the unit, and I meant it. We've handed it on to CID and they make the decisions now. It's not our problem anymore, so forget it, will you? You, Georgie Warrander, need to learn when to let go. Now, let's go out and catch us some lowlife.' She pretended to sniff the air. 'Bad moon rising. Hang on to your six-shooter, deputy. This could be a real showdown.'

Warrander smiled weakly and followed her bulky form outside to the car.

CHAPTER 3: CRUSHED

Wednesday, Week 1

Phil McCluskie scratched his head and frowned. He'd spent the morning combing through road traffic accident reports for the previous ten days but had got nowhere. Lots of RTAs had been reported, but none recorded the involvement of the Armitages' small, dark green Ford Fiesta. He'd started with just Dorset but had soon widened the search to include the neighbouring counties of Wiltshire, Hampshire, Somerset and Devon. Still nothing so he'd opted for the whole of the south of England, to be followed at last by a countrywide search. He leant back in his chair and yawned, running his hand once again through his thinning hair. He looked up to see the lumbering bulk of his boss, Stu Blackman, approaching. He shook his head slowly.

'Nothing?' the detective sergeant asked.

'Nope. Not the proverbial sausage. You?' He was aware that his boss had made a start on contacting the A and E departments of the region's main hospitals.

'Same. Nothing. It's a puzzle and a half, isn't it?' He perched on the corner of McCluskie's desk. 'Maybe we're on the wrong track. Maybe that pain-in-the-neck daughter was right after all. Maybe something has happened to them. Know what I mean?' He paused. 'Who would be your bet?'

McCluskie didn't hesitate. 'The son. He's a right waster and I wouldn't trust him as far as I could throw him. Should we get him in?'

Blackman smiled slyly. 'My thoughts exactly.' He glanced at his watch. 'But let's leave it till after lunch. Pub?'

A look of rapture crept across McCluskie's reptilian face. 'I thought you'd never ask.'

Rod Armitage wasn't brought in for questioning that afternoon. By the time McCluskie had finished his third whisky chaser and Blackman his second plate of cheesy chips, the urge to confront the younger Armitage offspring had dissipated.

'Let's leave it until the morning,' Blackman suggested, ordering another round of drinks. 'We'll be fresher then.'

'You're the boss,' his assistant replied, knocking the whisky back in one gulp and licking his lips. 'Maybe a bit more cogitation is called for.'

'Good one, Phil. Cogitation before confrontation. Like it.'

* * *

Sharon Giroux usually arrived home before her husband on Wednesdays. She should have been back by two o'clock at the latest, since Wednesday was her designated half day in lieu of the Saturday morning surgery she ran most weekends, but she invariably spent several hours catching up on paperwork and usually didn't arrive home until well after three.

She'd called in at her parents' house on her way home, hoping that they would be at the door, cheerfully waving to her as she walked through the gate, but the bungalow was as dark and silent as on the previous two days. Pierre had been right, there were no bedding plants out. She let herself in and walked through the silent house to the back door, then out into the garden. The lawn looked ragged, as if it hadn't been mowed for several weeks. She made her way to the greenhouse and her heart sank. There were her father's prized trays of summer bedding plants, dried up and drooping, forlorn in the warm, dry atmosphere. They clearly hadn't been watered for well over a week. She filled a watering can and gave the trays a soaking. Was it any use? Some of the plants, so carefully tended by her father since being sown in early March, looked dead already, stems and leaves wilted to a dull brown colour.

She returned to the house, sat down in the lounge and phoned through to the number left by the detective sergeant the previous morning. There was no answer, so she tried the mobile number, given as an alternative. The phone was answered on the fifth ring but she had trouble making out what the voice on the other end was saying.

'DS Blackman, is that you?' she asked. 'It's Sharon Giroux. Are you there?'

The voice speaking to her was still unclear. She could only make out about one word in three. 'Look, I can't hear what you're saying. Can you phone me back, please? Maybe we'll get a better signal with a second attempt.'

She closed the call and sat for a while, trying to analyse the sounds she'd heard on the phone. The voice had been indistinct but she was sure that she'd picked up other sounds in the background fairly clearly, including what had sounded like the clinking of glasses. Surely they weren't in a pub, drinking? She waited a further ten minutes but no call came through, so she called again. This time there was far less background noise.

'Why didn't you call me back as I asked?' she said.

'Out on investigations,' came the reply. His voice was slightly slurred.

'What have you discovered?' she probed.

'Early days still,' he replied. 'Be in contact at end of week.'

With that he'd ended the call, not giving her a chance to explain about the plants. Sharon began to cry, and she sat in her parents' kitchen for several minutes until the tears subsided. Finally she rose, dried her eyes on a paper tissue and poured herself a glass of water. The bastard. He'd been drinking, she was sure of it. She locked the front door behind her, returned to her car and drove home, her sadness giving way to frustrated anger.

* * *

That evening she called the number George Warrander had left on Monday evening, asking him for help. Within half an hour the concerned young uniformed officer was at her front door, although he looked tense. She asked him inside and started to tell him of her increased worries following the discovery of the dying plants in her father's greenhouse.

'Yes, Dr Giroux, I can see why you are still concerned. But your parents' disappearance is in the hands of the CID. There's very little I can do to influence things. Have you told them?'

Sharon told him of the afternoon's phone calls.

'They may have been interviewing someone in a pub, Dr Giroux. I'm sure they wouldn't have been drinking, not heavily anyway, not during an investigation. Look, I'll email this latest information to them when I get to the station first thing tomorrow morning. I'm on early shift. I'll also ask them to contact you later tomorrow. Can you suggest a good time?'

He left the house and nervously scanned the street before stepping out onto the pavement. He couldn't afford to let his sergeant know that he'd called to see the Armitage daughter. Rose Simons would hit the roof if she found out. He turned the corner onto the main road and instantly slowed. She was facing him, leaning with her back against her squad car, her face white with anger.

'You, my young friend, are in deep shit. Do you think this is the way to get on in my friendly and supportive little empire? Ignoring every instruction I give you? Who do you think you are? Some kind of go-it-alone maverick?'

'She called me because she was totally frustrated, boss. She phoned the unit this afternoon with some new information and she reckons those two detectives were drunk in a pub. They didn't listen to her.'

'Maybe they've already sussed her out as a timewaster. And so she's sucking you in. And you, fool that you are, fell for it.'

'Boss, with all due respect, I think you've got her wrong.' He glanced at his watch. 'Anyway, my shift finished twenty minutes ago. I was in my own time.'

'But in uniform, so still under my command. Don't try and worm your way out of this, you little creep. I'll remember this. Don't you ever go near that woman again. Do you hear me? Not unless I tell you to.'

She climbed into her car, slammed the door and drove off, leaving Warrander feeling humiliated and crushed. Was his career in the police already over, when it had only just begun?

CHAPTER 4: UPPERS AND DOWNERS

Thursday, Week 1

Sharon caught sight of her uncle as she walked through the surgery's reception area in order to collect a form from one of the secretaries. He waved as he saw her.

'I thought you'd like to know that the bungalow is crawling with people,' he said. 'There's tape across the front gate and vans parked in the street outside. They seem to be searching the place. I passed by on my way to a job.'

'About bloody time. They must finally be convinced that something odd has happened, though with those two detectives in charge it's hard to predict anything. Thanks for letting me know, Pete.' She glanced at the clock on the wall. 'Maybe I'll have time to call round. I've got a slack half hour due to a couple of cancellations.'

'Do you want me to come with you?'

'Thanks, but no. I can handle this, and you have a job to go to. Is Rod still with you?' She watched the look of concern cross her uncle's face.

'No. He walked out on me on Tuesday and didn't come back, so that's it, I'm afraid. I told him it was a final warning, but he still stormed off in a temper and didn't appear again. I've done all I can for him, Sharon. He was a liability.'

Sharon nodded. 'I know. Thanks for what you've done for him over the past couple of years. We all realised that it wasn't easy for you. I know Mum and Dad were grateful. Well, I'd better be off.' She hurried back to her office to collect her coat and bag.

* * *

Sharon parked her car as near to her parents' house as she could, then walked towards the bungalow, making her way through one or two clusters of people who were standing watching the goings-on. PC Warrander was standing at the entrance gate.

'What's happened?' she asked.

'Nothing to worry about, Dr Giroux. We're just following standard procedure. DC Blackman decided to arrange a forensic check, so that's what's happening. I'll take you in, if you like. You've timed it right. I think they'll need your fingerprints for elimination purposes. The forensic chief is here for a few minutes.'

They walked to the door and entered the hallway. It seemed to be a hive of activity, with half a dozen people inside the bungalow, all busy with kits of various kinds. A tall, good-looking, middle-aged man looked up as they entered.

'This is Dr Giroux, Mr Nash. She's the missing couple's daughter.'

'Hi.' He held out a hand and smiled at her, his eyes crinkling at the corners. 'Dave Nash. I'm the county's chief forensic officer. I only called in to check on progress but I have a few minutes to chat if you want to.'

Sharon realised that she was holding onto his hand for rather too long and suddenly let it go. 'Thanks. That would be useful. What can you tell me?'

'We've started a basic house check as a result of your parents being reported missing. Dusting for prints, looking for anything unusual or out of place, taking a few samples for auto-analysis. At the moment my staff are following a checklist and they don't need me here, but I always make a quick visit in person if I can.'

'So you're the top dog?' She looked surprised.

'Indeed I am. One of my team will need to take your prints, so if it's convenient it could be done here.'

She nodded. 'Of course. And my brother, he'll need his taken as well at some point.'

'That's in hand, Dr Giroux. It'll take a little while before we can start drawing any conclusions, but my team's a good one. There'll be no slip-ups.'

Sharon felt a weight lift from her shoulders. She gave him a smile. 'Thanks. That's what I need, some reassurance. It's what I've been looking for since I reported them missing on Monday, that my concerns are being taken seriously.' She paused. 'I've just got this feeling that something awful has happened to them. I know it's illogical, but it's with me all the time.'

'I can understand that.' Nash looked at his watch. 'Better be going. Look, if we do find anything suspicious, that's when Sophie's squad will be called in.'

Sophie's squad?'

'It's one of our pet names for the county's top investigation team. Let's hope they won't be needed.' He turned and left the house.

She turned to George Warrander. 'Thanks. I don't know how much of this was your doing, but I'm grateful, really.' She smiled, the first time he'd seen her do so since his first visit on Monday. 'What was that about this so-called top team?'

George picked his words carefully. 'Let's hope it doesn't come to that.' He didn't elaborate. 'Let me take you to one of the forensic people who can take your prints. It saves us a lot of trouble, you calling in like this.'

* * *

DS Stu Blackman and his sidekick, Phil McCluskie, were visiting Rod Armitage. It had been obvious that the younger Armitage offspring was in bed when the two detectives first arrived. It had taken several knocks on the door before it had been opened, and even McCluskie had been impressed by the dishevelled state of the man.

'Rise and shine, Mr Armitage, it's a beautiful day,' he'd said, with a smile on his face. 'My, my. We are looking a wee bit the worse for wear, aren't we? Heavy night?'

His boss took over at that point, leading Rod to a chair in the sitting area while miming to his assistant that cups of tea might be in order.

'No news yet, Rod,' Blackman said. 'I can call you Rod, can't I? Easier for us. But I'd like a bit more information from you about your parents and your relationship with them. Can you confirm when you last saw them? When was that again?'

Rod looked blank, scratched his head and yawned again. 'A couple of weeks ago, it was. I told you that days ago.'

'Yes. I want you to be a bit more specific. An exact day and a precise time would be helpful.' He looked over Rod's shoulder at his colleague, standing by the kitchen worktop, and silently indicated that Phil should have a quick look round while waiting for the kettle to boil. McCluskie nodded and started turning over some letters that were untidily piled on the worktop.

'Monday? Tuesday maybe? I remember you saying that it was soon after your sister had left on her family holiday. Does that help?'

'I think it was the Tuesday evening. I would have been about six thirty 'cause I joined them for their meal.'

'Right. What did you have?'

Rod looked blank. 'What?'

'What did you have to eat? Your mum cooked it, did she? So what was it? Chicken? Fish? Pizza?'

'Christ, how do you expect me to remember that?'

'Try, Rod. Please try. I wouldn't have thought it was that difficult. It was probably the last time you saw your mum and dad alive. It's important.'

'Spaghetti Bolognese, I think. Dad likes it. Not one of my favourites. Why is it important?'

Blackman ignored the question. 'That's a bit surprising, isn't it? If your mum knew you were coming round, wouldn't she cook something you liked? Or didn't she know you'd be arriving?' He was watching McCluskie who was quietly inspecting the contents of the drawers and cupboards in the kitchen area, finishing with a negative shake of his head.

'No. I was busy at the time so I called on the off-chance.'

'To borrow some money? That's what you told one of our uniformed colleagues.' Blackman waited a few seconds. 'How much was that then, Rod? How much did you borrow?'

'Fifty quid. Look, what is this? What's it got to do with you?'

Again the question was ignored. 'How much did you ask for? More importantly, how much did you actually need? And what did you need it for?'

'My rent was due and I was fifty short. That's why I asked for fifty and that's why Mum lent me it.'

Blackman nodded. 'So there wasn't any friction? Not from your dad?'

'He was outside. It's always easier talking to Mum alone.'

'You mean she's more of a soft touch? Whereas your dad isn't?'

At this point McCluskie, who had just finished checking the room, sat down on the other side of Rod. 'I bet you could really use a big slab of cash, couldn't you, Rod?' he suggested. 'I mean, not these petty wee amounts, but money that you could really do something with. Thousands, mebbe. Eh? God, what I could do with a few thousand. Holidays, women, the high life. We can but dream. Here's your tea.' He passed a mug of steaming liquid across to Rod and another to Blackman. 'Does your big sister approve of you going round and cadging money from your mother? I bet she doesn't, does she? I bet she tells your mum not to lend you cash. A bit of a meddler, is she? Bloody sisters, eh? Goody two shoes.' McCluskie sipped his tea and put the grubby mug down on the nearest surface. 'Tell us about that wacky baccy that's in the wee box under the sink, Rod. We'd love to know about it and where you got it.'

Rod didn't reply.

'Well now, my friend,' Blackman said. 'Here's how it works. We can have a good look round right now with your permission, and we'll leave the place tidy. If you make us get a warrant, then we'll come back with the team and we'll tear this place apart. The choice is yours, so which is it to be?'

Rod held his head in his hands.

* * *

If anything the room looked tidier after the two detectives had finished their search than it had done before. They'd dumped many of the mouldering food containers in a large plastic bin-bag, creating some much needed space in the cramped flat. On the low table in the middle of the room was a small collection of packets containing a mix of tablets, most of them voluntarily offered up by Rod. The search had only uncovered a few others that he'd forgotten about. They'd found nothing that seemed relevant to the disappearance of his parents.

'We can see that you're only a user of this stuff, not a dealer,' said McCluskie, who'd been a member of the drug squad sometime in the distant past. 'And I have to say, it's a real mix of junk here. Uppers, downers, the lot. Do you actually know what you're taking when you pop one of these?'

Rod shook his head ruefully. 'Nah. I'm usually a bit pissed.'

'Brave man. Or mebbe more accurately, stupid and foolish man. So what do we do now, Sarge?' He looked across at Blackman.

'We'll take the gear and look after it. But we won't charge you, Mr Armitage, not at present. Let's just say that we'll hang on to everything, waiting for co-operation and good behaviour from you. Am I making myself clear? You're not yet in the proverbial deep shit unless we turn up something else or you do something stupid. Comprenez, amigo?'

Rod nodded.

'I'm impressed,' McCluskie said as they lugged the bin-bag of rubbish outside with them, depositing it in a nearby wheelie bin. 'Getting both French and Spanish into a two-word phrase. Got to be a winner, that, boss. Worth a pint, I think.'

'And cheesy chips?' Blackman suggested.

'Whatever,' came the reply. 'It's your turn to pay, I think, boss.'

CHAPTER 5: MORDEN BOG

Friday morning, Week 1

Sergeant Rose Simons extended her baton and used it to tap George Warrander on the shoulder.

'Arise, Sir George, do-gooder extraordinaire,' she said. 'I have one rest day and I return to find you being talked about as if you're some kind of celebrity. By CID, no less. The wheezing Sergeant Blackman and the entirely sober Detective McCluskie, of all people.' She looked at Warrander directly. 'So you may have been right after all. But don't pin too many hopes on those two wasters. They're notorious.'

Warrander was puzzled. 'So why are they in charge of Missing Persons cases?'

She laughed. 'They're not. It's normally a three-person squad. The leader is away on a course, due to return next week. The second-in-command retired last month and hasn't been replaced. And the dogsbody third was in an RTA at the weekend and is recovering from her injuries. Our two illustrious detectives are the scrapings from the very bottom of the barrel, filling in for a week or two. So don't get your hopes up, young Georgie boy. You're not in the big league yet. Better stick with me for a while. I'm very protective of my young charges, as you have already discovered.' She smiled at him. 'Cup of tea? It's my treat. Take it as a sort of apology. I was over the top on Wednesday night. Too much responsibility on these slim shoulders of mine.'

Warrander relaxed a little. 'Thanks. Tea would be great.'

'When I said it's my treat, what I really meant was that you fetch the mugs and make us both tea, but use my tea-bags. Okay?'

Warrander grinned at her. 'Yes, ma'am.'

'Oh, and you should be able to get two mugs' worth of tea out of a single tea bag if you go about it the right way. No sense in you wasting my hard-earned money needlessly, is there?' She looked at her watch. 'Fifteen minutes before we're due out on the wild streets of Danger Land, so get a move on, Georgie.'

* * *

It was mid-morning, several hours later, that a call came through to their squad car to head south to the Morden Bog Nature Reserve. The call would normally have been taken by a local team from Wareham, but they were all engaged elsewhere and Simons and Warrander had just finished a visit to a small general store in Lytchett Minster, where the owner had reported a possible till theft. In fact there hadn't been one — the missing money was found in a small cash bag on a shelf beneath the till, overlooked by the elderly manager. The sergeant was making some typically laconic observations about senility when these were interrupted by her radio crackling into life. It was a request to visit the site of an abandoned car that had just been discovered.

They drove south to the bleak heathland destination and turned off the road onto a track where two forestry commission workers were waiting for them. Warrander followed their vehicle as it made its way slowly along a rough track into the desolate northern section of the reserve and finally reached the edge of a large copse of trees. They stopped in a clearing at the end of the trail and stepped out of their vehicles, following the two men in silence for a minute or two as they walked between thick outcrops of undergrowth. And there it was, as reported. A small green Ford Fiesta, half hidden in a thicket of greenery.

'It's not nice, believe me,' said one of the workmen. 'We'll stay back.'

Warrander followed the stocky form of Sergeant Simons as she walked towards the car. A flexible length of pipe, taped to the exhaust pipe, led in through a window, open only a crack. Rose peered in. Two bodies, upright in the front seats and seething with maggots. Warrander peered over her shoulder then turned away, walking several paces before he vomited into a clump of ferns. There was no other sound. Even the birds seemed to have abandoned this particular spot, as if they knew of the tragedy that had unfolded on the ground below their perches.

* * *

'We found them an hour or so ago. We do a quick ground survey about every six months, looking for any clearance work that might need doing. You know, gorse, rhododendrons, the kind of stuff that will choke other plants given half a chance. It's a pretty lonely part of the reserve up here. Most of the nature lovers stay further south or west where it's a bit more accessible. This track's rarely used, you could see that yourself driving up it. Even then, that car has been driven off the track and through the bushes to end up where it is. It might have remained undiscovered for a lot longer if we hadn't chanced on it.' The speaker, the older of the two forestry workers, shook his head. 'I don't know. Why do they do it?'

Rose shrugged. 'Not worth speculating at the moment. I'm sure we'll get to the bottom of it, but there's all kinds of reasons. Some of them even make sense. Try not to talk about the details to anyone, will you? Forensics should be here soon. We don't want people told any of the details, not until we're absolutely sure we know what we're dealing with. We'll need statements from you both. George here will get those a bit later, once someone arrives to take charge.'

The two forestry workers returned to the clearing to wait with the vehicles and Warrander walked the route between it and the death site, following the path that the small car must have taken. Larger vehicles would have had more difficulty squeezing between some of the trees. Even so it was relatively easy to spot the occasional broken branch and scraped bark where the gap had proved almost too narrow for the small Fiesta. Why make it so difficult to find? Was that a common feature of the suicides of elderly couples? He returned to his boss, who was sitting on a tree stump, deep in thought.

'Just had a radio message. Forensics here in five minutes,' she said.

'Why would they do this, boss? Why would they have driven all the way out here to the back of beyond and hidden their car this well before doing it?'

She shrugged. 'Don't try to second guess it, Georgie. It's not worth it. We'll wait for forensics, then the experts will pick it all over. There's no accounting for what people will do when the pressure's on them, trust me. I've seen it all and nothing ever surprises me now. It's not our job to speculate and if you see the family, don't get drawn in by the questions they'll fire at us.'

'Will we have to break the news to them?'

She nodded. 'Expect so. It's us who've been in contact with them, after all. And it'll be better for us to do it than those two cowboys from CID. Blackman and McCluskie — detectives from the Far Side.'

'Don't you mean the Dark Side?'

'No, I mean the Far Side. They're a joke.'

* * *

Dave Nash arrived a few minutes later and started directing his team to their varied tasks as each unit arrived, starting with photography and video. A tent was put up over the car, even though the weather was expected to remain fine for several days. He was joined within an hour by Benny Goodall, the county's senior pathologist, who'd driven across from Dorchester. The personnel all wore white nylon overalls and facemasks, and looked like ghosts as they moved quietly among the trees in the copse. Finally the car doors were opened and clouds of noisy flies flew out, sounding like a chainsaw. The two experts started to gently probe the bodies in the car, but access was difficult because of its position, jammed into the trees. At this point they were joined by a third figure, just arrived in a silver saloon and tying a mask around her head, a few wisps of blond hair blowing out from under the hood of her white overall. She was accompanied by a younger, ginger-haired detective, also busy covering himself in a forensic suit.

'Dave Nash called them Sophie's Squad when he mentioned them to the daughter yesterday,' Warrander said to his boss.

'Well, I'll need to ask them if we can go and let the family know. We don't want them hearing about the discovery here via the radio news.' She walked across to the assembled team and caught the eye of the blonde detective, who was clearly in charge of the crime scene.

'Ma'am, we're keen to inform the family as soon as you're happy for us to do so. As far as I can tell, there isn't much doubt, is there? The car is theirs and they look about the right height.'

'Okay, but stress that it's unconfirmed at the moment. I trust your judgement. You're Rose Simons, aren't you? Tell them that I'll call on them later, Rose. Which family member will I be seeing?'

'Probably the daughter. She's a GP in Blandford. She can be a bit uptight, but I'll tread carefully. There's a son as well, but he's a bit of a waster.'

The detective looked across the clearing. 'Is that George Warrander with you? Give him my regards, won't you? Tell him I'll have a chat later when there's time.' She waved across the clearing at the young PC, who didn't quite know how to respond and lifted his hand in a cross between a wave and a salute.

Rose walked back and the two uniformed officers made their way to the squad car. More squad car units were arriving from Wareham and from headquarters at Winfrith.

'Let's get out of here while we can,' Rose said. 'It's starting to turn into a real circus.' She waited until Warrander had navigated their car along the tracks and had turned out onto the main road before she spoke again. 'How did she know who you were, Georgie boy? Is there something you haven't told me?'

Warrander chose his words carefully. He knew that his boss was likely to make a joke about whatever he said. 'She's the reason I joined the police. She interviewed me a couple of years ago when a friend of mine was found murdered. I'd thought about it before then but had never done anything about it. It kind of spurred me on. I asked her about joining and she sent me some details. I didn't think she'd recognise me.'

'What, a handsome young man like you? And in my tender care to boot?' She remained silent for a minute or two. 'So she had that much influence on you? Seriously?'

He nodded. 'Yes.'

'Hmm. Friends in high places. I can see I may have to treat you with more respect.' There was a slight pause. Warrander waited to see what was coming next. 'On second thoughts, maybe not. I wouldn't want you getting big-headed.'

* * *

It was well after midday when Rose and Warrander arrived at the medical centre where Sharon Giroux worked. The morning rush had subsided, with only a handful of patients occupying the seats in the waiting area. Sharon was standing in reception talking quietly to one of the nurses. She glanced up as the two police officers came in through the main entrance door and fell silent as she caught their eye.

'Can we go somewhere private, Dr Giroux?' Rose suggested.

'My consulting room. Do you have news?'

Rose merely nodded, and followed the doctor through to her office.

Warrander chose to remain standing as the two women sat. Sharon was tense, her hands tightly linked. It was obvious that she had picked up on their sombre mood.

'I need to tell you, Dr Giroux, that we discovered two bodies this morning in a car, out in the depths of the Morden Nature Reserve. It's your parents' car, without a doubt. It had been there for some time.'

Sharon frowned. 'What do you mean? Had it been in a crash?'

Rose shook her head. 'No. It had been driven to a remote spot deliberately. There was a pipe leading from the exhaust to the inside.'

'What? What are you saying? That Mum and Dad committed suicide?'

Rose remained non-committal. 'It would appear so, but it's early days yet. We'll need to examine all the evidence.'

'Who's the medic in charge?'

'Doctor Goodall. He's come across from Dorchester. He'll do a thorough job.'

'I know he will. But it's just not possible.' Tears were escaping from Sharon's eyes and running down her cheek. 'They wouldn't. Why would they? It doesn't make sense. They were happy with their lives. It's beyond belief.'

Rose spoke softly. 'It's always hard to comprehend. I wish we could have come with different news, Dr Giroux, but we have to let you know. In all likelihood it will be reported on local radio as the afternoon goes on, and it will certainly be on the teatime bulletins. You need to be prepared for that.

Do you want us to tell your brother, or would you prefer to do that?'

Sharon thought for a few moments. 'I couldn't cope with it. I know I should be able to, but I just feel so empty.' She paused. 'Who's running the investigation? Not those two dim-wits still? Jumping to conclusions like they do?'

Rose shook her head again. 'Suspicious deaths always get referred to the top, especially when there are two together.'

Warrander interrupted. 'It's DCI Allen in charge, Dr Giroux. She's the best there is, trust me. You have no need to worry on that score.'

Sharon continued to wring her hands, her face ashen.

'Maybe you should consider going home, Sharon,' Rose said. 'Can I contact your husband for you?'

The doctor just nodded, overcome by sobs and no longer able to speak. Rose put an arm around her shoulder.

CHAPTER 6: A GRIM TASK

Friday afternoon, Week 1

The task was a grim one, but with both Benny Goodall, the senior pathologist, and forensic chief Dave Nash on hand, Sophie Allen knew that the in-situ examination of the two corpses would be thorough. She stood back, watching, as they got on with their work.

'Do you think there's much doubt, ma'am?' Her second-in-command, DS Barry Marsh, stood by her side. 'I've just checked back with the information built up this week from the missing persons inquiry. The car's theirs and the bodies look about the right age to my untrained eye.' He wiped some perspiration from his face and tried to scratch his ear, impossible under the nylon hood. A few strands of his ginger hair peeked out onto his forehead below the white material.

'You know me, Barry. Not one to make too many assumptions, but when the obvious is staring you in the face like this, it would be stupid to ignore it. Yes, it's them. But it's so peculiar. When old people take their own lives in some kind of pact, they tend to do it at home. They want to end it all in the place that means most to them, that most reassures them. It's a kind of comfort blanket. So they usually take pills and go to bed, because to them it's their final rest. Even if they do it this way, in a car using the exhaust pipe, it's usually in their garage at home. Why come out here to this remote place? Unless of course it meant something to them, if they first met here, say. Or maybe he proposed to her here while they were out walking all those decades ago.' She paused. 'We'll get Rae onto that line of enquiry once we get started, looking to see if there's some reason why they would have chosen this spot. It is very tranquil here, and beautiful while the sun's shining, so there could be logic behind it. We'll wait and see.'

Benny Goodall, who'd been carefully probing the two bodies, straightened up and backed away from the open car door. 'Okay, that's as much as I can do here. If you can get them out, Dave, we'll move them back to my place and I can start the serious work.' He turned to Sophie. 'No obvious wounds or injuries of any type. The next stage will be examination of some underlying tissue back at the lab. Carbon monoxide poisoning leaves evidence behind. Most obviously in skin colouration, but that's a no-no with this level of dermal decomposition. It's the heat and flies. All is not lost, though. There'll be other indicators left in deeper tissue and in the internal organs, and they'll show up during the PM. Their daughter's a local GP, you say?'

Sophie nodded. 'In Blandford.'

'Right. She'll want the medical facts, no doubt, so I'll bear that in mind. Keep her away at present, though, Sophie. Sometimes doctors think they'll cope okay with seeing bodies like this, but they're unprepared for the emotional impact when it's someone close.'

'That's helpful, Benny. Barry and I will drive up to see her later this afternoon. The uniformed lot have already broken the news. It seemed the best option because they've been involved with her since she reported the disappearance at the beginning of the week.' She paused. 'So how long do you think they've been here?'

He smiled grimly. 'You've waited a long time before asking me the obvious question. I wondered if you were losing your touch.' He glanced across at the bodies again. 'Much more than a week. I'd say it was closer to two weeks, maybe three. What do you think, Dave?'

The forensic chief removed his mask and hood as he stepped away from the car. 'I agree, but we'll need to look at the reference material on body decomposition before we can give you a more accurate timeframe.'

'But it was definitely before they were reported as missing on Monday? You can be sure of that?'

'Oh yes, undoubtedly.'

She turned to the senior uniformed officer, a sergeant from Wareham. 'I want a close search done on the immediate area, and everything picked up and logged. I know there'll be some bits and pieces of litter but we can eliminate those later. Same with the car, Dave. I know it'll go back to the depot for checking, but I want everything inside it logged as well. There's something not quite right here. Can we fix up some security devices to log activity at night? We can't afford to have someone stationed here overnight, but we need some way of monitoring the place in case anyone visits.'

Sophie walked back to her car with Barry Marsh. 'It's a relief that they've been there for two weeks or more. It means that anything those two plonkers running the missing persons inquiry did or didn't do was of no consequence. The old couple had already been dead for a couple of weeks.'

'Will we have to include them as part of the team, ma'am? Blackman and McCluskie, I mean?'

Sophie gave a snort. 'Over my dead body. I had a dispute with McCluskie when I first arrived here a few years ago and got him shifted off my interim team for being drunk on duty, among other things. He was a sergeant then. He had the ability, there was no doubt of that, but he was lazy and cut too many corners.' She unlocked the car doors and removed her white nylon overall, dumping it in the boot. 'He wouldn't want to work for me again, anyway. He blamed me for getting him demoted.'

Barry shut the boot after depositing his forensic suit inside. 'Did you? Get him demoted, I mean?'

'Dead right it was me. He's got the morals of a guttersnipe. It wasn't just the excessive boozing. He was hitting on any of the women witnesses who were half-attractive, and that could have put the prosecution case at risk. I decided to pay a second visit to one of the witnesses because something she'd said didn't quite add up and it was my first case here in Dorset. This was before this unit was set up properly. I felt uneasy with something in the statement she'd given him so decided to double check. I found them both half-clothed, ready to jump into bed. He'd got her so drunk she didn't know what she was doing. The powers that be at HQ have kept him out of my hair ever since.' She climbed into the driving seat and waited until Marsh was seated. 'In the only important sense, Barry, it wasn't me that got him demoted. It was his own actions, but I couldn't ignore them so I reported what he'd been doing. The decision was made at a much higher level.' She started the car and drove out towards the road, then headed north. 'I can't tolerate that kind of attitude. It goes against everything I believe in.'

* * *

They found both Sharon Giroux and her husband Pierre at home. Pierre showed them through to the lounge, where Sharon was sitting in an armchair, hugging her knees. Her eyes were pink.

'Dr Giroux, I'm so sorry for your loss.'

'Is there no room for doubt?' asked Pierre.

Sophie shook her head. 'We took dental x-rays at the scene with a mobile unit, and we've just had them confirmed with your in-laws' dentist, Mr Giroux, so it's now certain.' She turned back to Sharon. 'I'm DCI Sophie Allen, by the way, and this is my assistant, Detective Sergeant Barry Marsh. We'll be taking over the investigation into the circumstances of your parents' deaths in the initial stages. In the longer term, the nature of the investigation will depend upon my findings and subsequent recommendations.'

Sharon looked up at her. 'So does it seem to be suicide?'

'It looks that way. But I'm well aware that appearances can be deceptive, so I won't make any assumptions. The evidence gathering will be thorough and I'll keep an open mind until I see it all. One thing does puzzle me, Dr Giroux, and that's the place they were found. It's in the north-east segment of the Morden Bog Nature Reserve. It's very much off the beaten track. Can you suggest any reason why they would have been there?'

Sharon sipped at a mug of tea that had been sitting by her side. 'We used to have family picnics there when my brother and I were small. Dad was always keen on wildlife and it was a brilliant place for dragonflies and other marsh insects.'

Sophie nodded. 'So there is a sentimental connection?'

'Yes. He used to take photos of the wildlife and sometimes of us, standing in our wellies.' Sharon gave a gentle smile. 'We took sandwiches and flasks of tea, and used to stomp around the place for a few hours. Mum, Dad, Rod and me. Well, Mum used to sit with her back against a tree and read while we were pond dipping, then get the food out. She wasn't an enthusiast herself.' She replaced her mug on the low table beside her chair. 'It was what kicked off my interest in biology. Then from that to medicine, so I suppose what I am now is partly down to those summer afternoons on the edge of Morden Bog.'

Sophie listened carefully, trying to weigh Sharon up. She was obviously intelligent and perceptive, only to be expected in such a well-regarded GP. And she'd worked her way there from an ordinary, working class background. Good for her. Sophie had a great deal of respect for people who'd made it the hard way, through sheer effort and a dogged determination. Wasn't she the same? That's why she felt for this woman so much. She recognised a kindred spirit.

'What do you do, Mr Giroux? For a job, I mean?' Sophie turned her attention to the husband.

'I'm an academic editor for research journals in environmental science. I work from home for three days each week and in Oxford for two. The flexibility suits me. And it means I'm on hand for child-minding duties for much of the week. It works well.'

'So do you know the place, Morden Bog? If you're an environmental scientist? I realise that your work is academic rather than practical, but even so.'

'Yes, I do. As a much younger man I came across from France in a group of students to study Dorset's heathland habitat. It's quite famous. We spent a day or two at each of a variety of locations. That was when I met Sharon. My group was staying in a hostel in Blandford and we met in one of the pubs there on an evening out.'

'I do want to double check a few things with you both. I think you said that you were on holiday in Cornwall until the weekend. Is that right?'

'Yes,' Sharon replied. 'We were in St Mawgan, near Newquay. With Easter being so late this year we gambled on the weather being good, so took the whole fortnight. We rented a cottage. Neither of us was there for the whole time though.'

Sophie looked up. 'What do you mean?'

'I had a two-day medical conference in Exeter at the start of the second week. Pierre was in Oxford for a couple of days during the first week. It was partly a working holiday for him.'

'So did either of you come back to Blandford during your break?'

Both Sharon and Pierre shook their heads.

'Okay. I need to ask you about your brother, Sharon. He has a bit of a chequered history, including some run-ins with the local police over the years. How well did he get on with your parents? I'm aware that you've already partly covered this ground earlier in the week, but I do need to know.'

'He got on okay with Mum, less well with Dad. There was often friction between them. Dad had strict standards, something totally meaningless to Rod. He's never seemed to fully understand the difference between right and wrong. His own convenience is much more important to him.'

'He is known to us, Sharon.'

The doctor nodded wryly. 'Drug possession, petty vandalism and theft. The whole family knows about Rod and his inability to stay out of trouble. Dad was so frustrated he was sometimes reduced to tears. Mum was more phlegmatic about it. But he's never done anything violent, Chief Inspector. That's one thing I can say for him.'

The detectives left a few minutes later. As they drove away, Marsh said, 'So the family never knew about the possible GBH charge. It must have been dropped very early on.'

Sophie steered the car out onto the main road heading south. 'No independent witnesses and the victim, a very drunk young man, backed out of pressing any charges very quickly. He refused to say whether he was being intimidated, but the suspicion was there. There might be a nastier side to young Rod than his family have ever suspected.'

CHAPTER 7: SCAR

Saturday morning, Week 1

It was a beautiful May morning. The blue sky was dotted with a few small puffs of cloud, and the air was as fresh and clean as a newly cut lemon. Sophie Allen stood leaning against the car, listening to the sound of bird calls while waiting for her husband to finish tying his boot laces. In another hour the first of the morning's ramblers would probably be arriving, although they wouldn't be able to gain access to the area around the crime scene, still cordoned off by police tape. She loosened the neck strap of her camera, then handed a set of binoculars to Martin as he stood up.

'Which way first?' he asked.

'We're about a mile and a half south of where the car was found. I want to head north-west and get a feel for the area. I've got the map, so we shouldn't get lost. My guess is that we should get there in about half an hour or so, but it depends on what we find on the way.'

'Sounds okay to me. It's supposed to cloud over about lunchtime, so we've a good few hours.'

The couple started walking, heading along a well-defined path for the first few minutes before veering off onto a small track. They moved quietly, scanning the area ahead of them as they rounded each corner or reached the top of an occasional hillock. Insects darted between the bushes, birds were noisily singing in the undergrowth and a few squirrels were out seeking food in the shady areas under the sparsely clumped pine trees. They were both alert, Martin for birds, often identified first by their calls, Sophie for . . . what exactly? She didn't know. She just felt the need to explore the area, to absorb something of the atmosphere of the bleak heathland. It wasn't very bleak this morning, though, and she walked alongside her husband, stopping every so often at a bird cry or a picturesque scene.

The couple meandered slowly north-west, around small copses of pines, alongside clumps of heather and, further on, around boggy areas that seemed to attract clouds of insects. Sophie suddenly put her hand on Martin's arm.

'There's someone ahead of us,' she said. 'About three hundred yards. By that small clump of trees. Can you look through the binoculars?' She put the SLR camera to her eye and adjusted the lens to maximum zoom. The figure was still unclear but she took several photos. 'Can you make out any detail, Martin?' she asked.

'Dark brown trousers, olive green jacket. He blends into the surroundings. Could be a birdwatcher. I think he has binoculars. Yes, look, he's lifting them up to his eyes. Shall we get closer?'

They walked further along the rough path but lost sight of the distant figure as the track curved around a low, heather-covered hillock. When they regained sight of the clump of trees there was no one there. They made their way across to the spot and looked around them but they seemed to be alone.

'The woods start here,' Martin said. 'Once in the trees he'd be out of sight. It looks like they stretch quite a distance across to the west.'

Sophie extracted the map and opened it up, tracing the route they'd followed with her finger. 'I'd guess we're here,' she said, pointing to a spot on the map. 'You're right. Look. The woods extend across to the Sugar Hill Road, north of Coldharbour. The open heathland is mostly south and east of here. The terrain is much more mixed from this point north and west. Could you tell where he or she was looking?'

'I can't be sure but it looked as if it was over there.' He pointed.

'That's east.' She looked at the map again. 'That's where the car was found.'

She put the camera to her eye, again at maximum zoom. 'I think I can make out the taped-off area. Can I have the binoculars?'

She focussed, and scanned the view in front of her. Trees, bushes, a female sika deer with her two young offspring, police tape, two distant uniformed figures walking from a parked squad car. The deer ran into the undergrowth. Sophie handed the binoculars back to Martin.

'It may have been nothing,' she said. 'Whoever it was may just have been watching some deer. Shall we go on?'

They left the small copse and strolled towards the police area, reaching it about ten minutes later. They ducked under the tape.

'You can't come in here, past that tape,' one of the uniformed officers said when he spotted them walking towards the clearing.

Sophie held out her warrant card. 'I'm the SIO,' she said. 'Anything unusual to report?'

The officer shrugged his shoulders. 'Nothing, ma'am. It's been very quiet.'

'Have you seen anyone at all?' she asked. 'Particularly in the last half hour?'

He shook his head. 'No one.' He glanced at his watch. 'It's not ten yet. I expect we'll see a few ramblers before the morning's out. Especially with the weather this good.'

She nodded, then walked slowly around the immediate area, scanning the view in each direction. Other than some birds heading towards the distant trees, there were few signs of life. She took a bottle of water from the side pocket of her backpack and swallowed several mouthfuls, then returned to the centre of the clearing to speak to the officers guarding the site. 'Okay. We'll be off. These are for you, by the way. Leave some for the next unit, won't you?' She handed over a packet of biscuits, turned and rejoined Martin who had remained on the edge of the path.

'Where to now?' he asked.

'I think we'll head along the tree line, west,' she said. 'We've got the flask of coffee so we can maybe stop for a break in half an hour or so. Then loop round to the south and get back to the car late morning. Does that sound okay?' She passed him the water bottle.

'Fine,' he answered. 'I'm actually enjoying this. Some all too rare "us" time.'

'I feel the same, but I want to move a little bit faster for a while. Okay?'

They removed their jackets and set off west at a sharp pace, following a rough path that hugged the edge of the tree line, disturbing only the occasional squirrel. There were no signs of human activity. After about twenty minutes the path left the trees, turned south-west and crossed an area of open heath. Sophie could see a small car park ahead of them, with three vehicles on the gritty surface. Cars could be heard passing along the nearby Sugar Hill Road. A solitary figure was approaching the parked cars on a path south of theirs, about the same distance away. Sophie walked faster and Martin, despite being several inches taller, found himself being left behind.

'Is there a rush?' he asked, increasing his stride and coming up beside her.

Sophie laughed. 'Maybe. We'll get to the car park then turn south-east for the return path. There are a couple of bench seats by the look of it, so it might be a suitable place for our coffee stop.' She took a handkerchief out of her pocket and mopped her brow, but she didn't slow down.

They reached the picnic area just ahead of the person on the more southerly path, and Sophie stopped and looked around her.

'Good morning,' she said as the man approached. 'It's a lovely day, isn't it?'

The stranger nodded but didn't reply. He was tall, of average build and with his dark hair brushed back tightly. His eyes were hidden behind dark glasses. He didn't return Sophie's cheery smile.

Sophie waved vaguely towards the binoculars hanging around his neck. 'See anything interesting? We spotted a family of sika back there, and a few birds, but the sun's getting a bit too bright for them now.'

'Not much,' came the gruff reply.

As he looked towards her, Sophie noticed a thin scar that ran down the left side of his face. Not the kind of scar that would have been caused by a work accident, not to her knowledge. It was almost certainly a knife scar, caused by an extremely sharp blade run expertly down the facial skin. He turned towards a nearby black Range Rover fitted with darkened windows, and climbed in. Within a minute the vehicle was out on the road, disappearing around a bend leaving dust in its wake.

'What was that all about?' Martin asked.

'He was the man we saw earlier, watching the taped-off area. I spotted him as we made our way along the tree line. I just wanted the opportunity to see him close up.'

He laughed. 'You're incorrigibly nosey. I can't believe how suspicious you are.'

'Dead right I'm nosey. Two dead bodies, and we find someone hanging about in the trees and looking at the site? He was no birdwatcher, I'll bet you a bottle of wine on it. The real question is, what was he really looking out for?' She glanced back at her husband. 'Now I need that coffee. Shall we head over to that bench, the one in the sun? I'd suggest a pub lunch later, but are we still on for a meal out tonight?'

'Absolutely,' he replied. 'The Italian restaurant in Swanage, the one that serves great fish. So I think we should steer clear of too much booze just now. Agreed?'

'If you say so, O wise one. But there's a nice pub down at Coldharbour and I quite fancy a pint and a sandwich. But only if you agree.'

He waited until she'd finished pouring their coffees, slipped his hand inside her jacket and attempted to tickle her armpit. Sophie shrieked, scaring away the birds that had landed close to their table hoping for a few crumbs.

CHAPTER 8: FIDELIO

Late Saturday morning, Week 1

Tony Sorrento drove fast, heading north on the narrow Sugar Hill Road, then turning east onto the main A35 arterial road towards Poole. Why should he be feeling irritated? Moreover his scar itched slightly, a sure sign that he was tense. Again, why? The abandoned car had remained undiscovered for more than two weeks, far longer than his boss, Wayne Woodruff, had ever anticipated. The bodies inside would be badly decomposed by now, reducing the chances of yielding clues that might point to something other than suicide as the cause of death. So why was he still feeling tense? He couldn't identify the cause of his worry. Maybe some part of him had hoped that the car would remain undiscovered forever, however illogical such a hope would be. Woodruff had anticipated a lull of about a week, had hoped for ten days and had in fact gained over a fortnight. He should be feeling pleased, not knotted up like this. It had been a mistake to make the journey across this morning. What had he expected to gain from the visit, for Christ's sake? Police tape around the clearing and a couple of dozy coppers standing around not doing very much, that's all there'd been, and he could have predicted exactly that from previous encounters with the police.

His mind ran back over the hour or so that he'd spent tracking across the nature reserve. He'd been careful to park on the more remote west side, avoiding the obvious eastern entries that were closer to the scene. He'd seen nobody during the time he'd spent following minor paths across the heath, choosing sparse tracks that kept inside the tree line as much as possible. His only encounter had been with that woman just as he'd got back to the car. Maybe it was her manner that had made him feel uneasy, so alert and watchful despite her cheerful manner. He'd seen her eyes flicker over him and glance at the car. She'd had that look about her, observant, missing nothing. She might even have noted the vehicle registration. Maybe he'd get rid of this one, ask Gordy to trade it in for something new. Could it be managed within a week? Gordy would know. The exchange would have to be kept low profile though. He was a professional, after all, and followed the code meticulously. Get rid of anything that might conceivably end up giving the cops a lever, however small. It doesn't matter whether it's animal, vegetable or mineral. Just chop it, quickly and efficiently, leaving no trace. That was the code.

* * *

Gordon Mitchell was relaxing in his back garden when the call came through on his mobile phone. He glanced at the caller display and grimaced. His wife, Marilyn, was dozing in her recliner chair, her swollen pregnant stomach gently rising and falling in time with her snores. Their two sons were quiet for once, lying on a rug and reading books about space flight, in keeping with their latest choices of future careers: pan-galactic space warriors. Last month it had been yeti hunters. Gordon pressed the receive button as he walked into the cool shadow of the house.

'Yes, Tony?'

He listened quietly to the requests, becoming increasingly annoyed as his employer's series of demands mounted. That harsh, grating voice was fast ruining what had been a very pleasant Saturday afternoon.

'Of course,' he said as the caller finished. 'Leave it with me. Bye.'

Gordon poured himself another glass of chilled fruit juice and returned to his seat in the garden. He sometimes felt like cursing the day, eight years before, when he'd first found himself working for the Woodruffs. He'd been drinking heavily, gambling too much and getting into debt. The offer of work from Phil Woodruff and Tony Sorrento had provided a way out of the impasse facing him at the time, particularly since his largest debt had been with a gambling club they owned. Once they'd discovered his background in legal support work, the solution was obvious. He took the job they offered and felt extremely grateful at the time. But now? At times he felt like a trapped animal, unable to extricate himself from the tangled net of dodgy contracts, shady deals and dubious agreements that formed a large part of his work for the family business. And he'd developed a real flair for it, a knack of spotting ways to swing deals on the cheap. At least they'd never asked him to do anything violent, but he knew full well that his working life revolved around activity that teetered on the edge of criminality. He still marvelled at the way he'd managed to keep it all hidden from his family. Marilyn thought he worked for a legitimate property company. His elderly parents held him up as a paragon of virtue. If only they knew.

He glanced across at Marilyn, just beginning to stir from her slumber, and his two sons, still intently studying their space explorer books. Whatever happened in the coming years, they must be protected, kept in the dark about the true nature of the employment that kept them in such a comfortable lifestyle. He walked back into the house, starting the series of phone calls that would result in a new vehicle for Sorrento at the end of the week. As if Tony couldn't show some patience and wait a bit longer. But no, everything had to be done now, with a vehicle that matched his exact specification. No delay, no understanding that he, Gordon, might want a weekend free of work-related concerns in order to spend some precious time with his family. Just the usual, self-centred attitude from the gang's hard man, a man it was wise not to cross. Not if you valued your health and well-being.

The calls took well over an hour, spent wheedling with a series of bad-tempered individuals, all angry at being summoned from their leisure activities. Finally Gordon put down the phone and sighed. All done. But he still couldn't understand the need for so much hurry to replace the vehicle. Unless Sorrento had done something silly. He wondered if Wayne Woodruff knew about it. Maybe he should do a little bit of gentle stirring. He called Wayne.

Ten minutes later he made a pot of tea and took it out to the garden where his wife was now awake and reading. She smiled gratefully and blew him a kiss as he deposited the tray on the low table beside her.

'Biscuits and lemonade, boys,' he called.

* * *

Marilyn had been awake for far longer than her husband suspected. She'd been watching him though her half-closed eyelids, observing his nervous pacing in and out of the house. She knew a lot more about his work than he thought and, more importantly, the kind of people he worked for. And she knew that he had been on the phone to that hard man, Tony Sorrento. She'd been checking Gordon's mobile phone for some months now, reading his text messages, looking at his call logs and noting his contacts. And she'd discovered the nature of the work he did for his employers. At first she'd been dismayed and had wondered if they still had a future together. But, at heart, she still believed Gordon to be a good man. He idolised her and the two boys, and nothing seemed to be too much trouble for him as far as his family was concerned. She'd tracked back through their early married life and beyond, and spotted that his current employment had begun at a time when he'd been at a real low point. She was sure that at any other time in his life he wouldn't have touched a job offer from the Woodruffs with a barge pole.

She sighed and reached for the cup of tea that Gordon had placed beside her. He was unhappy and deeply so, she could see that. She could also see that he'd dearly love to find a way out of the clutches of the Woodruffs. Maybe that could be her role in life, rescuing her husband from his near enslavement, like a latter-day Fidelio. A smile came to her face with the thought. Marilyn Mitchell, fantasy heroine of the operatic stage. And five months pregnant.

CHAPTER 9: TICKLED TOES

Monday morning, Week 2

'Just here, look. There's a contusion to the back of the skull.'

Sophie looked at the position indicated by Benny Goodall's latex-encased finger. 'How significant? Would it have caused loss of consciousness or even dazing?'

The pathologist took a step back from the corpse of Ted Armitage. 'It would have made him see stars and resulted in extreme dizziness if nothing else. But at his age, there's a good chance that he'd have been reduced to unconsciousness, if only for a short time.'

'How obvious is it? What I mean is, could it have been missed if we'd assumed suicide and not been suspicious?'

'It's possible, I suppose. I don't think I'd have missed it, but . . .'

'Others might have?'

Goodall shrugged. 'We're all overworked, Sophie. We all find ways of cutting corners just to make our lives a bit more tolerable.'

'But some cut corners more than others?'

There was no response.

'What about the blood tests?'

'Slight traces of sedatives in both of them.'

'So they might have been drugged?' Sophie said. 'Then hauled out to the car, driven to that spot and the car rigged up to pour exhaust fumes in. So were their deaths due to carbon monoxide poisoning?'

'The signs seem to point that way, yes. It'll be another couple of days until we get back the accurate blood tests. That should be definitive, and give us the exact amount of sedative in their bloodstreams and should also allow us to extrapolate the carbon monoxide levels back to their approximate time of death. Then you'll be in a better position to draw definite conclusions.'

'But it's all pointing one way, isn't it, Benny?'

He nodded. 'Sadly, yes. Normally we'd have spotted the visual signs from their skin colour, but with the condition they were in, that was difficult.' He paused. 'When's the daughter arriving to identify the bodies?'

'Later this morning, when her surgery's finished.' Sophie looked across at Sylvia's body. 'You'll tidy them up, won't you Benny? She might be a doctor, but seeing them in this state would send her over the edge.'

'Of course. My staff are pretty skilled at camouflage.'

'What will you do if she asks to see their full bodies, like this, rather than just the normal head view?'

'Is that likely, even if she is a doctor? What would be the point?'

'Better to be prepared. I think I might stay, if that's okay. I'd like to be here to see her reaction. By the way, are there any clues as to how the sedatives were introduced? Pills? Or by spiked drinks? Maybe even an injection?'

'It's impossible to say. The skin tissue has started decomposing so we wouldn't be able to spot the tell-tale signs of any recent injections. As to the other methods, it's unrealistic after this amount of time.'

Sophie frowned. 'Okay. Sedatives would be easy for a doctor to get hold of, and administer as well. The parents would trust her, wouldn't they?'

'Possibly. So you think this might put her in the frame?'

'All options open, Benny. Let's have a coffee and wait. I've bought a pack of new stuff for you. Martin says it's the best instant coffee he's tasted recently. Worth a try? I've promised to tie him up and tickle his toes if he's wrong.'

Goodall looked aghast. 'And that's a punishment? What would you do for a reward?' He covered his ears and closed his eyes. 'No, don't tell me. I couldn't handle it.'

* * *

Sharon Giroux arrived an hour later with her husband. She was pale and seemed slightly unsteady on her feet. Sophie left the mortuary assistant to take charge and guide the small group into the viewing room. She stood back against the wall in order to watch the couple as they approached the two bodies. Sharon turned and nodded as each head was momentarily uncovered. Sophie then left the room in order to leave the bereaved couple alone with the dead parents. She stood outside, waiting for when they came out.

Sophie laid a hand on Sharon's arm. 'Is there anything I can do, Sharon? You must be feeling devastated by all this.'

The reply came as a whisper. 'I feel lost. They were always there, always in the background. They were the reason I am what I am. And now? I just feel adrift.'

'You need to know that we're treating the deaths as suspicious.'

'What?' Sharon stumbled and grabbed hold of her husband's arm.

'The pathologist picked up several irregularities. Nothing is certain yet because he hasn't got the results of all the tests, but it's looking increasingly likely. I don't want to waste any time, so I've already launched a murder investigation, although that fact won't be released to the press until tomorrow when the final blood test results are back with us.'

Pierre looked puzzled. 'Why blood tests?'

'We're fairly sure they were sedated.'

Sharon almost exploded. 'I knew it! I knew there was something wrong. I tried for days to convince those two clowns, Blackman and McCluskie, but they didn't believe me.'

'They followed standard procedure, Sharon. I checked when I took over. All police forces have a policy in place. Missing children are treated very differently, but with adults who are not deemed to be at risk there's always leeway given at first, simply because so many are just away for a day or two with good reason. I can understand why you feel angry and frustrated but remember what I told you. Your parents had already been dead for well over a week when you reported them missing.' Sophie was hiding her own feelings about the mishandled early stages. One thing was for sure, Blackman and McCluskie hadn't heard the end of the matter.

'I'll need to visit your brother, Sharon. Is he likely to be in later this morning?'

'It's probable. He tends not to get out of bed until nearly noon, so I'd say that the chances are good.'

'Who inherits, Sharon? Have you had a chance to find out if they left a will?'

'Not yet. I know they did leave one, and it will be with their solicitors, but I don't know the details. I think Rod and I inherit, along with something for Uncle Pete. They really appreciated his help in trying to keep Rod on the straight and narrow, so they always told us that he'd get something.'

* * *

'I've told all this stuff to those other two plods. They were here a couple of days ago.'

'Did I hear you use the word plods, Mr Armitage?' Sophie looked coldly at the dishevelled man standing in his doorway. He was attempting to tuck a grubby shirt into even grubbier jeans while holding onto a mug of tea. Barry Marsh stood to one side. 'Do you think it's a wise choice of words to use? I'm the SIO for this case. I can make life easier or more difficult for you, largely depending on the mood I find myself in. Words like that don't make me feel especially well-disposed. Maybe you'd like to rephrase?'

'Sorry,' Rod muttered. 'Those two other detectives. And the uniformed ones who called on Friday. That's all it seems to be. Questions and then more questions. And now you arrive. That'll mean more questions, won't it?'

Sophie nodded. 'Yes it will. But that's the only way we'll make any progress. Can we come in?'

She didn't wait for an answer but pushed past Rod into his small living room, Barry Marsh following close behind. The place was still moderately tidy following the search of a couple of days earlier. Sophie turned to Rod.

'I heard about how my two fellow detectives did an unpaid cleaning job for you. They'll be glad to hear that you've kept it more or less tidy since then.'

Rod merely shrugged and dropped into a nearby armchair. Sophie chose to sit on a hard-backed chair set to one side, with Marsh sitting beside her, notebook in hand. The sofa looked too stained to risk her clothes.

'So, Rod, you've had plenty of time to reflect on what you've already told my fellow officers and think about its accuracy. What day was it you saw your parents for that evening meal?'

'The Tuesday, nearly three weeks ago. I'm sure of it now.'

'And you said that you all had Spaghetti Bolognese to eat, is that right?'

He nodded.

'What clothes were your parents wearing, Rod? Start with your mum.'

Rod looked blank. 'How d'you expect me to remember something like that?'

'What about your dad? You told the others that he came in from the garden just before you ate. Was he in old clothes?'

'I think so.'

'The local weather records show it was raining lightly in Blandford for the first part of that evening. Was he in a jacket when he came in?'

Rod shut his eyes and grimaced, as if it was asking a lot of him to make him concentrate in this way. 'Yeah. He had an old jacket on, a sort of greeny colour. He hung it on the back of the kitchen door, I think.'

'And underneath?'

Rod shook his head. 'I can't remember.'

'How did you sit at the table? Who was where?'

A pause. 'I sat opposite Mum. Dad was at the top. He might have had a blue jumper on.'

'What about your mum? Can you remember anything now?'

'She might have been in blue as well. She was talking about her new jeans, I think.'

'How does she make her Bolognese? Was it ready prepared or does she make her own? You told my two colleagues that it wasn't one of your favourites but that your dad liked it. Is that right?'

Rod nodded. 'Mum makes her own, though she uses a jar of sauce. Dad gets on to her about making it properly with purée and other stuff, but she stands her ground.'

'What did you talk about? Other than the money that you borrowed, I mean.'

'Nothing much. Dad's a man of few words, and most of them are complaints.'

'TV programmes, maybe? Their plans for the summer?'

'If you must know, they spent most of the time talking about Sharon and how she might be enjoying her bloody holiday in Cornwall. That's all it ever is, all the fucking time. Sharon, Sharon, Sharon. How wonderful she is, how wonderful her kids are. What a lovely house she has. How important her job is. What a great husband she's got. It drives me fucking mental.'

Sophie watched silently as he sank back into his chair and closed his eyes. There had been real venom in Rod's voice. Interesting, and worth following up. Was it just envy of a higher-achieving sibling, or did it go deeper?

'How much money did you borrow from your mother, Rod?'

'I've already told your lot that. Fifty pounds.'

Sophie nodded. 'It's just that we noticed she'd taken five hundred pounds out of her savings account earlier that day. And you paid an overdue rent bill for that amount at about the same time.'

'Okay. It was five hundred, 'cause I needed it, otherwise I'd have lost this place.'

'So why didn't you tell us that to start with?'

Rod sighed. 'cause I didn't want Sharon finding out. She'd never let me forget it.'

'Did you speak to your parents at any later time? Even by phone?'

'No.'

'Did you try? Did you phone and maybe fail to get an answer?'

'Yeah, later in the week.'

'Go on.'

'Mum was still worried that I might be kicked out of here 'cause the landlord had threatened me with it before. So I tried to call her and let her know I was okay. But the phone just rang.'

'There's an answer machine at their house. Why didn't you leave a message for her?'

'I don't know. I hate the bloody things so maybe that's the reason. I s'pose Dad might have picked up on it, or even Sharon.'

'It would be helpful if you could remember the day, Rod. We'd have a clearer idea of the sequence of events. So?'

Rod ran his fingers through his untidy hair. 'Christ. You're stressing me out. Maybe the Friday or Saturday. I don't know.'

'It's important that you produce a list of your whereabouts each day that week. It shouldn't be too hard. You were working for your uncle, weren't you? Add who you were with, if you can remember.'

Sophie stood up. 'I'll leave DS Marsh here to give you a hand. We're trying to build up a timeline of the events that week. It will help us to home in on the probable date for their deaths. So it's important for you to be as accurate as possible.'

* * *

Rae Gregson, the unit's junior member, had spent the morning preparing an incident room at Blandford's police station, directing technical staff on the placement of computers, printers and scanners sent across from county headquarters. The systems were now being networked together as she finished off the details on the incident board, organised in her usual meticulous way. She was inspecting her work, hands thrust into her skirt pockets, when her boss arrived in the incident room.

'That looks good, Rae.' Sophie looked at the material that Rae had fixed to the board. 'Some of Rod Armitage's recollections match what we've discovered, by the way. There's an old green jacket hanging on the back door of their house with gardening gloves stuffed in the pockets. He remembered his father taking it off and hanging it there.'

'Doesn't prove anything, though, does it, ma'am?'

'Of course not, you cynic. We've taught you too well.'

'I traced that car you asked about. It's a company vehicle, registered in Bournemouth. Woodruff Holdings. I haven't taken it any further.'

'No, that's fine. I'll maybe get Barry to give Bob Thompson a bell to see if he recognises the name. Normally I'd just call Kevin McGreedie, but he's on leave at the moment. If anything interesting crops up I'll switch you back onto it. Can you continue digging into the family background? We need to find out if there are any skeletons in the closet. Okay?'

CHAPTER 10: GOING DOOLALLY

Monday afternoon, Week 2

Rae Gregson had already made some headway with her research into the background of the immediate family members, and her discoveries fitted in with what they already knew. Edward Armitage had been retired for ten years. He'd been the manager of the local bus station, having risen through the ranks from his first job as a bus driver. He'd been a stickler for detail, judging from the comments Rae had gleaned from the bus company, clearly judging that cleanliness and punctuality were what the travelling public most desired from their local bus services. Quite right, Rae thought. And maybe a similar approach to his family life had been the cause of the friction with his son. Although she hadn't yet had the pleasure of meeting the rather wayward Rod, Rae had collated all the information about him that had come in from the two previous detectives and the uniformed squad. Even at this stage of the investigation, it was looking increasingly likely that father and son had been at loggerheads for many years.

Edward had been seventy-five years old at the time of his death. He'd obviously been hard-working, and Rae guessed he must have been proud of his rise to a managerial role, having come from a family of farm labourers. Certainly the clues tended to suggest that he looked down a little on family and friends who had not progressed quite so well in their careers. Rae wondered if his attitudes, along with his motives for pushing ahead with his own career, had been formed because of his marriage to Sylvia. She had been well educated and was working in a bank when she'd met the young Edward. Her own family background had been in farming, but not as labourers. Her parents had owned a sizable farm several miles to the west of Blandford, and she'd attended a private school as a girl. Her prize possessions had included several gymkhana cups won as a teenager, still kept polished in a display cabinet in the elderly couple's bungalow. Sylvia had never returned to work after the birth of her two children. She'd received a windfall from a favourite uncle and this had helped with the purchase of the bungalow and the residual money had helped the family through some lean times as Ted was working his way through junior roles at his work. Sylvia had volunteered for support work with several local charities once the two youngsters had left home, and these duties seemed to have kept her busy. Rae did wonder about this. Sylvia had obviously been better educated and more intellectually able than her husband, yet seemed to have done little with her life in her middle and later years. Had she found fulfilment in her charity work? It was possible, but had it really been enough?

Sharon had inherited her mother's brains, but amplified several times. She seemed to have been a ferociously dedicated pupil while at school, winning prizes every year, finally securing a place to study medicine at Birmingham University. Her parents must have been overawed by their daughter's achievements, and probably used them as an emotional lever against the intransigence of Sharon's younger brother, Rod, the exact opposite in so many ways. Rae was beginning to understand the result. A family that might have seemed happy enough on the surface, but which bubbled with internal pressures underneath. Was this the ultimate cause of the tragedy that had happened several weeks previously? There was no way to tell at the moment. There were many families with similar tensions and comparable pressures, but they didn't dissolve into a whirlpool of brutal murder. And hadn't the boss always said that extreme family tensions tended to erupt into unplanned violence, bloody and messy? Usually easy to solve? The murder of the elderly Armitage couple didn't fit that description, for sure. So what extra forces had been at work? She decided to widen her background research and look into Rod's friends and acquaintances, then examine Sharon's own family situation. She had a short-list of people who had employed Rod during recent years. Maybe it was time to pay a few visits. And then a similar probe into the very different life of his sister. Was she just too good to be true?

* * *

'Ted was my half-brother. He was a good fifteen years older than me. His mother died when he was about ten and Dad remarried. I'm the result. We were almost different generations because of the age gap, but we got on well enough. He was a steady, reliable sort of bloke.'

Pete Armitage was in the small office from where he ran his decorating business. He employed a part time secretary, but she only worked mornings and had left an hour earlier. Rae was standing to one side of the desk as Pete sorted through the morning's paperwork, signing invoices and documents the secretary had left for his attention.

'What about Sylvia? How did the two of them get on?' Rae tucked a few loose strands of dark hair behind her ears as she spoke.

'She was lovely. Just the kind of woman most men would give their right arm for. She loved her home and her family, and she was so supportive of Ted. They doted on each other. It's a bloody tragedy, what's happened. I'm still in shock.'

'Can you think of any reason why anyone would want to harm them?'

'No. The idea's ridiculous. Your lab people must have made a mistake. No one would want to harm them. I know there's been friction with Rod, but he's got no violence in him. Take it from me.'

'But as you said, there has been friction,' Rae suggested. 'And stretching back some time.'

'Rod's always had a chip on his shoulder. It was there when he was still a small boy, it was there when he was growing up and it's still there now. But I still don't think he could harm anyone in his family.' Armitage paused. 'I suppose, from his point of view, Sharon seemed to have all the luck. The brains, the looks, the talent. What he always fails to see is that she's worked hard to get where she is. Okay, he was never going to match her in educational stuff, but he gave up too easily on everything else as well. I know she's naturally attractive, but he'd have been a lot better if he'd looked after himself and paid a bit more attention to his appearance.'

'So he resented her even as a child?' Rae suggested.

'Yeah. He'd even try to get her into trouble. It never worked though. His lying was always totally transparent, so we all knew to double check on what he said. And Sharon could outwit him anyway. She could see one of his half-baked schemes coming a mile off. It was sad in a way. It seems a bit disloyal of me telling you this, but you need to realise that he's useless at planning and scheming. He couldn't plan his way out of a paper bag.'

'It's just confirmation, Mr Armitage. We've already sussed the gist of what you're saying. Has Rod had any close relationships?'

'There were a couple of longstanding girlfriends, but he was never one for commitment, so they left. He only ever realised what he'd lost when it was too late. He'd mope for weeks after they'd gone, but what could he expect? That's what I told him. He never put himself out for them, so why would they bother? Plenty more fish in the sea. Tastier ones as well.'

'Did Rod have a reference when he joined you?'

'Are you joking? No one has ever given Rod a good reference as far as I'm aware. He's a bone-idle shirker. I've refused to give him one, now he's left me. My name would be mud around here if he got another job on the basis of a false reference that I'd given him. I have a good reputation in Blandford and I want to keep it that way, thank you very much.'

'But you've always got on well with Sharon? You sounded a bit in awe of her.'

Armitage looked up. 'I never thought of it like that. I suppose you're right. We Armitages are ordinary people. To have one of us get as far as Sharon has is really something special, so I suppose you're right. We're all a bit in awe of her, I expect. But she's very supportive of the family. We all know we can turn to her for advice. She's very approachable.'

'What about her husband?'

'Oh I like him. I know he's French, but he's a great bloke. They make a lovely couple.' He made a point of looking at his watch. 'Look, time's getting on. I need to be back at the current job, otherwise God knows what mess my new apprentice will be making. Can you just phone me if you need anything else?'

* * *

Rae's next visit was to the Giroux family home, a large detached house in an upmarket part of Blandford. Pierre answered the door and, after Rae had introduced herself, told the detective that his wife was still at work and wouldn't be home until well into the evening.

'It's you I came to see, Mr Giroux. Just for a few minutes?'

She followed him through the hall into a comfortably furnished lounge.

'I'd like the full details of your recent holiday in Cornwall, if possible taking it day by day.'

'So we're suspects?'

Rae gave a thin smile. 'I'm sure you watch enough crime drama to realise that we have to account for everybody close to the deceased. Don't jump to conclusions, Mr Giroux.'

She noted the details as he related each day's activities. He'd travelled to Oxford by train in the middle of the first week of the holiday to visit his office, something he did each week.

'But you normally drive there, don't you?'

'From here, yes. But it's not a long drive from Blandford, usually about two hours. Coming from Cornwall is a different matter. Besides, I managed to get a lot of work done on the train, so I saved time in the long run.'

'Which way did you go? Did you change at Reading?'

He nodded. 'I stayed in the same guest house I always use. I'm there for one or two nights each week. My contract requires me to be in the office for two days each week, and I'm happy to oblige. Working from home is all very well, but those of us who do it still need some contact time in the office. Much of my work is electronic though, so I use email a lot.'

Rae finished her notes. 'And when did Dr Giroux go to her medical conference? Was that in the second week?' She flicked through her notes, crosschecking.

'Yes. On the Monday and Tuesday of our second week. She took the train as well. We only took one car with us to Cornwall, you see. It seemed a sensible option to leave the car for the rest of the family in Cornwall.'

'Hers would have been a relatively easy journey, wouldn't it?'

'Yes. She was only away for one night.'

They heard the sound of the front door opening and both looked up.

'That'll be Sharon,' Pierre said. 'She often pops home to drop off some paperwork and have a quick cup of tea before she starts her evening surgery.'

Rae stood up as Sharon came into the lounge. 'Hello, Dr Giroux. I'm DC Rae Gregson, from DCI Allen's unit. I'm just visiting to fill in some background details.'

'Right. Anything I can help with?'

'I just wondered if you were aware of anything unusual in the weeks leading up to your parents' deaths? Anything out of the ordinary?'

'Not really. Their lives were pretty routine, as are most people's at their age. The only thing they mentioned was a bit of a mix-up at a funeral they went to at the beginning of last month. Apparently they ended up attending the wrong funeral service, though they extricated themselves before it really got going. I think Rod knows more about it than me. He happened to call on them the same evening and found them a bit upset about it.'

Rae frowned. 'He hasn't mentioned it, as far as I know.'

'He wouldn't, simply because he'll have forgotten about it entirely. Don't think there's anything suspicious in his omission. Things just don't stick in his mind.'

Rae decided to call in on Rod Armitage on her way back to the station.

* * *

Rod was sitting on the front step of his block of flats, enjoying the sunshine and sipping at a can of lager. He looked up as Rae stopped in front of him and showed her warrant card.

'Yeah, I know, I'm a lager lout. But it's not against the law, is it? Or aren't we even allowed to do this now? Bloody police state.'

'I'm not here for that, Mr Armitage. I'm part of DCI Allen's team and I've come round to ask you a few more questions about your parents. Well, one thing in particular. Your sister told me that your parents had some kind of funeral mix-up a while ago. Apparently you saw them later that evening, so you might know more of the details than her. What can you remember?'

'What? When was this?'

'She said it happened early last month, and that they were upset about it. Is that right?'

Rod looked blankly at her for a few moments before his expression cleared. 'Oh yeah. They went to some friend's funeral and ended up in the wrong one. How stupid is that?'

'Can you remember any of the details?'

'No! How would I know about some old codger's funeral? It made me think they were going doolally themselves.'

'Did they say where it was?'

'Poole, I think. They said it was a sunny afternoon and the people there were weird. That's all I remember. Maybe they'd had a bit too much to drink themselves. S'not likely, though. They were mean with the booze.'

'Well, if you do remember anything else, particularly the date, please contact us. You have our details, don't you?'

He nodded and raised his can to his lips, watching as Rae turned back to her car.

CHAPTER 11: RIPPLES ON THE POND

Monday afternoon, Week 2

Tony Sorrento was visiting one of the Woodruff-owned premises in Poole. He drew into the prime parking place at the Boulevard Casino Club and climbed out of the Range Rover. He cast his eyes over the vehicle. He'd asked Gordy for an identical replacement, but now wondered if a silver one might not be a better choice.

'Thinking of a new limo, Tony?' The speaker was a burly man with a pale face who had just come out of the staff door.

Sorrento turned and nodded. 'Let's go inside, Toffee. I need to get to the bottom of that problem you reported. Who was it again?'

'Jimmy Russell. He joined us two years ago. At the start his takings matched everyone else's, but the past eighteen months they're down one month in about every three. He's palming some of the bar money, I'm sure of it, but never when I'm around checking.'

'How much?'

'It probably totals a couple of thou. I'll show you.'

Sorrento followed the club manager into his office, where a spreadsheet displayed on a laptop screen showed the bar takings of recent months, broken down by staff member.

'Does he know that we monitor the takings like this?'

Toffee Barber shook his head. 'None of them do. It's what we agreed years ago, remember?'

'Of course I remember. I made the rule. It's just that it leaks out sometimes.'

'Not here in my club. No leaks.'

Sorrento thought for a few moments. 'Any other clues? New car? New home? New togs? New wife?'

Barber shook his head.

'Drugs, then?'

'Possibly. He's been looking a bit pasty at times, a bit spaced out.'

'I've told you not to employ druggies.'

'And I don't. He was fine when he started, and there's nothing obvious to spot.'

'Is he on tonight?'

'Yeah, from eight until two.'

Tony looked across at the club manager. 'I'll be back to see him as soon as he arrives. Don't let him know. And keep that parking slot free for me.'

* * *

Sorrento was back just before the seven o'clock opening, waiting in the manager's office. He watched coldly from behind the desk as Toffee brought a nervous-looking man into the room and indicated that he should sit at the desk. Toffee moved to stand near the door.

'Happy in your work, Jimmy?'

Russell nodded nervously. The dark suit he was wearing hung loosely on him, and he looked gaunt, strained and anxious. His thin, dark hair lay plastered to his head as if it hadn't been seen shampoo for days, or longer.

'Don't we pay you enough?' Sorrento leaned back and clasped his hands behind his head. He waited.

'Things are a bit tight, I s'pose. Could do with a bit more.'

Sorrento smiled thinly. 'That was a rhetorical question, Jimmy. Maybe you don't know what that means, so I'll explain it to you. You're not meant to answer it. I asked it to make a point. Do you understand now?'

Russell nodded nervously, looking confused.

'You see, I think we do pay you enough. I think we're more than generous when you take everything into account. Wages, bonuses, loyalty rewards. It all adds up, Jimmy. You earn more here than a brainless gimboid like you could expect anywhere else.' Sorrento paused. 'I had a look round the area where you live earlier. A bit grubby, isn't it? I hear you've got debts with one of the local dealers. That's not a direct problem for us, Jimmy, but it explains why you've been palming off some of our money.' He leant across the desktop and pointed his finger a few inches from Russell's face. 'I fucking hate thieves. Fucking vermin. Even worse, druggy thieves. Sewer rats. How much, Jimmy? We reckon that it's about two and a half grand. I want it back, so you've still got a job for the next few months while you pay us what you've thieved. Don't even think about doing a runner because I'll find you and I'll break both your legs. What you do when the debt's paid is up to you, but until then you're mine. Understood?'

All the remaining colour had drained from Russell's face. He said nothing.

'Oh, and that dealer who you owe? I had a quiet word with him and he won't be bothering you for a couple of months. He might come looking for his cash after that, but that's between you and him. He might look like a tough nut to you, Jimmy, but he'll do exactly what I tell him. Now get out of my fucking sight.'

Sorrento watched Russell leave the room, then turned to Barber. 'We'll take three grand off his wages over the next four months. That should leave him with just enough to live on. Once it's paid off, I couldn't give a running fuck what happens to him. Just get rid of him.' He stood up. 'It should never have got this far, Toffee. You should have spotted it earlier, and dealt with it sooner. I've got better things to do with my time than sort out your problems. Things aren't easy now that Phil's dead. Wayne's much too unpredictable and I have to watch over him all the time. I might have to pay a visit to Ricky Frimwell in prison to pick up some tips.'

'Who?'

'He ran a similar setup for a long time, and Phil was a pal of his. That side of Frimwell's operation ran tickety boo, but he was also into much darker stuff. That's what nailed him. I've been thinking for some time that we could make a move on some of his outfits, but Phil's illness put paid to those plans. I've got more influence over Wayne, so it's a good time to make a move. If it comes off, Toffee, there'll be a place for you in the setup, so keep quiet for now. Okay?'

Barber nodded. 'Yeah, of course.'

* * *

Sorrento drove the short distance to the Rising Moon pub. The Woodruff family had owned it for many years and it was still used as the headquarters of their business empire. The nerve centre was a group of offices on the upper floor, including one each for the three current leaders of the venture, Sorrento himself, Justin Griffiths and the surviving Woodruff son, Wayne. A smaller office was used by Gordon Mitchell, their legal expert. The largest room, previously occupied by Phil Woodruff, had been empty since the patriarch's unexpected death the previous month but no one yet felt powerful enough to claim it, not even Phil's son, Wayne.

'Okay, Tony?' Wayne called from his open door as Sorrento passed along the corridor.

Sorrento decided it was time to discuss his expansion plans with the nominal leader. He switched direction and walked into Woodruff's office, closing the door behind him.

'Yeah, fine,' he replied. 'Listen Tony, there's something I was talking to Phil about just before he fell ill, but we didn't move on it because he got bad so quickly. You ought to know about it because I think it was a great idea and would add to our reach.' He sat down opposite Wayne and waited.

'Okay, tell me.' Wayne leant back in his chair, removed his reading glasses and scratched his bristly skull.

'We've got the five pubs, the three nightclubs, three massage parlours and the casino club. Plus the hotel. We were talking back in the winter about ideas for expansion, remember?'

Woodruff nodded. His face gave little away so Sorrento rarely knew exactly where he stood. He'd always got on well with old Phil, but his son was far more unpredictable. And moodier with it.

'There's an easy route to double our holdings without much effort and I mentioned it to your dad. He was thinking about it just before he died, but didn't get to consider it in detail. He was interested and cautious at the same time, and I can understand why.'

'Tell me.'

'We take over some of the places that Ricky Frimwell owned. Phil knew him and Charlie Duff, but steered clear of them for obvious reasons. The thing is, Wayne, Duff won't ever get out. He'll die in prison. Ricky got twenty years. He'll be an old man when he's released. I got Gordy to trace the current legal owners of their properties, and the details were all over the place. But he stuck at it, and apparently it's Frimwell's mum who owns the main interest nowadays through some kind of trust, and she's a bit doolally. Those cafes are in prime locations. They're a bit rundown now but if we bought them we could really do something with them. We might get them at a knock-down price.'

Woodruff paused. 'Yeah, I do remember it being mentioned. I'm not sure, Tony. They're a bit tainted, aren't they? And what about the other stuff? The sex shops? The car workshops? The hotels?'

'We only buy what we want and what we think we can cope with. And only if it adds value to what we've already got. I was thinking that I could go visit them in gaol. Find out a bit more and talk them round if we decide to run with it. Frimwell's mum would probably do whatever he told her. It would double the size of our operation and wouldn't cost us that much. It's you and Sue, me and your mum to decide, Wayne, and I think it's worth looking into a bit more. I'm happy to do the leg-work but I need your agreement.'

'Why would they want to sell?'

'Frimwell's mum's a bit low on ready cash at the mo, and this might cause her to start selling up. But she'll probably only do it if she gets the nod from him. I might be able to talk him into it. I knew Ricky years ago.'

Woodruff thought for a few moments. 'It can't do any harm to do a bit of digging, can it? Okay. But keep a low profile while you're doing it. Those two bastards were nasty, sadistic even, and I don't think we should be making too many ripples on the local pond. I don't want the cops to notice us. That might ruin everything.'

Tony grimaced. 'Come on, Wayne. You know me. We've got our nice friendly insider who'll let us know if we pop up on the cops' radar. It's all sweet.'

CHAPTER 12: MIND PROBE

Monday afternoon, Week 2

Barry Marsh decided that Rae should continue with the visits to friends and family of the Armitage couple while he did some of his own checking. The name Woodruff, mentioned by the boss, meant something to him, he knew, but he couldn't remember any details. It came from the dim and distant past, maybe as far back as the days when he was a newly appointed detective, working in Poole. Bob Thompson, now a DS in Bournemouth, had been his work partner. Would Bob remember more? He'd been second-in-command in DI Kevin McGreedie's unit for several years now, and would probably have access to local intelligence.

He called Thompson and asked if he remembered the name Woodruff.

'Not that I recall, Barry,' came the reply. 'Leave it with me and I'll ask around, but don't hold out any great hopes. Could it be from somewhere else? Didn't you spend a year or so in Weymouth on the beat? Maybe there?'

Marsh wasn't convinced. True, no local Woodruff had shown up on the central criminal database, but he still felt that the name was somehow familiar and, for some reason, had a Bournemouth link. He walked to the coffee machine and made himself a cup. The problem was, the more he thought about it the less likely it was that he would remember. He needed to switch to a different task and maybe then the memory would come back into focus, when it wasn't being forced. He gazed out of the window across to the trees on the opposite side of the road, looking for inspiration. None came so he returned to his desk in order to follow up the next line of inquiry, the quirky story of the Armitage couple's funeral mix-up. Rae had been unable to gain any details from the son but had reported the incident. The two detectives had identified a possible week in late April when it could have occurred. He phoned Poole Crematorium, but to no avail. The administrative officer didn't seem to understand his request. Finally, in frustration, he decided to visit the place and look through the records himself. It was only a twenty-minute drive and he needed to get out of the office for a while. Some fresh air would do him good. He'd check the calendar in the Armitage bungalow before driving to the crematorium.

* * *

'I don't quite understand,' the secretary said. 'How could anyone attend the wrong funeral? We print out a list of the ceremonies each day and post it outside in several prominent positions.'

'That's what I'm here to find out,' Marsh replied. 'I'm looking for the name Georgie Palmer. Do you have a record for a funeral in that name for April the twentieth?'

'Yes, we do. At four in the afternoon.' She pointed at the list for the date in question. 'You can see that the previous service was an hour earlier. Did they get the time wrong?'

'Not as far as I'm aware. They arrived a bit early, that's all I've been told. And this is the complete record for that day? There's nothing missing?'

'Ah well, you see, this is for the full-length ceremonies. We slot in short committals as and when we can if they're needed in a hurry. You know, if someone has a church funeral and just needs five minutes here. They don't go on the main list that we pin up outside.'

'But there's still a record? There must be, surely, if someone's cremated?'

'Oh, yes. The short committals are very quick because they're not always cremated at the time of the ceremony. It's often done later or the next day. There might have been one because of the hour gap before the Palmer funeral.'

She checked her computer records. 'Yes, there was. It looks as though there was a five-minute committal that day. Let me check the name.'

Marsh waited.

'Here we are. Philip Woodruff.'

'What?' He leant across the desk to look at the screen. There it was, in clear lettering. 'I want every single detail associated with that ceremony printed out. Who organised it, who booked it, who paid for it. Nothing missing. Do you understand? And don't breathe a word of this to anyone.'

* * *

'What does it mean, ma'am? It's so unexpected. I don't know what to make of it.'

'Nor do I at the moment, Barry. Let's not speculate too much until we have more facts, so we need to follow it up in more detail. And you still can't remember where you came across the name years ago? Or the context?'

Marsh shook his head. 'I thought it was in Bournemouth, but Bob Thompson thinks otherwise. It'll come to me soon enough, particularly when we start digging.'

'Let's check over what we know. In late April the Armitage couple went to a funeral at Poole and ended up attending a committal by mistake. A few weeks later they're found dead, apparently a case of suicide. I spot someone behaving suspiciously near the scene, and his car is registered as being owned by a company that shares the same name as the deceased person at the mistaken funeral. It could be dismissed as coincidence if the name were a common one like Smith, but Woodruff? How likely is that?' She paused. 'Go and see both the Armitage offspring. We need to push them to remember every detail about that odd funeral mix-up, particularly Rod. What his parents told him will be in his brain somewhere. It's a pity we can't insert a mind probe and download the information direct. Stuff gets completely mashed up in that fuzzy brain of his.'

'Sounds too sinister for me, ma'am. I don't know whether I'd want to be in the police if we could do that. Imagine the other stuff we'd come across at the same time if someone's brain was being wired up.'

'We'd see all their erotic daydreams, I expect. Fascinating.'

He looked horror-struck.

'Only joking, Barry. You shouldn't take everything I say quite so seriously. By the way, Dave Nash called in with an interesting snippet. There was no trace of a reel of tape, either inside the car or outside on the ground.'

'So it proves they didn't tape the hosepipe to the exhaust themselves?'

'It's the kind of mistake that's so easy to make. Someone made what they thought was a really good job of it all, but the devil is in the detail and that's what they've mucked up on. Whoever it was taped the pipe and pocketed the reel afterwards rather than leaving it lying around. A simple error, but it gives us confirmation. Dave's team has combed the whole area and nothing has shown up.'

* * *

Matt Silver, Sophie's boss at headquarters and now a chief superintendent, visited in the late afternoon accompanied by Bob Thompson, a detective sergeant from Bournemouth who was in line for promotion to DI rank. Sophie guessed that Silver was visiting the various investigation units around the county in order to find a home for Thompson once he'd gained his promotion. Would this create a knock-on effect? Would it create a situation where she might lose Barry? She fervently hoped not, but she guessed that Kevin McGreedie, the current DI in Bournemouth, wouldn't want to wait too long before filling the vacancy created by the loss of Thompson. Her own position was a rare one. The rank of DCI was slowly being phased out. Heaven knows what she'd do when they got around to examining her role. She chatted with the duo for several minutes in front of the incident board, before heading to the canteen to buy a drink. She spotted George Warrander sipping a coffee, alone at a table, so she went to join him. He attempted to rise as he spotted her, but she waved him down.

'No need, George. I thought I'd join you for the chat I promised you. How are you getting on?'

'I'm really enjoying my job, ma'am. It's been great so far.'

Sophie sipped her peppermint tea. 'No regrets, then? You must have taken a salary hit.'

'Yes, but I'm sure it will even out in the long run. Anyway, there's no comparison in terms of the value of the job, so I don't have any regrets, not yet anyway.'

Sophie noticed that he still had the same spiky hair style, albeit slightly shorter, that she remembered from two years earlier, when she'd interviewed him during the Donna Goodenough investigation. 'Did you follow the trial?'

'Yes, as much as I could. And the next big one you were involved in, that Duff character. It must have been a strain for you.'

She nodded. 'But everything worked out well in both cases. That's all we can ask for, isn't it? I'm glad you seem to have made such an impressive start, George. I know that Rose can appear to be a bit of a cynic, but she's got a heart of gold underneath that hard-bitten exterior. Why don't you pop up to the incident room sometime in the next day or two? Rae, our DC, has almost finished putting together what we know so far. You and Rose, as the first squad involved, may have some suggestions. I'll let Barry Marsh know.'

'That would be great, ma'am. Thanks. I'd better go. The sarge will be expecting me in a minute or two. I really appreciate your help, ma'am.'

Sophie sat pondering for several minutes, sipping her tea, then returned to her office. It had been a good day. The Armitage deaths were now confirmed as murder rather than suicide, which gave her team something substantial to work on. She now needed some thinking time, to consider how the newly discovered facts fitted in with her mental picture of the events surrounding the Armitage deaths. She knew little about the small town of Blandford Forum, so she had an early evening walkabout of the Georgian town centre, admiring the buildings grouped around Market Place. The buildings looked their best in the sunshine.

'It looks beautiful when it's like this, doesn't it?' Sophie turned to see Pierre Giroux. 'I spotted you admiring our little town, so I thought I'd come across for a chat.'

Sophie smiled at him. 'Yes. I was reading about the history of the big fire here. It must have been terrible when it happened, but the result is an attractive town centre like this.'

'I'm an outsider, and even I love it. You ought to visit the museum sometime. It's fascinating.'

'How's Sharon? Many people go and see their GP when they've lost their parents in a tragedy, but she's hardly likely to do that, is she? I hope one of her colleagues is keeping an eye on her.'

'I think so, and I do my best, Chief Inspector. We talk, but there's not much more I can do. She's taken it hard and isn't sleeping at all well, but I suppose that's to be expected.'

'You just have to give her time, Mr Giroux. But then, the same will be true for you and your children. You'll all be in shock still.'

He nodded. 'It's all too unreal. I keep thinking, this can't be true, this can't have happened. But it has. Once we've had time to calm down, I plan to take them on a short break to France to stay with my family. We all need some normality, even if only for a short time.'

CHAPTER 13: SMARTIES

Tuesday, Week 2

'Now, Georgie boy, don't go getting yourself into any bother out here in the wilds. I'll be back later in the morning to check up on you, and I don't want to find you asleep under a bush.'

The two uniformed officers were back at the Morden Bog Nature Reserve, where George Warrander was scheduled for a morning guarding the incident site. Not that there was much left to guard. The final clear-up of the scene was planned for later in the day, with the removal of all barriers to public access. The car had been taken away, along with all other debris found in the vicinity. In reality he was merely watching over the lengths of "Crime Scene Do Not Cross" tape that still encircled the area and were flapping gently in the breeze. Good job it wasn't raining. That would have turned boredom into misery.

Warrander watched his sergeant, Rose Simons, drive away. Then he took a slow walk around the outer edge of the site, trying to remember exactly how it had looked a few days earlier when they'd first been called to the tragic scene. The scars on the young saplings, formed as the small car had wedged itself into the undergrowth, were still evident. The ground had been churned up by the trailer used to transport the abandoned vehicle to the forensic depot for further examination, and much of the undergrowth had been cleared in the search for evidence. He returned to the point where the track ended as it reached the clearing, and sat on a log. This is quite pleasant, he thought. There was no one about to disturb the serene atmosphere. He watched as a group of rabbits appeared and started to nibble at the tufts of grass and a small weasel-like creature dashed across the path. Warrander took a mint from his pocket and popped it into his mouth. He sat for about fifteen minutes before setting off for another stroll, this time across the centre of the clearing, approaching the area where the car had been found. A thick clump of heather, its flower heads not yet open, lay to one side with some bushy shrubs beyond. Warrander picked up a stick and began to idly poke around in the undergrowth. He stopped suddenly. There, half hidden by the leaves and heather, was a reel of sticky tape. Grey sticky tape, the same shade as the tape used to fix the length of tubing to the exhaust pipe on the Armitage car. How had it been missed by the search teams? He used his walkie-talkie to radio back to the station, then sat down to wait.

Dave Nash was on the scene within half an hour, along with one of his most trusted forensic officers. Sophie Allen and Barry Marsh were not far behind. Nash was clearly puzzled. He looked annoyed.

'It can't have been missed,' he insisted. 'We went over this whole zone inch by inch, and not just once. We even searched it again yesterday, once the car was removed. It's inconceivable that it's been there all the time.' He turned to Warrander. 'How noticeable was it? You've obviously moved it slightly.'

'About an inch. There was just one small part of it showing through. I thought it was a stone at first, but the colour was wrong, and it glinted. That's why I poked it a bit.'

'So a part was definitely visible?'

'Yes, but just a tiny bit. It would have been easy to miss.'

'By you, maybe. But not by my team.' Nash sounded enraged, almost ready to explode. Sophie laid a hand on his arm.

'George didn't mean that the way it sounded. Didn't you have close-up photos taken of the whole area? Maybe they need to be checked before we jump to any conclusions. When you've finished with the first set of photos, get George to poke the reel back into the position he found it in. Get some more shots, then we can compare them with the ones taken on Friday.' She looked again at the roll. 'This looks brand new, as though it's never been used. See the yellow tab at the end? Surely that's the manufacturer's original. Doesn't it look like it to you?'

Nash and Marsh were less sure. The area was searched and photographed again, and the two detectives walked back to their car, reaching it just as a squad car arrived. Rose Simons hurried out.

'What's going on?' she asked.

'George spotted a reel of sticky tape. Forensics are back at the scene,' Marsh explained. 'Maybe you'd better get him away or stay here with him. It's nearly caused Dave Nash to have a heart attack.'

Rose laughed. 'That boy of mine, he's something else, isn't he? I'll put a stop to his smarties ration if you want me to.'

'Maybe you should double it, Rose,' Sophie answered. 'There's another interpretation here, not just the obvious one of a negligent search team. Let's wait and see.'

* * *

Sophie and Marsh watched for a while then drove to the forensic centre.

'It could make quite a difference to us, couldn't it ma'am?'

She nodded. 'Oh, yes. Whatever way you look at it, it's a bit of a game changer. Interpretation one, that the forensic search missed it and it's been there all the time. It appears to make the case for suicide stronger. Interpretation two, that it's been planted overnight. It means someone's just realised their mistake in not leaving the tape and has been back to correct the error.'

'But if that's the case, it's too late, surely? We'll have the photos to show it was planted later. If anything, it will add to the evidence.'

Sophie shook her head. 'No. Think in the long term, Barry. It weakens any potential court case. Any half decent defence lawyer would use it to cast doubt on the competency of the forensic unit, arguing that they must be inept because they missed it. And if they're inept on this issue, what other mistakes have they made? That's how the argument will proceed. It's very clever. Look, we all know it was murder because of what Benny discovered in the post mortem. That was backed up by the missing reel. Now it's turned up, it leaves the medical evidence only. What bothers me is how they knew. Was it just coincidence and they realised their mistake in the last few days, then chose last night to plant it there? Or is it linked to us realising it wasn't there on Friday? The thing is, hardly anyone knew about it. Dave only confirmed that no reel of tape had been found yesterday afternoon. When did Rae post that information on the incident board?'

'It was there when I came back from Poole, so maybe mid-afternoon? Why?'

'Because Dave swears that none of his team would talk, and no one apart from him knew of our hunt for the reel of tape anyway. So who could have seen it on the incident board?'

'The chief super was in yesterday afternoon with Bob Thompson. Blackman and McCluskie called in to drop off a report. Pete Armitage was in because he's putting in an estimate for repainting the inside of the station and needed to see all the rooms. I passed him downstairs as I came in. And there could have been others that I don't know about. Some of the uniformed squad have been in and out. I suppose we'd have to include the cleaners too.' He paused. 'Don't you think this is all a bit ridiculous, ma'am?'

'Maybe. But I'm a bit paranoid, Barry, as you well know.'

* * *

It was as Sophie had expected. The photo evidence taken on the day of the gruesome discovery showed no evidence of any discarded reel of tape in the place where Warrander had found one. Warrander was adamant that a small part of the reel was showing, but this was not the case in the originals, so they now knew that someone had visited overnight to plant the evidence. The problem was compounded by the fact that no new tyre prints were evident, nor had any vehicle stopped in the vicinity during the hours of darkness when there had been no police presence. A small video camera set up to record traffic movement on the nearby road had shown that no cars had stopped at the side of the road, yet the activity sensors had recorded movement, although this could have been wild animals snuffling about in the undergrowth. The chances were that someone had made a long walk in the dark to the forensic site. It was puzzling, and disturbing in its implications. Was someone playing games with them? Or was the explanation simpler than that? Did the culprit not realise the detailed level of photographic evidence that is now made of a crime scene? But in that case, why had nothing been captured on the videos?

She spoke quietly to both Nash and Marsh. 'Keep this to yourselves. The fewer that know about it, the better. If someone was there last night, we don't want them to know that we've found the tape. Let's continue to keep the place under surveillance. Do you think it might be worth doing another quick check of the area? Assuming someone came by car, they may have left traces. Footprints maybe.'

Nash agreed. 'I'll do it. As you say, the fewer that know about it the better.' He returned to his car.

Sophie called Rose Simons, who was still at the nature reserve with Warrander, and explained the situation, emphasising the need for total discretion.

'I know my job, ma'am,' came the reply. 'Others may blab after their second drink, but not yours truly. It takes at least five with me, and they'd have to be doubles. If you want me to, I can tape up young George's mouth when he goes off duty tonight. That roll of sticky tape he found needs to be put to some useful purpose, don't you think?'

Sophie rolled her eyes as she slipped her phone back into her bag. 'I don't envy George Warrander. Rose Simons is a brilliant cop, but her humour can get just a bit too much at times.'

* * *

The two detectives returned to Blandford police station and found Rae Gregson entering more details onto the computer system.

'I went with Sharon Giroux to her parents' solicitor, ma'am,' she said. 'The will is fairly simple, but there was a surprise. She and her brother get fifty percent of the estate each, but that's after twenty thousand has gone to Pete Armitage, her uncle. Apparently it was in appreciation of his efforts to keep Rod on the straight and narrow, mainly through giving him his apprenticeship ten years or so ago.'

'Any idea how much will be involved?' Barry asked.

'Possibly about three hundred thousand in total. The bungalow should get about a quarter of a million, and they had some bank investments and insurance. Not all the details are in yet, though, so that figure might change.'

'That's a lot of money for someone like Rod,' Rae suggested. 'A hundred and forty thousand or thereabouts? How did Sharon react?'

'She wasn't surprised, if that's what you mean. I think she already had an idea of the bungalow's value and the savings were about what most people would expect. I expect it'll be Rod who'll be a bit shocked.'

'Is it enough to kill for, though? And they both knew they'd be getting it at some time.'

Sophie spoke. 'It might have been whittled down a lot over the coming years, particularly if care bills had come into play. It's possible that in another decade the amount might have dropped by half. Care homes aren't cheap. And Sharon would know that. She'd make enough calls on elderly people to know exactly how much it costs.' She paused. 'The problem is, if it was Sharon, why would she go to this much bother? It was very elaborately set up. Surely, as a doctor, she'd have access to simpler ways of doing it?'

'They always get caught, though, don't they, ma'am?'

'We don't know of the ones that don't, Rae. So we can't be sure of the extent of it.'

CHAPTER 14: PARANOID

Wednesday, Week 2

Marilyn Mitchell had widened her investigation into the Woodruffs' business empire. She now had a fairly clear idea of the extent of their reach across south Dorset. They owned pubs, cafes, hotels and massage parlours in most of the major towns in the area, although most were in the Bournemouth-Poole conurbation. She already knew the hierarchy within the organisation, with her husband at number five, below the family members and Tony Sorrento, but she guessed that Gordon's official status was for official documentation only. In practice he was a mere employee with no direct input into the making of important decisions. Those discussions would be family only, with the addition of Gordon's boss, Tony Sorrento and the other mainstay, Justin Griffiths. In fact, following the death of Phil Woodruff, it seemed probable to her that Tony would be moving into the top slot, judging by the messages she'd seen coming Gordon's way.

She sat back and looked at her laptop screen. Mind-mapping software was just wonderful for displaying complex connections like this. There was the whole empire laid out in front of her, businesses and people, assembled slowly over the past couple of days. Her own work as a commercial property specialist had trained her in the methodology of this type of research and she always set password access to her work files. Gordon need never know what she was researching. She sipped her coffee and pondered. She needed to identify a weak point that would allow Gordon some get-out leverage, and at the same time find him another job somewhere. Maybe they'd have to move away from Dorset, but anything was better than staying here and watching her husband slowly lose his self-belief. It was up to her to create an escape route for him before things deteriorated further. She'd seen what he'd spent the previous day working on from his emails. Arranging for Sorrento to visit Ricky Frimwell in prison, apparently to discuss a business deal. Maybe even seeing Charlie Duff as well. Marilyn had no great knowledge of the criminal underworld, but even she had heard those names and was aware that they were in jail for multiple murder, rape and human trafficking. Up to now the Woodruff gang had restricted itself to operating in a shady area just outside the law, and they had steered clear of any serious criminality, as far as she knew. But now? Why would Sorrento want to talk to that evil duo?

* * *

Tony Sorrento sat in the visitors' room and watched Ricky Frimwell walk towards him. He still had that arrogant swagger, his eyes still darted around the room, observing everyone but giving nothing away. He nodded as he sat down. Tony pushed one of the cartons of coffee across the table. He'd been allowed to bring the two coffees across from the machine after intense checking by the guards, even though he'd already been searched on entry. Remind me never to end up in jail, he thought. Not under any circumstances.

'This is an unexpected pleasure, Tony,' Frimwell said, with heavy sarcasm. He swigged from the cardboard carton.

'It's business, Ricky, pure and simple. Some of your old premises are sitting empty, gathering dust. They're not doing anyone any good, 'specially your mum, who's the main owner now, I guess. We want to do a deal with her 'cause we could use the cafes and clubs. I thought it would be better to see you first to sound you out.'

Frimwell didn't hurry to answer. He took another sip of coffee and stared coolly across the small table. 'You did right,' he finally said. 'I'd have been fucking angry if I heard you'd seen her without talking to me first. I might be in this fuck of a place, but I've still got some influence. I hear what's going on outside.'

Sorrento nodded. Privately, he thought Frimwell was little more than a violent, sadistic thug with no business acumen whatsoever. That had been plain at his trial a year earlier, where the evidence had shown that the co-leader of the Duff gang was a psychopath with no real grip on reality. And as for his uncle, the even more twisted Charlie Duff, well, maybe there was no need to see him at all if this visit went well. Sorrento knew that the duo had murdered one of his own contacts, Blossom Sourlie. It took all the self-restraint he had to remain calm and appear to be pleased to be in Frimwell's company when all he really wanted to do was to hit him hard in the face and break his nose.

'We can both come out on top, Ricky,' he said. 'Well, in your case it'll be your mum, what with you stuck in here for a while yet. But the money could be waiting for you when you get out.'

'Buy or rent?' Frimwell asked.

'We'd only be interested in buying them,' Sorrento replied. 'We don't do renting. And it's not all your places. I'd need to map them out and see what would work for us. But we wouldn't cheat you, Ricky. We'd offer a fair sum. Your mum'll be in clover.'

Frimwell sat brooding, silent. He was powerless and Sorrento knew it. This was all bravado, the pretence that he still had influence over the world outside the prison walls. Even before his arrest, in the last few years of his gang's existence their self-indulgent ways had put them on a slippery, downward slope. Sorrento knew that his own contact in the Duff gang, Sourlie, had tried to instil some order into their activities, but had failed miserably. It had been impossible to work with such out-and-out psychopaths.

'I did wonder whether I'd need to speak to Charlie as well as you. What do you think?'

Frimwell shook his head. 'Don't even try. As far as I know, he's hardly spoken a word for a year. He's in and out of the nutters' ward like a fucking yoyo. They probably keep him drugged up to the eyeballs.'

'Okay.' He hid his relief. He knew psychopathy wasn't contagious, like measles, but the fewer murdering thugs he had to mix with, the better. Thank God the Woodruffs had never shown the same addiction to violence that Frimwell and his deranged uncle had displayed. 'So, do we have a deal?'

'Yeah. But don't cheat me, Tony. You'd fucking regret it.'

'I'm legit, Ricky. I push hard for good prices, but I don't cheat people. Your mum'll have no complaints.'

He left after a few minutes more of small talk.

During the three hour drive back to Bournemouth, he considered the various options. If he could get this deal to work and, despite his promise to Frimwell, at a bargain price, then he'd cement his position as the real brains behind the Woodruff operation. Of course he'd need Gordy's help, but there should be no problems there. The one person he could always rely on was his assistant, Gordon Mitchell.

* * *

Back at the Rising Moon pub, Wayne Woodruff was sprawled in an armchair, a tumbler of scotch in his hand. They were seated in Justin Griffiths's office. Griffiths attempted to smooth down his hair with his hand, forgetting once again that he was almost completely bald.

'So you don't think much of Tony's plan?' Griffiths said.

'It's not the plan, Griffy. He always comes up with good plans and this one is probably as good as his others. It's just that I can't help thinking he's up to something. With Phil only buried last month, the right thing to do is to let things calm down for a while. Stop and take stock. But no, not Tony. He has to push on with everything at top speed. There's no let up. Today Bournemouth, tomorrow the world. I mean, do we really want to nearly double the size of the operation?'

'More dosh for us all, Wayne, if it works well. And Tony's ideas usually do.' He sipped his drink slowly. He couldn't see the problem. 'You're worrying over nothing, Wayne. Tony's never let us down. He's the hardest grafter here.'

'I just wonder if he's getting too ambitious.'

'Okay. You think he's making a move on your role?'

Woodruff nodded.

'Well, with your dad gone, that does just leave the three of us working the business, doesn't it? I s'pose someone has to be top dog, and it sure ain't me. I kind of assumed it'd be you, and I'm sure Tony feels the same. Aren't you being a bit paranoid?'

'I told him to keep a low profile, yet he's off up to Long Lartin to visit Ricky Frimwell like a shot. Won't that set off a few alarms?'

Griffiths shook his head. 'No reason to. He knew Ricky and his mum. Could be totally legit as far as the clink's concerned. And we're not on anyone's radar, are we? So why worry?'

Woodruff finished his drink. 'Okay, if you say so. I was just a bit worried, that's all. Don't breathe a word of this to Tony.' He got up and left Griffiths's office.

Griffiths ran his hand over his head again and leaned back in his chair. That had gone well. He'd let Sorrento know of the meeting once he returned. Tony's plan was beginning to come together, judging by the text message he'd received from him just a few minutes ago. He, Justin, had suspected for some time that Wayne was far more unpleasant than anyone supposed and might even be involved with some recent cases of intimidation and violence. If Tony had really found a way to oust their new leader, then he was all for it, but it wouldn't be easy. After the death of Phil, Wayne was the majority shareholder now, surely?

CHAPTER 15: A BLESSING IN DISGUISE

Wednesday night, Week 2

Bournemouth's central gardens is a long ribbon of lawns and flower beds that runs south towards the beach area and cuts through the centre of the town, following the bubbling water of the Bourne Stream as it flows towards the sea. On a warm, bright evening the paths are used by a large number of people as they make their way towards the bars and clubs near the waterfront. Not so tonight. A chilly wind had set in from the east. Tony Sorrento, sitting on a secluded park bench set amid shrubbery, yawned and stretched out his legs. He looked up as a dark figure approached and sat down beside him.

'Why the need for this?' Sorrento asked. 'I bloody hate having to come out at night. It makes me feel like a fucking criminal. It had better be important.'

'It is,' came the gruff reply. 'You've cropped up on the radar.'

'What?'

'You heard what I said. Woodruff Holdings is now on the official investigation list. I hope you're squeaky clean.'

'How the hell did that happen? Jesus. This is unbelievable.'

'A black Range Rover was parked near Wareham Forest on Saturday, and there was some kind of mix-up at a funeral last month. Neither by themselves would be worth a second thought, but when they generate the same name someone's likely to show an interest, particularly when a double murder is involved.'

Sorrento looked angry. 'It was never meant to be murder, that's what I was led to believe. It was meant to be some kind of weird suicide pact. I only found out about it when it reached the papers.'

The visitor shook his head. 'It was murder alright. They were drugged, then driven to that spot. It showed up during the post mortem. And some clever-clogs taped the hosepipe to the exhaust and pushed it through the window, but then took the tape away with them. How stupid can you get? The crazy thing is, it got put back Monday night after I got a message to Wayne about it. Who did that? What's going on here, Tony?'

'Jesus, I knew nothing about any of this until they discovered the bodies. I just got a message a couple of weeks ago that the problem had been sorted and the old couple wouldn't talk. I had no idea they were dead. I thought they'd just taken a sweetener of a couple of grand. Then I got word that they'd killed themselves, but that all changed when it hit the papers so I went for a look-see on Saturday. That's when my car must have been spotted.'

'It was yours, was it?'

Sorrento nodded. 'But it's registered to the company. I parked a mile away, way over west. And there were other cars there. Why mine, for God's sake? Who reported it?'

'Only the bloody SIO. She was there that morning, snooping around, and you must have set some alarm bells ringing in that suspicious mind of hers.'

Sorrento cast his mind back a few days, trying to remember the scene. 'Blonde? Middle-aged?'

His visitor nodded. 'That's her. Allen. Detective Chief Inspector Sophie Allen. She whistles and everyone dances to her tune.'

An awful realisation hit Sorrento. 'Christ. Isn't she the one that nailed Frimwell and Duff?'

'That's right. Why are you so interested in them?'

'I visited Frimwell today in prison. I drove up to Evesham with a business proposition for him.'

'As long as you didn't use the name Woodruff you should be okay. It's that name that's surfaced, not yours.'

Sorrento calmed down. 'And the other link was the funeral?'

'Apparently the oldies went to Phil's funeral by mistake. Is that right? They must have told someone in the family about it, which is how we got to know.'

Sorrento nodded.

'Why was that a problem? Why weren't they just left to forget the whole thing? They were probably half senile, for God's sake.'

'That's what I told Wayne. But he'd handed over a wodge of cash to our friendly, bent councillor right slap-bang in front of them. I bet they didn't even notice, but someone obviously got paranoid about it. Christ, talk about over-reaction.' He remained silent for a few moments, thinking fast. 'You know, this might not be a disaster after all. As long as it's Woodruff's name that's hit the lights, it might all work out in our favour.'

His visitor looked at him shrewdly. 'Do I sense some devious plotting going on, Tony? Are you up to something?'

'No need for you to know too much. You'll be well looked after if it all turns out okay. Try and deflect any interest, but if things do start to go pear-shaped, make sure it's all directed at Wayne. If you must know, we're planning a bit of a coup, and this could help it on its way. In fact the whole episode might be a bit of a blessing in disguise.'

'I'm hanging fire on the whole thing, Tony, because I don't really know what my position is now that Phil's dead. I had a deal with him that stretched way back. I don't like Wayne, which is why I contacted you rather than him. He's too unpredictable and I can't afford that, not in my position.

The last thing I can afford at this stage in my career is to get involved with an impulsive thug like Woodruff Junior. The deal I had going with Phil was fairly low level, and it was never going to be noticed. But with Wayne? Who knows what direction he'll eventually head off in. And Phil would never have got himself mixed up in murder. What you're saying about taking over makes me feel a wee bit better, but I still need time to think about it. I'll do what I can, but with her tenacious ladyship in charge we might all have to ease off until this mess gets sorted. I'll be back in touch after that, okay?'

He got up and disappeared into the night.

* * *

Marilyn Mitchell waited for Gordon to come off the phone before tackling him.

'Was that Tony Sorrento?' she asked.

He nodded.

'Listen, Gordon, it's time you got a completely different job and severed links with that crew. I know what they're like and I know the type of work you do for them. If you don't do it soon you'll become more and more embroiled, and it'll get harder to make a clean break. Are you in debt to them still? Do they have any hold over you?'

Gordon shook his head and sat down beside her. 'No. I finished paying them what I owed a couple of years ago.'

'In that case, what's holding you back?'

'It's the money. I couldn't make anywhere close to what I earn now, not if I shifted elsewhere. I never got any proper qualifications for my line of work, even though I'm good at it. That means no one would take me on, not at my age. I'd have to pay my way through a couple of college courses and get some certificates.'

She reached across and took his hand. 'But why would that be a problem? You could do it if it was necessary, Gordon. It would only be a year or two, and we could make ends meet for a while. Maybe you could get a job locally while you did the college course. Or I could, once the baby's here.'

'Even if I got some qualifications I could never earn as much as they pay me. And that worries me.'

'Do you think that really matters to me? I hate to see you as unhappy as you've been in recent months. I want my happy, contented husband back, and I'm willing to make sacrifices to do it. Can I make it any clearer to you?' She leant closer and kissed his lips, curling her fingers around the back of his neck. 'It might be now or never, Gordon. I'm worried that things are going to get worse for you while you're with them. I can see that you've been worried sick for the last few weeks. Can you talk about what's bothering you?'

'Tony's manoeuvring to take over. He doesn't trust Wayne's judgement. He says that Wayne can veer between being ultra-cautious one day and a real loose cannon the next. Tony wants things tidied up so we know where we are. If he succeeds in his expansion plans, then it'll be more money for all of us, he says, but a helluva lot more work too. It worries me. I was getting sick of all the in-fighting before this latest business, and I feel even more negative now.'

Marilyn felt the baby move, and stroked her stomach. 'It's different now, Gordon, with this one being a girl. I keep thinking that when she's born it will mark a turning point for us, and I want it to be the right kind of change. I want you to feel proud of who you are and proud of us. And I want her and the boys to be proud of you, and none of this can happen while you're with the Woodruffs and that man Sorrento. Please, for my sake, start planning the break. I'll help in any way I can. Trust me.'

CHAPTER 16: SLEEPOVER

Wednesday evening, Week 2

Barry Marsh, the detective sergeant in Sophie's unit, had a cautious and careful approach to his work. He took some time to assimilate new ideas, particularly when they had the potential to derail a line of inquiry that he'd spent some time working on. Sophie's suggestion that someone might have leaked the news about the missing reel of tape had really shocked him. His first thought had been, *surely not.* But he'd come to see that the only other explanation was coincidence, that the killer had realised the error on that precise day, having forgotten about it for more than two weeks. How likely was that? Coincidences happen for sure, but in this particular case the chances were slim. Which left him with the unpleasant alternative. Someone with access to the incident board from mid-afternoon on Monday was somehow involved and had passed the vital information on.

He glanced again at the list he'd constructed and thought through the possibilities, weighing up the people involved. Sophie, himself and Rae — not unless the world had gone mad. The chief superintendent, Matt Silver, and DS Bob

Thompson — certainly not. Blackman and McCluskie, somewhat slapdash detectives — unlikely, although McCluskie could have an axe to grind, and the duo certainly seemed to operate in a world of their own. A couple of local officers, but they all seemed so reliable. The dead man's brother, Pete Armitage — he'd been around the station, but no one had seen him enter or leave the incident room unaccompanied. But even if he was involved, what would he gain? Barry had already spoken to the member of the cleaning staff responsible for the incident room and felt fairly sure that she wasn't the type to gossip.

His mood wasn't helped by the fact that he still hadn't remembered why the name Woodruff seemed to stir up something in the dusty recesses of his mind. It was something from long ago, he was sure of it. But he just couldn't come up with anything. He'd just have to wait and hope that he would remember at some point. He needed an evening off, just to relax. He sent a quick text message to his girlfriend, Gwen, who lived in Southampton, suggesting a meal out. Her reply was quick in coming. 'Curry,' it read. 'And stay over please.'

He relaxed. He'd been working nonstop on the case since the discovery of the bodies, and a short break would be very welcome, even if it was just a single night. Was curry a good precursor to sex, though? Maybe he should forego his usual chicken madras in favour of something a bit milder.

* * *

'That's not your usual choice, Barry. Lamb bhuna? What's come over you? Should I be worried?' Gwen Davis took another bite out of her crispy popadum, lavishly covered with mixed pickle.

'Of course not,' he replied indignantly. 'Worried about what, anyway? I just fancied a change.'

'That's what I mean. Does this mean the writing's on the wall for us as a couple? I mean, where's it all going to end, this strange wish of yours for new experiences?' She looked across at his perplexed face and winked at him.

'Don't do that, Gwen. It worries me. The boss winks at me sometimes, and I never know what it means.'

Gwen laughed again. 'I bet you do really. It just signifies a bit of gentle teasing. What confuses you is that it's coming from a woman, and that's the bit men find hard to deal with. It's okay for men to wink at women, but you can't cope when it's the other way round. You're a sorry lot, perpetually hung up on your lost power. It was all fine when you men had the upper hand, as if it was yours by some god-given right, but it's not so easy now, is it?' She winked again.

Barry sighed and took a swig of lager. 'Can we talk about something else now?'

'I like your new shirt. Very sexy. Good choice of colour for you.'

'But you chose it, Gwen. It was one of your Christmas presents to me.'

She giggled again. 'Did I? That's good. I was worried I might be losing my sense of style.'

She slid her right foot out of her shoe and started to run it up his leg, but Barry's embarrassment was cut short by the approach of a waiter bringing their starters. 'Onion bhaji. Bliss,' was all Gwen said for the next five minutes.

'How long have you been a curry fan?' he asked, as Gwen laid down her fork.

'Centuries, I expect. I must have had several previous incarnations in Indian palaces, being fed fine food by my own personal slaves. I just love it. What about you?'

'It was when I was a beat copper in Bournemouth. Bob Thompson and I used to get a takeaway sometimes when we finished our shift. Only once a week, mind. I suppose it was a bit of a bachelor thing. Curry and beer. To be honest, I never enjoyed it much then, but our local takeaway was pretty crappy, though we didn't realise it at the time. It's only when you've been to a few good places that you realise how good curry can be.'

'It's like everything else, Barry. Quality matters. Too many people stuff themselves stupid with cheap junk and then feel bloated for days afterwards. It's much better to come to a place like this that doesn't overfill your plate but gets the taste right. So you never went to a restaurant?'

'No, not often. We'd have a couple of pints in the pub and then go to the takeaway next door. We shared digs only five minutes away, so we'd go home, put our feet up, switch the telly on and tuck in. The takeaway lost trade when an Indian restaurant opened in the area which served up better food, and it finally closed. The place is an organic cafe now, and it's meant to be pretty good. The pub's still there. Interesting name — the Rising Moon.'

'I was never into takeaways,' Gwen replied. 'I like the whole experience with the music and the decor. It's even better when the staff are in authentic dress.' She waited. 'Barry? Are you okay?'

His mind was elsewhere. The Rising Moon pub. That was it! It had been owned by someone called Woodruff. What was the first name? Phil? A slightly dubious character, who used to boast about his over-ambitious plans for expansion. Pie in the sky, that's what he and Thompson had thought. He felt a sharp kick on his leg.

'Barry. For goodness sake! Either put that forkful of food in your mouth or back on your plate. It's not a pretty sight hovering halfway, with your mouth hanging open.'

'Sorry. Just thought of something.'

'You don't say? I'd never have guessed.' Gwen rolled her eyes.

CHAPTER 17: FOLLOW THE MONEY

Thursday morning, Week 2

Marsh was whistling a tune as he made his way up the stairs to the incident room next morning. As he entered the office, he saw that most of the occupants were looking at him. He blushed slightly as he made his way to the incident board.

'Whatever that was, it sounded cheerful,' was Sophie's comment. 'It's not often we hear whistling around here. Do it more regularly, Barry. It helps break up the morbid atmosphere. Did you recognise it, Rae?'

'Auld Lang Syne? God Save the Queen? The Ace of Spades? Can't be sure.' Rae kept a straight face.

He decided to laugh it off. 'To be honest, I don't know what it was. I was just feeling a bit more cheery than normal. I remembered where I'd come across the name Woodruff before, ma'am. It was ages ago when I was a beat cop in Bournemouth. Phil Woodruff ran a pub in the Pokesdown area called the Rising Moon, and it's still there. I passed it on my way in this morning and took a look. The Woodruff name is still above the door, but with a different initial. It's probably run by someone else in the family, now that he's dead.'

Rae looked puzzled. 'But it must be coincidence, ma'am. It's been niggling me since we made the link. Why would the fact that the Armitage couple mistakenly went into the wrong funeral have caused them to be murdered? This isn't the backstreets of downtown Chicago. It's too bizarre. There must be some other connection, surely?'

Sophie was still looking at Marsh. 'You passed Pokesdown on your way in? To Blandford? Where were you coming from? Ah, now I know why you feel like whistling. I'm not a detective for nothing, you know.'

Rae looked from one to the other. 'I don't understand this conversation.'

Barry opened his mouth to reply, but saw that his boss's attention was elsewhere. Was it his imagination, or did she look a little on edge?

'I want to bring Blackman and McCluskie in closer,' she finally said. 'I know it seems to go against my previous decision, but I want them where we can keep our eyes on them. And we don't post anything else on the incident board about the Woodruffs or anyone connected to them. We'll keep that line to ourselves. Agreed?' They all nodded. 'Rae, remove that second reference, the one about the car I saw. That'll leave just the one, the funeral mix-up.'

'Why, ma'am?' Rae asked.

'I want to see if its disappearance causes either of them to comment. Tell me if that happens, won't you?'

* * *

Blackman and McCluskie appeared in the incident room mid-morning, sober and smartly dressed. Marsh met them and took them into Sophie's office. Both seemed slightly nervous.

Sophie's tone was cool. 'I need someone to log and cross-check all of the forensic details, so that'll be your job. Barry here is my second, so you report to him. I want to know all there is to know about the car, the crime scene and how and when they might have got there. You might need to cross check with the uniformed squad that found the car, Rose Simons and George Warrander. Don't contact the family in any way without my say so. I have Rae Gregson from my own team liaising with the two of them, and I want it to stay that way. You'll need to get up to speed with what we already know from the forensic team, but more information will trickle in on a daily basis and we'll adapt what we're doing accordingly. You'll work from here, in the incident room.'

Blackman frowned. 'Do we have to, ma'am? I mean we have our office downstairs. Can't we just use that, as normal?'

'Why would you want to do that? The whole point of a murder investigation is that you keep abreast of what's going on, so I want you in here. We work from eight to eight. And every time you go out it gets logged on the system. Time out, time back in, where, what and why. Check with Barry before you go anywhere. Have a rundown ready for me at the end of each day. Clear?' She smiled thinly.

Marsh showed them their work desks and went to have a chat with Rae.

'Christ,' was all Blackman could manage.

'Ditto,' McCluskie replied. 'Welcome to the workhouse.'

* * *

The full autopsy report arrived mid-morning. Sophie sat down with Marsh and ploughed through the details. There was nothing new, and they weren't expecting anything, but they still had to double check.

'It doesn't make sense, ma'am. The deaths, I mean. I still can't imagine any scenario that would justify murdering that couple in such a calculated, planned way. It's just so weird.'

Sophie finished reading the final page and looked up. 'I know what you mean. We're missing something. Whatever it is, it'll be some little snippet that will make everything fall into place. The family are all mostly sensible people. I even wonder if Rod isn't more capable than he appears to be. Okay, so we haven't had time to make any real progress yet on the possible link to this Woodruff person, whoever he was, but I still can't see how a mistaken visit to a funeral could end up in a double murder. It's what Rae said earlier, we're not in gangland Chicago. Even there, I doubt whether a couple like the Armitages would ever find themselves victims of violence as senseless as this. So it isn't senseless. It can't be. Someone, somewhere, either gains a lot from their deaths or was in danger of losing a lot with them alive.'

'Follow the money?'

'It's the best way. It's what my gut instincts tell me. I've always said, Barry, there are crimes of passion, usually easy to solve, and crimes of greed and cover-up, often more difficult because they've been planned very carefully. This has all the markings of the latter.' She paused. 'Deep Throat deserves a medal for that phrase. It's become a cliché, but a lot of the time it's true.'

Marsh shook his head. 'You've lost me.'

'*All the President's Men.* My favourite film of all time. As far as I know, that was the first time it was used. Deep Throat was the insider, feeding information to the two investigative journalists, Woodward and Bernstein. He advised Woodward to "follow the money" at one of their secret meetings.' She looked at the clock. 'How do you fancy a pub lunch, Barry? Across in Bournemouth, maybe?'

* * *

The Rising Moon was a large, red-brick building dating back to the years after the Second World War. It had a car park to one side and a garden at the rear, surrounded by hanging baskets and small flower beds, all full of colourful blooms. Inside, the two detectives looked around them. The place was clean, carpeted and well furnished. A few people sat at the scattered tables, and two men propped up the bar.

'Is it how you remember it, Barry?'

'No, not at all. It used to be a bit of a dive, to be honest. It was split into two bars, as a lot of pubs were back then. This open-plan decor is much better, and the whole place has a more comfortable feel.'

Sophie ordered a pint of ale and a glass of orange juice from the barmaid, and collected two lunch menus from the counter. As always, the fruit juice was put down in front of her and the beer pushed towards Marsh. She pointedly switched them over.

'Sorry,' said the young woman. 'Unusual, though.'

Sophie smiled. 'I know I am. In lots of ways. Even so, you should have asked.' She saw one of the men smirk. 'I'll have the chilli and rice. What about you, Barry?'

'Ham, egg and chips, please.'

The barmaid put through the order. The two detectives chose a quiet table set in an alcove that gave them a view of the room.

Sophie sipped her beer. 'Tell me what the place was like ten years ago.'

'It used to have a dividing wall down the middle of this room. The bar was in the same place and served both rooms. We used the public bar. That was in the other section. This area was the lounge and was a bit nicer, but not that much. I never came in here if I was out with a girl. It was too naff. We used to go to the bars close to the seafront. Much livelier. This place was convenient 'cause it was close to my digs. I never liked the staff very much either. Maybe they knew I was a copper. Let's hope the food's better than it was then.'

'Pub food is always a bit chancy, isn't it?'

'They used to have curry on the menu, trying to compete with the takeaway, I guess. That place wasn't great, but the curry here was total crap. They should have just stuck to sausage and mash. At least that was edible.'

Sophie laughed. She looked up as a staff door opened on the other side of the bar. Three men entered, and made their way to the bar, where they helped themselves to some sandwiches laid out ready on a plate and sipped gin and tonics, which the barmaid poured as soon as she spotted them.

'The shorter one reminds me a bit of old Phil,' Barry said. 'I wonder if it's his son.'

'I can top that,' Sophie replied. 'One of the others, the one with the scar on his face, is the man I spotted up at Morden Bog last weekend. Well, well. Aren't things getting interesting?'

They watched the men chatting to the barmaid until a bell rang behind her. She disappeared through a doorway and re-emerged with two plates. The group at the bar watched as she crossed the room and laid the plates down in front of the two detectives.

'I think I've got it right this time,' she said.

'What is it about men and chips?' Sophie replied. 'A whole day's calories on one plate.'

The barmaid tilted her head. 'Not so much the ones we serve. They're cooked with just a spray of oil. Probably no more calories in his meal than yours.'

Sophie smiled. 'Well, that's good to hear from his point of view, but you've got me worried.'

The young woman looked her up and down. 'I'm sure you don't need to worry too much, with your figure. I only hope I'm half as slim at your age.'

They were part way through their food when the man Barry thought he recognised came across to them. 'Everything alright?' he asked.

They nodded.

'It's fine, Mr . . ?' said Sophie.

'Woodruff. I'm the licensee here.'

'No complaints, you'll be glad to hear. And the beer's good too. How long have you had the pub, Mr Woodruff?'

'It's been in the family for years but most of that time it was my dad's name above the door. He died early last month. We own a few other pubs and clubs in the area. Are you local?'

'No. We're based near Dorchester and were just passing by.' She glanced across to the bar, but the other two men had their backs turned. Woodruff walked back to join them and all three left.

'Do you think he recognised you, ma'am? The one with the scar?'

Sophie shrugged. 'I couldn't tell. To be honest, I couldn't care less. And anyway, all I am is some woman who spoke to him on Saturday morning, nothing more than that. And if he did recognise me, and found out who I am, it might put more pressure on him, and that might lead to a slip up. He either has something to hide or he doesn't. If he does, we'll get to the bottom of it. Let's finish up. We should get back so I can needle Blackman and McCluskie a bit more.'

* * *

'So who is she?'

'Only the fucking chief inspector in charge of the murder investigation, that's who,' Sorrento replied.

He and Woodruff were standing at an office window, looking out through net curtains onto the car park below.

'What? What's she doing here?'

'Maybe you can tell me. On second thoughts, I don't want to know, in case it makes me some kind of accessory. If you did have anything to do with those deaths, Wayne, you'd better get your thinking cap on, because she seems to have picked up your scent. But one thing you need to know is that the rest of us won't agree to you putting our insider at risk by leaning on him to find out. For years he's been useful in keeping the cops out of our hair, and we want it to stay that way. He's got to stay hidden. We don't involve him, apart from asking him to keep us informed, even if you think he might save your hide. We have our futures to think about, and we don't want them going down the pan.' He looked out of the window again as the detectives drove away, the ginger-haired man behind the wheel. 'Yeah, that car was parked along from mine on Saturday morning. It's her alright. Look, Gordy and I'll find out what we can and keep you posted. Just don't do anything hasty. It'll all probably blow over if you give it time.'

Once Woodruff had returned to his office, Sorrento took out his mobile phone and sent an urgent text message. 'Need to meet again. Important.'

CHAPTER 18: FAMILY QUESTIONS

Thursday afternoon, Week 2

Sophie sipped her tea and looked around the lounge of the Giroux home.

'Have there been any developments?' Sharon asked.

'Yes, fairly substantial ones, but I can't tell you any more than that, Dr Giroux, certainly no details at this stage. You must realise that there are a number of puzzling aspects to the case and we're in the process of trying to link them all together.'

'So there isn't an imminent arrest?'

'You just have to be patient. We don't move until we're fairly sure.'

'In that case, why are you here?'

'Because I need more information from you about your two-day visit to Exeter during your holiday. You told us it was in the middle of your second week in Cornwall. I need the full details. Times. Where you stayed, what you did, who you were with. It's a necessary formality, Dr Giroux.'

'Your DC could have asked me for that. Why you this time?'

'Because I have a suspicion that you're holding back on something. So, to start, I want full details about the conference.'

Sharon sighed. 'It was at Exeter University on the Monday and Tuesday of our second week in Cornwall. It was a catch-up for GPs on the latest information about prostate cancer diagnosis.'

Sophie looked at her. 'That was on the Monday, and it was a single day according to the organisers. It didn't spill over to a second day.' She waited.

'On Tuesday there was a symposium on the latest treatments for patients with CPD, so I stayed on.'

'That was in the afternoon, from two onwards.' Again she waited.

'What are you implying?' Sharon asked.

'I'm not implying anything, Dr Giroux. I just need to know where you were during those two days. Look, why don't you start from the time you set off from your holiday cottage? The Monday morning, wasn't it? What time?'

'I left shortly after six thirty. I'd booked a taxi to take me to St Austell station. The session was due to begin at ten, so that gave me plenty of time for the journey. I checked in and dumped my bags in the overnight room I'd been allocated, then I freshened up. It also gave me time to grab a coffee before the session started.'

'Did everyone arrive at about the same time?'

'About half of us. Some of the people from further away had travelled the day before. Anyway, the session went on until six. It was meant to finish earlier, but there was a lot of discussion about a couple of points.' She fell into silence.

'Many of the delegates left at that point. Am I right?'

Sharon seemed reticent. 'Most. Only a few were staying over for the session on the following day.'

'So what did you do that evening?'

'I went out for dinner with a few other doctors and then on for some drinks.'

A very minimal answer. Sophie again sensed that Sharon was nervous and holding back on something.

'Is there something you want to add to that?'

'No. Why should I? It's what I did. I've answered your question.'

'I'll need names, for corroboration purposes.'

'For heaven's sake. This is ridiculous.'

'It isn't, Dr Giroux. We're investigating a double murder, as you well know. Every single item of information we're given is double checked. That's standard procedure. If I went back without taking any names from you, it would be a dereliction of duty. You need to tell me who you were with.'

Sharon pursed her lips. 'I don't know that I can do that.'

'Well, let's come back to it. You led us to believe that you were fully involved in a conference the next day, but it was only in the afternoon. So what did you do in the morning?'

'I did some shopping in Exeter and wandered around the cathedral.'

'Alone?'

Again the pursed lips. 'No. I was with someone.'

'Was this someone in the group you spent the Tuesday evening with?'

Sharon nodded.

'And at the conference?'

Sharon looked trapped. 'Look, there was nothing in it, but I don't want Pierre to know.'

'So it was some kind of liaison?'

Sharon sighed. 'He was my boyfriend when I was at university. We split up just after we graduated. We've kept in touch but at a distance. Those two days were the first time we'd seen each other since we were students. We just wanted some time together to catch up on each other's lives.'

'So you weren't out in a group?'

'We were for the meal, then the two of us split off and headed to a different pub for a quiet drink. I think we were both curious to see if the old spark was still there.'

'And was it?'

'It was different compared to the old days. Look, I value what I have. My husband and family mean the world to me and I wouldn't dream of doing anything that would put our future at risk.'

'It's not my place to judge you, but I will need his name and a contact number. As I said, everything has to be corroborated. But I can assure you that we will be totally discreet.'

'Okay. I think I trust you and your team, but I'd have had problems with those two cretins who came round initially. I wouldn't trust them further than I could throw them. They make me shudder.'

'None of this will go on the incident board, Dr Giroux. It will be kept tight between myself and my immediate team. I may not even tell them unless it opens up a new avenue.'

'Well, it won't, I can assure you of that. I didn't kill my parents, if that's what you mean.' She wrote a name and telephone number on a slip of paper and handed it across to Sophie.

'Does your husband know? That you stayed in contact?'

Sharon shook her head and tears appeared in the corners of her eyes. She lowered her head, but then looked up again. 'It's just escapism. You must know, surely? Sometimes life seems to be just one gigantic juggling act. Family, work, house, elderly relatives. All those responsibilities piling up, all clamouring for attention. Even on holiday there was the pressure of keeping the kids amused. I just needed to escape from it all for a day or two.'

Sophie covered Sharon's hand with hers. 'I know the feeling all too well. I said not to worry about it and I meant it.'

Sharon gave her a weak smile.

'We'll need to see Pierre, to go through the same questions with him. Is he home at the moment?'

'No. Today's his day in Oxford. He's due back mid-morning tomorrow.'

'Okay. If I can't make it, I'll send one of my team round.'

* * *

Rae was putting the finishing touches to her report on the family finances. She'd discovered some unexpected aspects. Much of the financial history was as she would have expected, and showed a careful approach to managing their money. Their main bank account was jointly held, and the same had been true of their house mortgage until it had been paid off some years earlier. Sylvia had also maintained a savings account in her own name for many years and this account now held a sizable sum. The regular withdrawals from it seemed to have all gone to charity and were fairly small.

Rae looked again at the details. Her boss had said often enough that money matters were at the root of so many family murders. People saw that the chance of gaining a large sum of money might be slipping away from them, and decided to act before they lost what they often saw as theirs by right. Maybe Sylvia had started talking about giving more of the money away to charity, and the son or daughter may have decided that their future inheritance was being put at risk. But which one? Sharon was far better off financially than Rod, but her overheads would be much greater. A larger house, two children, an expensive lifestyle. Rod was poor, almost destitute, but his needs were few. What if the two of them had acted together? What if the friction between them was a sham, put on deliberately to divert suspicion?

She put the report aside and started on the details for Pete Armitage, Ted's brother, included because he benefitted from the will. Rae only had access to a few documents at this stage but she could see that Pete's decorating business was not exactly in the best of financial states. It appeared that the work had dried up a little in recent years with income only just matching his overheads. Maybe some more probing was required. Rae collected her jacket and walked across to Barry Marsh's desk.

'I'm just off to have a chat with Pete Armitage, boss. There are a few gaps in our knowledge of his financial background. Okay?'

* * *

Rae found Pete at home on a late lunch break, so they talked at the kitchen table while he munched his way through some ham sandwiches. He lived alone since an early marriage had failed within a year of the wedding. He'd become so used to pleasing himself in his daily routines that he couldn't imagine having to adapt to a shared life.

'I hope you don't mind me asking you these questions, Mr Armitage. As I explained on the phone, it's necessary because you're a beneficiary from the will.' She took a sip from the mug of tea that he'd poured for her. 'I know I've only seen preliminary figures, but it looks as though income for your business has slumped a bit in the past couple of years. Is that right?'

'The crash hit everyone. I nearly went to the wall, and a lot of other people in the building and decorating trade didn't make it. Trade's picked up a bit since then, but it's still not healthy.'

'You've been employing Rod. Do you have any other workers?'

Pete shook his head. 'I used to have someone full time and at least one apprentice, but that's all changed. I've just got rid of Rod too. He was a liability and I only employed him as a favour to Ted and Sylvia. That's one of the reasons I've been losing money. His work was poor and he only turned up when he felt like it. I've just hired a new apprentice starting next month, and I hope she'll turn out to have a better work ethic than Rod.'

'So any money coming your way will be useful?'

'If you're talking about the money Ted and Sylvia left me in their will, then yes, it will be useful. Obviously. But if you're suggesting that I was involved in their deaths, then you've got it wrong. That money was a thank you for giving Rod a job when he needed one. And I've been doing it for quite a few years now.'

'But you've got rid of him pretty quick, haven't you? Now they're dead? How do you think that looks?'

Pete looked at her angrily. 'That comment doesn't even deserve an answer.'

'Did Ted or Sylvia give or loan you any money a few months ago?'

'Why would they have done that? My business is fine, thank you very much, and I don't go around asking for handouts.'

'So is that a no?'

'It's a no. Now I have to get back to work. I have a job to finish.'

CHAPTER 19: DENSE AND SUBSTANTIAL

Thursday afternoon, Week 2

DS Stu Blackman sighed, stretched back in his chair and put his hands behind his head.

'Christ, this is tedious stuff.'

'Isn't there a way we can swing a quick visit out somewhere?' asked McCluskie. 'I need some air. I need to stretch my legs. You're the boss. Can't you think of a reason?'

'Need to lubricate your throat as well? The problem is, Her High and Mightiness made it clear we have to get clearance to go out. That means the reason has to be a good one. And my brain has gone dead.'

'So you do have one, do you? It's just that sometimes I wonder. Like now, for instance. Why can't we go and see those two uniformed squaddies who found the car? Just to double check that we have all the details and they match with forensics? Doesn't that sound convincing enough?'

'You're a genius, Phil.'

'No I'm not. It's just that you have a brain the size of a pea. How you made it to detective sergeant beats me. Marsh has just come back in, so let's try it.'

Blackman tightened his slightly grubby tie and left his desk, followed by McCluskie.

Two minutes later the pair were back in their seats.

'Christ,' Blackman said, loosening his tie again.

'Ditto,' replied McCluskie. 'Doesn't it make you want to weep? Her High and Mightiness and the Ginger Gremlin. What a duo.'

'Treating us like that! It's not as though we're bloody prisoners, is it?'

McCluskie looked at him shrewdly. 'That's exactly what we are. She's keeping us here so we can't get up to any mischief. So the key question, Mr Mastermind, is what mischief are we in danger of getting into? What are we supposed to have done? 'cause she hates having me within half a mile of her, believe me, I know. I reckon there's been a glitch in the investigation, maybe a leak, and we're on the suspect list for it. Better to have us on the inside pissing out than on the outside pissing in. If I'm right and, let's face it, I'm rarely wrong, we've stumbled onto something interesting. Let's try to find what that glitch could have been.'

'Then what?'

'Manipulate a better deal for ourselves. What else?'

* * *

'So who might resent the potential loss of inheritance money? You say she'd mentioned it to Sharon, Rae?'

The whole team was assembled in the incident room for the late afternoon summary. Rae nodded.

'Yes. I called her and she said that her mum had mentioned the possibility. I suppose the people most affected would have been Sharon herself, Rod, her brother Pete and Pierre, Sharon's husband.'

'And you spoke to Pete earlier this afternoon?'

Rae nodded. 'It was mainly because I could see that his decorating business is not very profitable. He can only just be making ends meet, and he's just given Rod the sack. I wanted to question him about that, but I did ask him if he knew about any charity donations Ted and Sylvia were making. He denied it.'

'And did you believe him?'

'Not sure. He got a bit uptight when I mentioned it. He also got angry when I suggested his sacking of Rod was a bit soon after the deaths. I think he's got a shorter fuse than I first thought.'

'The other thing we don't know is how well the parents got on with their son-in-law, Pierre.'

'He's next on the list to interview again,' Sophie added. 'He'll be back from Oxford late tonight, so one of us can see him in the morning. He seemed a very pleasant and co-operative man when we spoke to him last week. You see him, Barry. He won't try to use that Gallic charm on you.'

Barry grinned. 'Every reason to suspect him then?'

'We don't know a lot about him. It might be worth doing some background checks. If Sharon was the apple of her dad's eye and Pierre was in need of money, he might have approached Sylvia on the quiet. It's a thought, isn't it? Anything else, anyone?'

'We got on well with Rod, ma'am,' McCluskie said. 'We discovered his liking for certain illegal substances, so if he needs to be interviewed again we'd be good to go.'

Sophie was non-committal. 'I'll bear it in mind.'

'It would be good for us to visit the scene, ma'am,' continued McCluskie. 'We're going through all the forensic stuff and crosschecking it, but it would make sense for it to be in context. Can we do that?'

'Okay, but contact Rose Simons first and arrange for her to go with you. She can take you through what she spotted. And keep me in the frame.' She looked at the clock. 'She's just about to come on duty. You could go now.'

Sophie waited until Blackman and McCluskie had left the room, before turning to Marsh. 'That went well. Thanks for prompting me with Blackman's request. I just need to get a message to Simons and Warrander before they head off with our transparent 'tec duo.' She fished her mobile phone out of her bag.

* * *

George Warrander and Rose Simons led the way south to the crime scene, then took Blackman and McCluskie through their discoveries of the previous week. All except one: the missing roll of tape that had mysteriously reappeared.

Blackman shook his head. 'Sounds bloody horrible. I'm glad it was you that found the bodies and not us. Who'd do such a thing?'

'You're the detectives,' Rose answered. 'That's for you to discover, not us to speculate. And how come you're back in favour all of a sudden? That's a bit of a turn up, isn't it?'

McCluskie grinned. 'We're just too good to be kept out of things for long. And it was our case originally, remember. Maybe she saw sense.'

Rose nodded slowly, apparently serious. 'Yes, I can see the undoubted strengths that the two of you will bring to her investigation. You'll fill a real hole. Don't quite know what you'll fill it with, but if something dense and substantial is required, you're the two for the job.'

McCluskie took a step forward, arm raised and anger on his face.

'Don't try it, sonny-boy,' Rose responded. 'By the looks of you, you'd have trouble swatting a fly. Whereas me, well, I heave drunks into the back of vans all night long. I could floor you with one punch and without breaking sweat. We've done what you asked and now we need to get back to some serious policing. So if there's no other information you need, let's go.'

They made their way back to their cars. Warrander driving, he and Simons followed the two detectives out onto the road north.

‘What was that all about, boss?’ Warrander asked.

‘Those two make me sick. At least your pet DCI has the sense to keep them where she can see them. But they’re not happy bunnies, and my guess is that’s because they’re actually expected to do a decent day’s work for once. She’s up to something with them, that’s my guess. Particularly since she asked me not to mention the missing tape turning up.’

‘Why are they still in the force?’ asked Warrander. ‘And how come a moron like Blackman’s a DS?’

‘Well, that’s a story and a half. Contacts, Georgie boy. His uncle was a chief superintendent when rules were there to be broken. He used his influence just before he retired, or so it’s said. Blackman was okay for a while, but he buddied up with McCluskie when they were DSs together, and fell under his influence. When McCluskie was demoted a couple of years ago Blackman stuck by him. Misplaced loyalty. Now he’s under McCluskie’s thumb even though he’s the senior officer. McCluskie is a shrewd operator, way beyond Blackman in ability. He’s clever in a sly sort of way, but he’s got a huge chip on his shoulder. Anyway, I’ve talked too much. Let’s get back to civilisation, shall we? Or at last what passes for civilisation in the Wild West town of Blandford Forum. Mafia thugs look out. Here we come.’

Rose sent a quick text message to Sophie.

CHAPTER 20: DOUBLE CHECKING

Friday morning, Week 2

Pierre Giroux showed Barry Marsh into the sitting room.

'This shouldn't take long, Mr Giroux. I just need to get all the facts about your trip to Oxford from Cornwall, and then confirm all the other details about your holiday.'

Pierre settled his tall slim frame into a chair facing Marsh. 'I just took the one week's leave from work, the second week of the holiday. My normal work pattern is to work from home for three days each week and to be in Oxford for each Wednesday and Thursday. I managed to spread my work across the two weeks, apart from those two days. I worked most mornings and joined Sharon and the children on the beach after lunch.'

'Except for the two days she was in Exeter,' Marsh added.

'Yes, of course. Those two days were cloudy with some light rain, so we visited Truro, then the Eden Project. That was the Monday and Tuesday of our second week. Sharon was back with us in time to put the children to bed on Tuesday evening.'

Marsh checked his notes and nodded. 'Right. Now, take me through your two days away. What time did you set out?'

'At six thirty in the morning, the same as Sharon the following week. The local taxi picked me up and took me to St Austell to get the train to Reading, then I changed for Oxford. I worked on the train. I was in Oxford for the afternoon and stayed overnight in my usual hotel. I was in the office all day and most of the evening, then got the first train I could to get back to St Austell the next morning. Sharon and the children picked me up from the station at lunchtime.'

'Doesn't Newquay have a train service? It's a lot closer to St Mawgan, so why not travel from there?'

'It would have been ideal, but the service is terrible. Trains don't start running until mid-morning. It's a lot easier to go direct from a station on the main line.'

Marsh made a note to check this information.

'You appear to have been busy all the time you were in Oxford. Didn't you have a few hours free at some time? Maybe an evening?'

Pierre shook his head. 'No. I did as much work as I possibly could in those two days. It meant that I had more time with my family when I was back in Cornwall.'

'I can see the sense in that, but I will need some names, Mr Giroux. People who can corroborate what you've told me. And have you kept your tickets? That would be useful.'

'The one to Oxford was kept by the machine, but I still have the one for my return home. They make ideal bookmarks.' He crossed the room to a pile of books, pulled a ticket out and handed it to Marsh.

'Did you go out at all in Oxford? Maybe for meals, or to socialise?'

'Not until mid-evening. I had lunch in the office canteen. I had a pub meal each evening in the Lamb and Flag on my way back to my hotel. It's on St Giles. They have some good wines there, and I use it most weeks.'

* * *

'It all checks out, ma'am,' Marsh reported to Sophie. 'I even phoned the pub and spoke to the manager, who confirmed his account. At the moment there's no reason to doubt his story. The same with his wife, I expect.'

Sophie shook her head. 'Her story is not quite so innocent, but I don't think she was up to anything that was linked to her parents' deaths. It all hangs together and she has good alibis. So, at the moment, I think we can remove them both from our list of suspects. But I'm still a bit uneasy about them. Sharon is more of an emotional wreck than I suspected and Pierre is just a little too smooth for my liking.'

'Maybe that's just because he's French, ma'am.'

Sophie raised her eyebrows. 'I don't think so. I've got French cousins and I get on with them really well.' She paused. 'What intrigues me is Rae's idea that the murders might have pre-empted a large charity donation. Apparently Sylvia had a regular standing order out to a cancer support charity, ever since her own mother died a couple of decades ago. What if she was thinking of making a large donation that would have reduced someone's inheritance, maybe significantly? We've also got to bear in mind the possible link to this Woodruff family who, let's face it, might be just a wee bit shady in their operations. And then there's this new thread. There doesn't seem to be a link, but could there be one? We need to know more about the Woodruff lot. Hasn't anything come back in from Bournemouth yet?'

Marsh shook his head.

'Maybe I'll pop across and see Kevin McGreedie now he's back from leave. It'll give me an opportunity to find out how Jimmy's getting on in his new job.'

Jimmy Melsom had been Marsh's assistant in Swanage. The young detective constable had worked with Marsh on three of Sophie Allen's earlier cases, but had moved to join Bournemouth CID when Marsh joined the Violent Crime Unit as Sophie's permanent number two. Kevin McGeedie was a senior detective in Bournemouth and was a longstanding friend of Sophie's.

'It's been almost a year now, ma'am.'

'Do you miss him, Barry?'

'Of course I do. He was a good lad. Not suited to the kind of insight we need, but in general CID work he'll be fine.'

'My thoughts exactly. And he should do well, working for Kevin.'

* * *

Sophie walked in through the swing doors of Bournemouth police headquarters and showed her warrant card to the security officer. She took the stairs up to the CID offices, pausing to admire the view across Bournemouth from the lobby windows before entering the place she referred to as "Kevin's Lair."

McGreedie was just coming out of his office. 'Well, to what do we owe this pleasure?'

She gave him a hug and a peck on the cheek. 'I haven't seen you for ages, and I've missed you.'

'Hah! You're up to something, I can tell.'

'Well, that as well. I hear you were away last week. Anywhere nice?'

'Just back to Selkirk to see Laura's mother. We had a good rest though.'

'How's Laura?'

'She's got breast cancer. Really badly. That's why we went to see her mum.'

'Oh, Christ. Kevin. I don't know what to say.' She reached out and touched his arm. 'Is it really that bad?'

'Afraid so. Apparently it's unusually aggressive, so the omens aren't good. She's just about to start a course of treatment, so we're all trying to keep our hopes up. What else can we do?'

'I'm glad I came across now. Why didn't you let me know, for goodness sake?'

He shrugged. 'Laura didn't want it bandied about before she had confirmation, which was only a few days before we went away. She hates fuss and bother, as she puts it. She really can't cope with pity.'

'Knowing her, I can understand that. You must give her my love and let her know that I'll help in any way I can. And I really mean that.' She thought for a moment. 'How would she feel about an evening out, across at our place for a meal? Maybe Saturday? Matt and Tracy are already coming and it'll be no bother to have two more. I'll get Martin to cook. You know how he loves to pretend he's a chef, complete with mock French accent.'

'Thanks, Sophie. I'll suggest it, but I can't say any more than that. Cup of tea?'

They walked across the main CID room to his office, where McGreedie switched on a kettle.

'How's Jimmy getting on?' Sophie asked.

'Fine. He's out on a burglary case at the moment but should be back soon. He's a solid, reliable grafter, and is making good progress on this sequence of break-ins that we're dealing with.'

'Barry taught him well. I'll have a word with him if I'm still here when he comes back. What I've really come across for, Kevin, is to pick your brains about this Woodruff outfit.'

'I saw your request for information, but only a day or two ago, so there's not been much time to get anything in detail.' Reaching for a sheet of paper, he didn't notice Sophie frown. 'Jimmy put it together. It's still a bit thin, but we'll get more to you as soon as we can.'

Sophie scanned the paper. It showed little that they didn't already know. 'But Jimmy's new to Bournemouth. I would have thought it would have gone to one of your longer-serving people.'

He shrugged. 'Maybe they were really busy. I can't comment because I wasn't here. Even now, we're run off our feet. You know what May can be like in a town like this. It's the start of the silly season.'

Just then the door to the main office opened. Melsom walked in and made his way to a desk. 'Hello, Jimmy!' Sophie called, and waved as he looked across.

He smiled and then looked awkward, as if he didn't know whether to wave back or salute. Sophie walked across to his desk. 'How are things?'

'Great, ma'am. I'm enjoying my work here. Is Barry still with you?'

'Of course. I'm hoping he'll do his inspector's exams soon. Rae's fitted in really well, so we're going great guns. Jimmy, I wanted to ask you about this information on the Woodruff outfit. It's a bit sparse.'

He looked worried. 'I was only asked to supply some background, ma'am. Nothing detailed unless a second request came in. I could get you more if you want me to, but I'd have to pick a few brains.'

'That would be really good, Jimmy. We're a bit stymied at the moment, so any useful information would help. Don't publicise it though, will you? DI McGreedie knows, but let's keep it as low profile as possible.'

Melsom looked puzzled. 'Okay. I'll do everything I can.'

On her way out of the office Sophie scanned the duty rosters for the current and previous weeks, still pinned to the notice board on the wall. Interesting.

Her phone rang. What she heard made her turn pale.

CHAPTER 21: THE BODY IN THE WOODS

Friday morning, Week 2

Alice Llewellyn was the senior ranger for Wareham Forest, and her responsibilities included the Morden Bog Nature Reserve, situated in the north of the designated forest area. She loved her work, which involved being outdoors in all weathers and seasons. She enjoyed working with anybody who shared her enthusiasm for the natural environment and its animal and plant life. Most of her time was spent in the southern part of the forest, which had an activity centre, nature trails and observation walks. The Morden Bog SSI was off-limits to visitors. Not only was the bog itself dangerous for the unwary, but its rich diversity of animal life would have been put at risk if too many visitors and ramblers tramped through it. Just occasionally, on wet days like today, Alice liked to visit the reserve, to check that all was well. She had heard about the discovery of the two old people the previous week, when she'd been away on holiday, and was thankful. After those dreadful discoveries of two years before, she never wanted to see another dead body again.

She parked her van in a clearing, donned her waterproofs and set off on foot into the marshy land, picking her way along a narrow footpath. Today was the first wet day after several weeks of dry weather. The plants and animals were all in need of some moisture, and she was glad to see rivulets of water draining off stony outcrops and feeding into the network of small, black pools. Enough rain had fallen overnight to offset any concerns about the tinder-dry undergrowth, although the rain was easing rapidly. Maybe the clouds would clear by the afternoon, leaving the air much fresher and cleaner.

A group of crows drew her attention, flying in and out of a dense thicket, their noisy clatter disturbing the quiet solitude. Alice moved nearer, taking care that she didn't slide into the dank pools that lay around the copse. She moved some branches aside . . . and fell back in shock. There on the ground, still partly hidden by the bushes, was the body of a middle-aged man. Or at least she guessed it was a man. The crows had been at work on the face, so it was difficult to be sure. Her hand went to her mouth and she stumbled back, retching violently.

* * *

Sophie drove to the scene directly from Bournemouth, arriving some fifteen minutes after Marsh and Rae. The trio made their way along the network of paths, directed by a uniformed squad who were fixing marker posts in place to indicate the safest pathway to the crime scene. Already the area was a hive of activity, reminiscent of the previous week when the Armitage couple had been found. The rain was now a light drizzle and even that was fizzling out as they trudged across the damp ground.

'The call came in from Alice Llewellyn, ma'am. Do you remember her from a couple of years ago?' Marsh said.

'Yes. Tall, fair-haired. Sensible and reliable, if I remember right. Don't tell me it was her that found the body?'

'Afraid so. It was pure luck that it wasn't her who found the car last week. Anyway, she called in right away, so there's been no time lost. Forensics are on their way, and the pathologist.'

'Have you had a chance to see the body yet?'

'No. Apparently it's a good ten-minute walk from where we left the cars. I knew you wouldn't be long so we waited. There's a uniformed squad from Wareham at the scene, but they know not to touch anything.'

They continued walking, following the meandering track deeper into the reserve.

'This is a good bit further south than where the car was found,' Sophie remarked. 'Martin and I were on firmer ground than this when we explored on Saturday. I think it must all drain down into this area. It's a bit dismal, isn't it?'

'I'd imagine it looks much better when the sun comes out, ma'am,' Rae answered. 'It's always the same with heathland like this. Drab in the rain, but really pretty when it's bright.'

They spotted the cluster of people ahead. Sophie made her way over to the ranger and spoke to her. 'Alice. What can I say? I've got a flask of coffee with me. Have a cup, it'll help you feel better. We'll take a look, then Barry can have a brief chat. I think it would be better if you went back to your office after that.'

Alice merely shook her head. She was holding a tissue to her face. 'It's too awful. I thought I was okay last time, it didn't seem to bother me too much. But this . . .' Her voice trailed away and she began to sob into the tissue.

'Two years ago you didn't see the bodies. That's what makes the difference. It's the direct visual evidence that gives us the shock.'

Sophie poured out a small cup of coffee from her flask and handed it to the ranger. Alice sipped it while Sophie and Marsh went to the thicket. They pushed some branches aside and looked down at the body. Black trousers and a black leather jacket, skull caked in blood from a massive wound to the side of the head. Dried blood covered the face and neck.

Sophie pulled on latex gloves and felt around in the pockets of the jacket and trousers. Nothing. She looked again at the badly stained face, scanning every inch of it. 'Could that be a scar on his face? Under the streaks of blood?'

Marsh peered over her shoulder. 'It might well be, but it's difficult to be sure without cleaning the muck off. What could it mean?'

'It opens everything up, doesn't it, Barry? Let's wait for the team to arrive. You go and talk to Alice while Rae and I have a short wander around.'

* * *

Sophie was sitting on a log when the forensic unit arrived, soon followed by Benny Goodall, the county's senior forensic pathologist. She watched the team take the initial photos and set up a tent over the corpse. Benny entered the tent and Sophie stood up and followed him inside. She watched as he started his examination of the corpse.

'Do you think it was the head wound that killed him?' she asked.

Benny was probing the victim's head. 'Probably. It's certainly bad enough. That whole side of the skull is caved in, with bone fragments pushed into the brain. Something very hard hit him with a lot of force. We'll know more when we get the body back to the lab and pick out the bits. It's just a mess at the moment. And there could be other wounds elsewhere.'

'Benny, can you clean up the cheek a bit? It looks as if there might be a scar there and if there is, it's very significant.'

Goodall cleared away the blood and dirt from the side of the victim's face, depositing the cloth into an evidence bag. 'Yes. An old scar running vertically. Why? What does it mean?'

'It links this death with that of the Armitage couple. Beyond that, I really don't have a clue. I was thinking about it just now, when you arrived. We're more than a week into the investigation into their deaths and we've got nowhere. Now this.'

Marsh stepped into the tent. Sophie looked up at him and nodded.

'Who is he, ma'am? Why's he here like this? I can't get my head round it.'

Sophie was frowning. 'We were beginning to think it was something bigger than it first appeared. Now we know it is. We have a leak, Barry. I'm saying nothing else at the moment. The only people who know are you, me, Rae, Benny here and Dave Nash. I want to keep it that way. No one else must know what we suspect. Is that clear?'

'Do you know who it is?' asked Benny Goodall.

'I don't know, but I have a strong suspicion, and that's all I'm willing to say at the moment. Barry, don't take offence but I'm not sharing my thoughts on this with you. Trust me, will you?'

'I could do the initial examination tomorrow morning, if you think it's urgent enough. Just for you, mind,' Goodall said, quietly.

'Benny, you're a sweetheart. But you knew that already.'

Sophie went outside and found Rae. They stood talking for several minutes and then Rae left. Marsh watched from the doorway of the tent, looking troubled.

* * *

'He wasn't killed here. We know that from the way the body's lying, and the absence of bloodstains on the foliage. There are drag marks through the bushes at the back of the copse, and some tyre tracks close by. There appear to be bloodstains close to those tracks, so it looks as though he was driven here, got out of the vehicle and was struck by a hard blow to the head. Then he was dragged through the bushes and hidden. All of this is still to be confirmed by forensic checks, but I think we can work on this assumption for now.'

Sophie was talking in low tones to the police team. They'd been joined in the clearing by a large group of police sent from headquarters, who were experienced in searching for clues. Many had been involved in combing the area a mile further north the previous week, after the discovery of the bodies in the abandoned car.

'We need to examine the whole area meticulously. Look for anything that seems out of place, however insignificant it might appear to be.'

The group fanned out and started the search. Sophie stayed near the tent, with Barry Marsh.

'Where's Rae?' he asked.

'I've sent her back to the office. I want her to do some digging. If we have a mole, I want to find out who it is, and she's the ideal person to do it. It's in our remit. Her inquiries will link closely with all this.'

'Shouldn't it be me? I have the rank.'

'I asked you to trust me. Rae's still relatively unknown on the force, so she can work unobtrusively. Don't worry, Barry. I know it's not you.'

'Are you sure there's been a leak?'

'Yes I am,' she snapped. 'And more than one. It's been systematic. Now give it a rest and let's get on with the job at hand.'

* * *

The search of the surrounding area was thorough, with every stray item logged, photographed and then taken away for forensic examination. A trail of blood spots led from a small clearing to the copse where the body had been hidden, a distance of about twenty yards. Faint tyre tracks could be seen both in the clearing and across some scrubby undergrowth at the edge of the nearby forest track. The body had been dumped before the previous night's rain had started.

Marsh phoned several local weather stations to find out when the overnight storm had begun.

'Eleven yesterday evening,' he said to Sophie. 'So sometime before then. It doesn't get dark until nine or thereabouts. So what do you think, ma'am? Between nine and eleven?'

'Could be a bit earlier. Whoever did it wouldn't want to use lights to see their way out. Too easily spotted from a distance. So possibly about eight. Would there have been anyone around who might have spotted them? Birdwatchers? Ramblers?'

'We could ask Alice. She'd know how likely that would be. We have to take her statement anyway.'

The two detectives drove to the activity centre, where they found Alice Llewellyn in the rangers' office, talking to one of the junior staff. She was pale and her eyes were red.

'We need to pick your brains, Alice,' Sophie said. 'We're fairly sure the body has only been there since yesterday evening, probably at dusk or thereabouts. Could anyone else have been around who might have spotted something?'

Alice shook her head. 'None of the staff. And we don't have any observation projects ongoing at the moment, so none of our known volunteers would have been out. There's a chance there could have been other visitors, maybe dog walkers and the like, but they tend to stay down at this end of the forest. We try to keep people away from the bog because it's a designated nature reserve.'

'So it's unlikely?'

'From my experience, yes.' She looked at her colleague, who nodded. 'We've sometimes had organised evening groups up there, but I don't think we've ever run into strangers at that time of day. It's too dangerous. Slipping into one of those pools could be fatal.'

'Okay. We won't do an urgent public request specific to the reserve. Instead we'll include it in a general request for possible witnesses. We need to take your statement, Alice. So if your colleague can leave us, we can get started.'

Alice looked grim. 'I've been through it before, so let's get it over with.' She looked at Sophie. 'It was all rather exciting then. It seems a lot worse this time.'

'It's what I said earlier. You didn't see any bodies then, Alice. That's what makes the difference.'

CHAPTER 22: MOLE HUNT

Friday afternoon, Week 2

Rae got down to work immediately. She started by summarising the information that Sophie had given her, following her visit to Bournemouth that morning. Rae used mind-mapping software rather than a physical incident board, and built up a web diagram on her laptop, securely protected with a new password. The boss had been right. There were just too many suspicious events. It wasn't only the possible leak of information from the incident board early in the week. There was now a trail of suspicious activity. Requests for information had been delayed or played down, legitimate queries sent down blind avenues or cleverly diverted.

At least she now had a name to work with, but she would have to be careful. The diversions had all been done so cleverly that he might notice any investigation. The mole's link to the Woodruff family business seemed pretty logical, but were there other connections?

The starting point must be that funeral. She thought so, and so did the boss. Something had happened there that had led to the deaths of Sylvia and Ted Armitage, who'd been present only by accident. She needed to know who had been present, apart from the Woodruff family themselves. But she couldn't afford to set off any alarm bells. Not even a glimmer of what she was up to must get back to the mole.

Why had the Armitage couple been there? Because they'd been early for the next funeral, the one they were planning to attend. Rae sat thinking. Wait! Maybe the two groups of mourners had intermingled, just slightly. Maybe a person at the later funeral recognised someone attending the Woodruff service as they left the crematorium. She re-examined the notes Marsh had made after his visit there, then phoned Sharon Giroux for confirmation. Rae then identified the funeral directors, and then the family member who had arranged the later funeral, that of Sylvia's friend, Georgie Palmer. Rae was up and running.

* * *

Rae drove south to Poole and spent an hour with Georgie Palmer's son, Colin, an assistant bank manager and keen local historian — as she soon discovered. Eventually Rae came away with a long list of names, addresses and telephone numbers, with those Colin considered most reliable marked with an asterisk. Colin himself had been too preoccupied with his mother's death to notice whether there were still people lingering from the previous service, but he was sure that at least a few of the guests would have been more observant.

Rae returned to the office and started the long task of contacting the guests. The first eighteen calls generated nothing, the people weren't even aware of the committal just a few minutes prior to Georgie's funeral. It was nearly six in the evening and Rae was beginning to feel despondent when someone volunteered the first key item of information.

This was Shirley Willis, a former work colleague of Georgie's. 'I saw Councillor Blythe coming out. I know him because he's on the development committee and I've been to a few planning meetings.'

'Did you speak to him?' Rae asked.

'No. I was still making my way from the car park and he seemed to be in a bit of a hurry.'

'We may be back in touch to get the details, Mrs Willis.'

Rae continued working through the list. A couple of people recognised a pub landlord from Bournemouth and the manager of a casino in the area. Rae thought the former could be the Woodruff from the Rising Moon pub. There were several false sightings, including one elderly woman who claimed that she'd spotted Sean Connery, still looking like the James Bond of Goldfinger days. Two people remembered a man with a scar on his face and several recalled the Armitage couple saying that they'd attended the earlier service by mistake. Finally Rae reached the end of the list. As far as she could see, the person of most interest was the councillor. She would need to discuss this with the boss before she went any further.

She didn't have long to wait. 'It was a fairly small congregation, ma'am. I've got these three to follow up, but my guess is that there weren't even twenty people there.'

'It was a committal, Rae. The full service had already taken place elsewhere, probably in a church. This would have been for family and close friends only.'

'Should I try to find out about that? We might get better information.'

'Make it indirect, and don't approach anybody yet. Just find out where it was for the time being. Meanwhile, visit these three and find out what they remember. Do a bit of digging into the background of this councillor, but keep everything low key. We can't afford to let any of this out at the moment.'

* * *

Rae worked until late. The councillor was certainly a man of interest. He'd served in a variety of roles during his time on the council, stretching back several decades. Planning and development, licensing, highways and byways, Councillor

Blythe had been involved with most aspects of council work over the years. Why would he have attended the committal for Phil Woodruff? The boss had said it would have been for immediate family and possibly extremely close friends. She left that line of inquiry for the time being and scanned through the online records of the local newspapers. Sure enough, just before the short service at the crematorium, there had been a church funeral for Phil Woodruff in St Bede's RC Church. Surely the councillor would have gone to that service rather than to the committal? She checked the council website, tracking back through the planning meetings. There was the reason — the timing. It clashed with a cabinet meeting discussing future hotel development plans. The meeting was recorded as having finished at the same time as the main funeral got under way. So the councillor had gone directly to the crematorium. Rae printed everything out, including the agenda for the meeting. This was becoming very interesting.

She then switched her attention to their suspected mole, and checked his record in the police force. There wasn't a lot. The problem was that she couldn't access the detailed service records without authorisation, and without the search being logged. She'd have to give up on that and think of a more subtle method. Social media? She checked his profile, using a made up one of her own. Keen on pubs and varieties of beer — no surprise there from what she'd heard. Hobbies included fish and chips, pizza and Manchester United FC. Why the latter? There's no accounting for a person's footballing preference, she thought, wearily. A few bigoted postings about gays and women, but she'd seen worse. Nevertheless, it was a little troubling when it was all put together. This man was a police officer, and supposedly respected by the community he served. Could she respect someone who posted such small-minded comments?

Rae sat back and thought, then connected to the Registry of Births, Deaths and Marriages, selecting the historical marriage category. She keyed in "Blythe, Thomas. Married between 1970 and 1990 in Dorset." And there it was. In 1989 the councillor had married Carol Frimwell. A feeling of dread came over Rae. She knew what that name meant to the DCI. Marsh had told her about it soon after she'd begun. He'd warned Rae never to mention the names Frimwell or Duff to the boss without good reason. And now the name had cropped up. What was his name? Ricky? He'd be somewhere in the prison system now. Out of curiosity she entered the name Woodruff into the same set of records. Bingo! Up came an entry for the same district, along with something unbelievable. Wayne Woodruff had married a Susan Frimwell six months later. Could that be right? She kept searching, and there it was. Susan and Carol Frimwell, twin girls born in 1964. She looked at the clock. After nine in the evening. Time to go. She had plenty of leads to follow up the next day.

CHAPTER 23: BARBECUE

Friday evening, Week 2

The Mitchells had been invited to a barbecue party at Wayne Woodruff's luxurious home, a villa in an upmarket district of Poole. A local catering company had set up a large barbecue unit on the rear patio, and dishes of salads, cheeses and cold meats lined a long trestle table. A smartly dressed waiter manned a bar, handing out glasses of champagne and chilled wine.

'Is there a reason for this party?' Marilyn asked. 'It was a bit short notice, wasn't it?'

Gordon shrugged. 'We're about to expand, apparently. The preliminary deal's been agreed, so by next month we should own twice the number of premises we do at the moment. It's a celebration party.'

'I always feel uneasy with these people, Gordon,' she whispered. 'You know that. Why did we have to come?'

'They've offered me better terms. I'm thinking of accepting.'

She turned to face him. 'What? I thought we'd agreed that you were going to get out?'

'It's been very quick, everything's happened in the last couple of days. And we're moving into total legitimacy.

Everything completely above board. I insisted on it and Wayne's agreed. I'll have a new role. I won't be Tony's dogsbody, not any more. It's a better opportunity, Marilyn. And my earnings will double.'

'Double?'

'Exactly. I couldn't turn it down, not under those terms. The money's more than we ever dreamed of.'

Marilyn still looked troubled. 'It was never the money, Gordon. I told you that. I just thought you deserved better than having to run around after that Tony Sorrento.' She looked around. 'Where is he, by the way?'

'No idea. I expected him to be here. He hasn't been in since yesterday.'

She sniffed. 'Well, maybe I can relax and enjoy the evening after all. He always seems to be watching people, calculating how to manipulate them, working out how to get the upper hand. I can't say that I particularly like Wayne either. He seems a bit moody and unpredictable. I always feel that his eyes are all over me. But Justin's okay.' She looked across at Griffiths, standing by himself on the lawn. 'Don't you think he looks a bit worried? He seems on edge. Let's have a chat.'

Close to, Griffith's face was pinched with worry. 'Are you okay, Justin?' she asked.

He appeared to shake himself. 'Yes, fine. Sorry, just worried about a few things at home. Nothing important.'

'I was saying to Gordon, I'm surprised Tony's not here. Not that I miss him.' Marilyn had never hidden her dislike of Sorrento, even to the man himself.

'I haven't seen him all day,' Griffiths replied. 'It's not like him. He's always at work, rain or shine. And he always gets a message to you if he's elsewhere, doesn't he, Gordy?'

'I haven't heard anything from him either,' Gordon said. 'I wouldn't worry though. He can look after himself. He might seem a bit abrasive but he's a good bloke underneath. He's never let me down.'

'Gordon's just been telling me about his new job offer. I don't know whether to offer congratulations or hit him,' Marilyn added.

The effect on Griffiths was unexpected. He looked at Marilyn as if she'd just spoken in a foreign language, then switched his gaze to Gordon. 'Jesus,' he muttered, and walked away.

'I take it he didn't know?' she said.

'Obviously not. I thought Wayne had told him. I don't think it matters. I'll maybe go and have a few words and smooth things over.'

Gordon followed Griffiths into the house. Marilyn stood alone, sipping her glass of water. Soon she was joined by Wayne's wife, Sue, a curvy blonde who'd rarely given her the time of day before. Sue brought a glass of bubbly and asked how she was. What on earth was going on?

* * *

At the end of the evening, Justin Griffiths walked to his car, ready for the drive home. He was a careful man, predictable and unadventurous. He'd only been in his current role with the Woodruffs for three years, having been one of their more successful pub managers before that. He was uneasy. Sorrento had been the decision-maker, the man of ideas. And now he'd disappeared. It wasn't like his boss to just vanish without leaving a message. There had been no answer to his phone calls and no response when Justin had visited Sorrento's house that morning. But what really worried him was Wayne's lack of concern. He didn't seem remotely interested, suggesting merely that he, Justin, should ensure that all Sorrento's current tasks were dealt with, either by Gordy or himself. He'd even suggested how the work could be divided.

It was unlike Wayne to be that organised. He'd usually panic at the approach of any crisis, leaving it to one of his three assistants to sort out the mess. But this had been different, almost as if he'd been prepared. Maybe some information had passed between Woodruff and Sorrento the previous day. Gordy was concerned too, judging by what he'd said in their brief chat. No one liked Sorrento much, but he got things done and that was important in a setup like theirs.

He climbed into his car, yawned and started the engine. Time to go home. He could think things through next week, in the office. Maybe Sorrento would be back by then.

* * *

In his cell in Long Lartin prison, Ricky Frimwell was re-reading a short letter from his younger sister, Sue Woodruff. He couldn't help but smile. Maybe it was time he changed his opinion of her. She seemed to be a real canny operator, underestimated by everyone who came into contact with her. He had decoded her carefully worded message and judged the new state of play. Her ideas seemed good and would bring some benefits to the Frimwell family. If some of Woodruff's mob of fuckwits thought they'd take over most of his old operation then the joke was on them. He knew where the real power lay and, with Sorrento no longer on the scene, he could start flexing his muscles, even from his prison cell. Life was beginning to get more tolerable.

And then the downside hit him. All his efforts had channelled power towards his half-sisters, Sue and Carol. Carol had always been a bit of an air-head, easily manipulated. But what about Sue? She'd always resisted him in the past. Would she do what she was told now? If she didn't, it would be a problem. Not just a problem, more like a fucking catastrophe. She had the shares. What if she went her own way at the last minute? Fuck.

CHAPTER 24: SANITISED

Early Saturday morning, Week 2

When Barry Marsh arrived in the incident room with Sophie, Rae was already there and hard at work. She was so engrossed in a phone conversation that she didn't even acknowledge his wave, so he made his way to the kettle and made a coffee. He'd only just sat down at his desk when he realised that she'd sidled across, and was glancing sideways at the DCI's office.

'Can we go out for a walk, boss?'

Marsh looked up at her serious face and decided not to make a joke of the invitation. 'Okay.'

'Separately? Meet you in the car park in a couple of minutes?'

He watched her leave, then followed her, catching up with her outside. 'What's with the skulduggery?'

Rae took a deep breath. 'Wayne Woodruff's wife is Ricky Frimwell's sister. Her name is Susan. They married in 1989. You told me never to mention the name to the boss, so I'm bringing it to you.'

Marsh stood open-mouthed.

'And it doesn't stop there. Susan has a twin sister, Carol. She married Thomas Blythe, also in 1989. Thomas Blythe is now Councillor Blythe. And guess what? I have a witness that spotted the good councillor at that ropey funeral, the one the Armitages went to by mistake.'

'Christ. Give me time to get my head around this.'

'I can't, because I haven't finished. I found out that Ricky Frimwell is in Long Lartin Prison so I contacted them first thing. That's who I was talking to when you came in. I asked them if there's been anything unusual in his behaviour recently. There hasn't, but he's had several unexpected visitors this week, including, on Wednesday, a man with a scar on his face. He signed in as Tony Sorrento, from Bournemouth. I think I've found your man, and a whole lot more besides.' She paused. 'I'm out of my depth. I don't know what to do.'

Barry remained silent for what seemed to be an age. 'We have to take it to the boss. It's way beyond me as well. The name fits, by the way. The boss was just telling me that she was on the phone to DI McGreedie in Bournemouth last night, and the facial scar rang a bell. He came back to her with the same name early this morning.'

'How will she react?'

'It should be okay. It was Duff that killed her father, not Frimwell. There wasn't a problem when we nabbed Frimwell. Duff was a different matter, though.' He thought back two years to that horrific case. Surely nothing could ever be as bad as that again? 'She'll be alright with it, I'm sure.'

'What are they like? I need to know, boss.'

'They're both violent, manipulative psychopaths. I heard Duff has completely lost his marbles and is in a secure unit, so we probably don't need to worry about him. He was the worst. Frimwell is his nephew. Nasty, devious and angry. Not a good combination.' He paused. 'Okay. Are you ready for this?'

Rae nodded.

'Let's go then.'

They walked back inside and climbed the stairs to the incident room and Sophie's office.

'Ma'am, we have some important developments for you. Rae's made several breakthroughs, but they involve a name that you might not want to hear.' Barry sounded tense.

'I wondered. I saw the two of you sidle off, hoping I wouldn't notice. Okay, get on with it, Rae.'

She sat listening intently as Rae recounted her story, occasionally closing her eyes. 'There's no chance of a mistake here, Rae? Is there any way you can double check?'

'I'm pretty certain, ma'am. But I'm limited as to what I can use to verify it all. Ideally I'd like to meet them somehow, but we can't do that yet, can we?'

'No, but you're our secret weapon, Rae. You're new to the area, and they haven't met you yet, whereas Barry and I are known to them. I'm not going to trust this to Blackman and McCluskie. It's too sensitive.' She thought for a while. 'Barry and I will go and pay another visit to that pub, this time officially. It's the registered address of Woodruff's business and seems to have the company offices on the upper floor, according to Kevin. I want to find out more about Sorrento and his place in their operations so, now we know he's dead, we have an ideal opportunity to ask some awkward questions.' She paused. 'How did you get on to all this Rae? I thought you were investigating our mole?'

'I was. I had the idea of identifying people at the funeral in case he was there. Then this just fell into my lap.'

'Well done, whatever you were up to. You get back to work and we'll visit Pokesdown. You can drive, Barry. I need to think.'

Marsh led the way back out to the car park. She'd taken that news well, he thought. But the implications were huge. Was there some kind of link between the Woodruffs and the old Duff gang? Please God no, he thought. But there was a sinking feeling in his stomach. He could remember a group of friends and family who'd attended the Frimwell trial occasionally. Had there been two women who looked alike? He couldn't remember. It had been a trial that he'd tried hard to forget.

* * *

It was too early in the morning for the pub itself to be open, but Marsh spotted a side door marked "Private" with a bell beside it. He rang and they waited.

A freckle-faced man in his late thirties opened the door, not one of the three they'd seen in the bar a few days earlier. Marsh held out his warrant card. 'I'm Detective Sergeant Marsh and this is Detective Inspector Allen. We're investigating the suspicious death of Tony Sorrento. We understand he worked here.'

The man's mouth hung open. 'Christ. Tony's dead? Surely there's been a mistake?'

'Middle-aged? Tall with dark hair? A thin scar down the left side of his face?'

'That sounds like Tony,' the man replied.

'Can we come in? It really isn't convenient standing out here like this.'

The look of confusion was replaced by one of wariness. 'Of course. I can find an empty office. There's no one else here at this time on a Saturday morning. I've only come in to do some filing.'

The two detectives followed him up a flight of stairs.

'And you are. . ?' asked Sophie.

'I'm Gordon Mitchell, the company secretary. Look, this is a total shock. Tony was my boss. I had no idea.' He stopped at an office and ushered them in, moving a few chairs aside so that they could sit down.

'Is there a photo of Mr Sorrento available?' asked Marsh. 'We're having trouble tracing his family or friends.'

'He was single and, as far as I'm aware, his parents are both dead. I'm not surprised you can't find anyone.' He opened a drawer and pulled out a framed photo of two men at what appeared to be a formal reception. One was him, the other was Sorrento.

'Can we keep the photo? It does look to be the person who was found dead yesterday.'

'Whereabouts was this? What happened?'

'We're not at liberty to say at the moment, sir. Not until we've traced a next of kin. But there are some questions we need to ask. First off, what was Mr Sorrento's role in the company?'

'He was one of the three directors. There were four, until the founder died a couple of months ago.'

'That would be Phil Woodruff? And the company name is Woodruff Holdings?'

Mitchell nodded.

'Can you tell us about the company?'

'It started here when Phil bought this pub. He expanded over the years and at the time of his death it owned five pubs, three nightclubs, three massage parlours and a casino.'

'What does it own now, Mr Mitchell?' Sophie gazed steadily at Mitchell.

'Well, we're in the process of expanding. We're in negotiation to purchase some more commercial properties, including a couple of hotels.'

'Would that be outright purchase or a merger of some type?'

Gordon hesitated. 'Probably more of a merger.'

'And can you tell us who you might be merging with? A company name maybe?' She spoke quietly. Marsh thought she sounded quite casual.

'I don't have the full details. But it's only at the negotiating stage at the moment. It isn't a done deal. It's with a property company called Midwinter Tide.'

'And was Mr Sorrento involved in the talks?' she said.

'Yes, very much so. It was his idea.'

'So would his death put a stop to the plans?'

Mitchell shook his head. 'I wouldn't think so. We were broadly in favour. Our current boss is Wayne Woodruff, Phil's son. He's keen, but the deal has to be the right one.'

Sophie nodded and looked at Marsh.

'We need some personal details about Mr Sorrento. His address would be a good start. We'd also like to see his office and check through his belongings. Would that be okay?'

'Do you have a warrant?'

'No, we don't. But it's a suspicious death, Mr Mitchell. Your help would be very much appreciated to avoid having to wait for a warrant.' She gave him a thin, challenging smile. He remained silent.

* * *

They left the Rising Moon an hour later, with a minimum of personal information about Sorrento, and little else.

'His office has been sanitised, Barry,' Sophie said. 'Nothing out of place, everything tidy. No suspicious letters or notes anywhere, nothing that would give us a lead. I bet that's why our friendly and helpful Mr Mitchell was there early on a Saturday morning. He'd just been through the place.'

'Well, at least we've got an address. And a key. That's helpful.'

Sophie snorted. 'We'll find the same thing at his house. At the same time that Mitchell was going through Sorrento's office, someone else will have been doing the same at his home.'

She phoned the county forensic team, passing on the address and asking for a search unit to be despatched.

The luxurious Bournemouth villa was deserted. The two detectives let themselves in and took a walk through the property, taking care not to touch anything of forensic importance. The furniture was modern and expensive-looking. Artwork lined the walls and a high-quality audio-visual system had pride of place in the lounge.

Sophie looked through a shelf dedicated to DVDs of opera. 'Verdi and Puccini. Not quite your typical lowlife thug. Certainly different to Frimwell, if it's his bunch they're planning to merge with.'

'He's dead, ma'am. Maybe he didn't fit in the new scheme of things. But it's a bit odd if they bumped him off just after he'd come up with this new plan.'

'Power struggle. With the father dying there'd be a vacuum at the top and maybe he trod on some toes while he was trying to fill it. I also wonder if he underestimated Frimwell. If he was assuming that nasty piece of lowlife was helpless in prison and was trying to cheat him, then he made a serious error. And with what Rae found out about Frimwell's sisters, he would have been skating on thin ice.'

'But surely he'd have known? If he was a director, wouldn't he have found out ages ago that his boss's wife was a Frimwell?'

'Not necessarily. You and I investigated Frimwell a couple of years ago. Did we know about his twin sisters? No. They've obviously kept a low profile. Wouldn't we if we were in their place? Sisters to an evil psychopath like him?'

Marsh was silent.

'His company's name was Midwinter Tide. Could you find out what happened to it after he was convicted? How come it still exists?'

They walked through the rest of the property, but found little of interest. The address books kept in a bureau cupboard had no obvious family names, nor did a calendar fixed to the kitchen wall. While Marsh waited for the forensic unit, Sophie visited the neighbours on each side. She returned after only a couple of minutes.

'There was a van here in the early hours of yesterday morning. One of the neighbours spotted it when he took his dog out at six. It had gone when he returned twenty minutes later. I don't think we'll find anything directly incriminating.'

Sophie was right. 'We'll leave Blackman and McCluskie to run this scene. It's been sanitised, so it's just routine from here on.'

Marsh looked troubled. 'But what if one of them's the mole, ma'am? Do we want them so closely involved?'

'Two things, Barry. Sorrento's death is clearly murder, so it's too major to keep under wraps. They'd know about it pretty quick whatever we did. And second, the mole probably isn't one of them, at least I don't think so. It's odd in a way. They're lazy, inept and, in McCluskie's case, immoral. But I never thought he was bent. Anyway, they're ruining the atmosphere in the incident room, with their gloomy faces. They're like a couple of kids who need a trip outside every now and again to let off steam. So let's give them this opportunity.' She looked at her watch. 'Post mortem in an hour. Time to get back to Dorchester.'

CHAPTER 25: COOL SMILE

Late Saturday morning, Week 2

'What do you have for me, Benny?' Sophie and Barry walked into the pathologist's theatre, where the autopsy examination was already under way.

'No surprises yet. Nothing unusual so far in the blood tests, but it's early days. I took a sample yesterday as soon as we got back here, and put it in for checking immediately. He was healthy and fit, and there were no obvious drugs in his bloodstream. There don't seem to be any other injuries, so it's likely that he was killed by that single blow to the head.' He returned his attention to the prominent head wound of the body on the bench.

'Any idea what caused it?'

'There are traces of grit at the sides of the wound so it could have been a lump of rock. The shape of the skull fracture fits that idea. Whatever caused it, the weapon would have been covered in blood, bone fragments and brain tissue. The assailant too. There would have been a spray of blood.'

'He was a tall bloke, Benny.'

'A couple of inches over six foot. The blow looks as though it came from above. Make of that what you will.'

'Maybe he was hit while getting out of a car.' She looked at Marsh. 'Maybe he was lured there, and someone was waiting.'

'I'd go with that,' he replied. 'I don't think it was spur of the moment. It's got that deliberate feel to it. And if it was a lump of rock, our chances of ever finding it are slim. That place is full of boggy pools. Whoever it was probably chucked it into one, and it's sitting hidden in six inches of slimy ooze at the bottom.'

Sophie nodded. 'That fits with the fact we found blood stains a few yards away, where the tyre tracks were. We need Dave Nash's analysis of them. Maybe someone was already there, waiting.'

'We were lucky that the ranger came across the body so quickly. It could have lain there for a lot longer, seeing how well it was hidden in the undergrowth.'

'It's difficult to be sure, Barry. Crows are noisy birds and their racket would have caught the attention of anyone passing by. And where he was found wasn't that far from the road, unlike the old couple last week. Alice said that she'd been walking for some time when she came across Sorrento's body, but when you look at the map she'd nearly completed a circuit. She was almost out of the bog area and close to several of the footpaths that are used by ramblers and dog walkers, so my guess is that someone would have stumbled across the body within another day or two if Alice hadn't spotted it. I don't think whoever did it was too worried. They only needed a day, just enough time to clear anything incriminating from his office and house.'

They left when the surgical procedures got under way. For some reason that she couldn't fathom, Sophie had a total abhorrence of scalpels, particularly seeing them cut through skin. She'd fainted at the very first autopsy she'd attended as a young detective. She hoped that her fear hadn't been inherited by her younger daughter, Jade, presently preparing her application to study medicine at university.

'Barry, we need to make another attempt to get Rod to remember what his parents told him about that funeral, especially now we have this new information Rae's discovered. It would be useful to know whether they recognised anyone there, particularly this councillor. But we can't afford to push him too hard. Can you see him again? Maybe a few gentle nudges might unlock some memories.'

* * *

The Armitage son was just leaving his flat. He was wearing an olive green waterproof jacket and walking boots caked in dirt.

'Going out for a breath of air. I need to get my head straight. I was going to walk along the river bank.'

'Can I come with you?' Marsh asked. 'There's a few questions I need to ask. Nothing too serious, though. Maybe walking might help you remember. Do you often go out for walks?'

'Not recent-like, but I used to years ago. Sometimes me and Sharon used to walk when we were kids. Down by the river, through the woods, that kind of thing.' He sighed. 'I've got to get myself together. Losing Mum and Dad shook me up, even if Sharon doesn't think so. Maybe it didn't show, but I felt it. Then Pete sacking me. I kind of thought, can I go on like this? It's kind of like reaching a point where something's gotta change, or I'm just gonna sink lower. I've gone all week without any junk or booze, and things ain't so fuzzy now. Being out helps a bit.'

They reached the nearby riverside path and started to walk beside the flowing water.

'I came to see if your parents might have mentioned anything about that funeral, Rod. You know, the one they went into by mistake. We wonder if it might be linked to their deaths, that they saw something or someone. Maybe they didn't realise what or who it was, but someone else did. So far we just know that they told you about it that same night. While you were across having a meal with them, maybe?'

Rod looked at him. 'Sounds as if you already know more about it than me. How d'you know I was across to eat?'

'I don't. It was only a suggestion. You told us that you went across most weeks, so I was just guessing.'

'Prob'ly right. Mum used to feed me up. Said she thought I guzzled too many pizzas and burgers.'

'If it helps, that day was really warm, Rod. For late April, I mean. There hadn't been a cloud in the sky.'

Rod's expression cleared. 'Oh God, yeah. I remember now. Dad moaned about all the time he'd wasted being at the funeral when he could have been in his precious garden. It really pissed me off. He was a slave to that garden. Bloody stupid. Then he moaned 'cause Mum had only done oven chips. She usually got the chip pan out and did them proper like, but she wasn't feeling well. It was the funeral that did it. She had a bad headache. What is it? Flashing lights and stuff?'

'A migraine?'

'That's it. She had a migraine, but she still had to do food for us. She was a bit of a martyr was Mum. If she'd phoned and told me, I'd have gone a few days later, or got fish and chips on my way over.'

Marsh waited.

'She said they arrived at the funeral early and had to hang about a bit. Then a coffin arrived and they followed the people inside, but they twigged it was the wrong service. Mum got stressed over it.'

'Anything else?'

Rod shook his head. 'That was it. They went back out and waited. People started to arrive for the next funeral, the one they should have been at. That's what Mum said.'

'And they were people she recognised? The ones for Georgie Palmer's funeral?'

Rod's brow was furrowed in concentration. 'They didn't know the people for that one either. The dead woman moved away years before. They were the only people from Blandford who went, so they didn't know anyone. Mebbe that was why they got confused. They only talked to one person there. That's why Dad was in a mood, even later on when I saw them. He said it was a complete waste of time. Him moaning made Mum even more miserable.'

Marsh thought back to Rae's list of people from the Palmer funeral. So the couple had talked to someone there. Who could it have been?

'This is all very helpful, Rod. I've got some checking to do, but what you've said fits with another witness.'

Rod stopped and turned to face Marsh. 'What? You think what happened was something to do with that funeral? Christ. That's weird.'

'We don't know. We have to check everything. I'll keep you posted.'

Marsh walked back to the police station and phoned Shirley Willis to check she was in. He then drove over to Poole.

* * *

Shirley was a bright, alert seventy-year-old. It soon became apparent that little escaped her notice.

'Yes,' she said. 'Councillor Blythe was in a hurry coming out of the crematorium building. And he was most definitely in the previous one, not Georgie Palmer's. He seemed to be in a bit of a mood, and didn't apologise for nearly knocking me over when he bumped into me.'

'Did he talk to anyone else?' Barry asked.

'Not really. The people I was talking to had to step back sharpish. The husband seemed to be a bit quiet after that.'

'Who were they, Mrs Willis?'

'I'd never met them before the funeral. They were looking a bit lost so I just started talking to them. I think they said they knew Georgie from when she lived in Blandford.'

Marsh nodded. 'That ties in. I just needed to double check with you. It might be a key piece of evidence.'

'Your colleague didn't say much when she phoned, but I've been wondering. Were they that couple found dead in the nature reserve?'

'Yes, and we're treating their deaths as suspicious. Can you keep all this to yourself, Mrs Willis? It's a very sensitive investigation and we don't want to release too much to the press at the moment.'

She nodded. 'Of course. They seemed a nice enough couple. They didn't strike me as the types who would commit suicide.'

'What did you talk about?'

'Mainly how we knew Georgie. The woman, I think her name was Sylvia, used to play badminton with her. She was a bit nervy, but I'm not surprised, after having just found themselves in the wrong place. I sat with them during Georgie's service and she was much calmer when that finished. They didn't come to the reception, though. Her husband wanted to get back to Blandford before the rush hour traffic, so we didn't chat for long.'

* * *

Marsh drove back to Blandford, and called at Pete Armitage's small office. He was in, checking through a pile of invoices.

'The curse of running your own business, Sergeant,' Pete said. 'I sometimes think I'll drown in paper.'

Marsh laughed. 'It's a curse for everyone these days, Mr Armitage. It's unbelievable how much we have to do in the police, but prosecutions would fail if it wasn't all done properly.'

'How can I help you?'

'I wonder if there's a chance either Sylvia or Ted talked to you about a funeral they attended back in April? In Poole?'

'No. I don't remember it. When was this?'

'Towards the end of the month.'

'I was away on holiday then. Took a break in Barcelona to see the sights and fit in a football match. Had a great time.'

Post dropped onto the floor of the lobby, and Pete walked through to collect it. Marsh was left looking at the invoices and the computer screen. His eyes ran idly down the list, and a name jumped out at him. Woodruff Holdings. Pete must have done a decorating job at one of their properties. Marsh was about to lean forward to gain a clearer view when he heard Pete's footsteps. He stood up, said goodbye and left.

* * *

'I didn't expect to see you back so soon, Chief Inspector.' Gordon Mitchell was still in the Woodruff Holdings company offices above the Rising Moon pub. He looked warily at the two detectives standing in the doorway.

Sophie gave him a cool smile. 'I need to see your company records, Mr Mitchell. There's a chance that Mr Sorrento's death may be linked to his work, so I'd like access to the records of other organisations and businesses that he'd have been in contact with. You currently own, what, twelve premises?'

Mitchell nodded.

'And Mr Sorrento did most of the day to day management? Apart from the legal aspects, which were your own concern. Is that right?'

'Yes.'

'So he would be dealing with a lot of people on a regular basis?' He nodded. 'We need to check in more detail. We glanced at the company records this morning, but little more.'

She unlocked the door to Sorrento's office. 'Has anyone else been in here since we left this morning?'

'Just the cleaner.'

'I thought I said no one was to come in? Wasn't that clear enough for you?'

'Sorry,' Mitchell mumbled.

Sophie and Marsh left him in the corridor and closed the door. Marsh switched on the computer while Sophie started looking through the large ring-binders on a shelf behind the desk. Both yielded the evidence they were looking for. Pete Armitage was obviously the main decorating contractor for all the Woodruff premises. He'd invoiced for two already this year, and three the previous year. They photographed each page.

'They might have had time to sanitise anything that could have linked them to Sorrento's death,' Sophie said, 'but this stuff wouldn't have appeared suspicious. It's just ordinary company records. Run of the mill stuff to them. But gold dust to us. Well, would you believe it? Could our nice, friendly Pete Armitage be a wolf in sheep's clothing?'

They left the office, taking the stack of folders with them.

'Useful, Mr Mitchell. Gives us many of the people he'd have been in contact with. You'll get them back when we've finished with them, probably in a couple of days.'

They walked back to the car.

'He'll be panicking round about now,' Sophie said. 'He'll be back in that office to see exactly what we've taken, then he'll be on the blower to his bosses. Someone, sometime, will think of our man, Pete. If he is involved, they'll start to worry.'

'Do you think he might be in danger?'

'Only if he is involved somehow. If it's purely coincidence, then he's got nothing to worry about, has he?'

'But we don't know yet.'

'No. Do you think we should put Blackman and McCluskie onto surveillance, just to keep him safe? They'll do a good job, won't they? Two solid, reliable, hard-working coppers.' Sophie laughed.

CHAPTER 26: WILLY-WAGGLING

Saturday evening, Week 2

A thin drizzle was falling, creating halos around the lights along the footpath. The figure in the dark coat had turned up his collar and lowered his umbrella as he approached. Mitchell couldn't make out his features.

'Listen, Wayne. Don't tell me anything I don't absolutely need to know. And that includes what you and your pals have been getting up to, because it makes me an accessory. The less I know the better. And who's this guy with you?'

'Gordon Mitchell. He's been doing our legal stuff for years now. We've just promoted him, so he'll be doing some of Tony's jobs. You need to be able to recognise him, just in case.'

Gordon stepped forward and held out his hand. It was ignored.

'Recognise him? Christ, what do you want from me now? Listen, this has gone far enough. I'm not some little snitch, at your beck and call. I looked after your dad's interests as a favour. All I did was to tip him off if the police were visiting one of his places. As far as I'm concerned, that stopped when he died.

That's what I told Sorrento. And the stuff you've been up to in the last few days turns my stomach. I don't know why the two of you fell out, I never asked him for details. But what you did was way beyond what was necessary. What is it with you? First that old couple, now one of your own top people. Are you fucking mad? Talk about a hornets' nest. Why did you do it?'

'He was double-crossing me and my family. It was either him or us. No alternative. And I've got Frimwell to keep sweet, now he's involved. He won't put up with any dissent. And as for that doddery old couple, do you think it was me that topped them in case they'd seen something? I'm not some psychopathic nut-head like Frimwell. There was more to it than that, trust me.'

There was a snort. 'Frimwell? That mad bastard? He's inside, locked up safe and sound. For life. What can he do?'

'He's still running things for his family. His sisters get a load of dosh each month from their mum's trust fund, and it's that same trust that owns the properties we'll be buying. I want Gordon here to take over the running of that trust, then start to make changes. Access to it will give me a helluva lot of flexibility. But I've got to keep the Frimwells sweet, all of them. They're a close lot.'

The man was slowly shaking his head. He was deliberately standing in deep shadow, and Gordon still couldn't make out any of his features.

Woodruff continued. 'And I know you did more for my dad. I know you pulled strings and made contacts for him, so don't try and bullshit me. I won't ask you to do any more for me than you were doing for him, so don't get high and mighty. I'll make it worth your while. We'll all be in clover once I get our business merged with the Frimwells.'

Gordon had never worked this closely with Wayne before, he'd always had Sorrento as a go-between. His new boss wasn't as canny as he'd imagined. Gordon was learning a lot from this exchange but he was worried about the implications of what he'd heard. Was Wayne behind the recent deaths, as this cop had implied?

'So it's a merger now? Sorrento was talking of just buying some of their properties.'

Woodruff sighed. 'It was all so unnecessary. He never realised that I'd always planned this. He thought up his little scheme all by himself, and just didn't twig that he was treading on my toes. I had a far bigger project in mind.'

'Isn't it chancy getting involved with the Frimwells? Do you think you'll be able to control them?'

Wayne laughed. 'You don't get it, do you? You cops think you know everything, but you fucking don't. I know it'll work because I've got an insider. I don't just have you and that greedy council bloke who acts like he's some bigwig but does everything I tell him. Shall I tell you his weakness, apart from the money I give him? He likes snorting crack in the presence of a couple of busty babes. He can't resist the white powder and the big tits. And if the trail of crack is spread out on the big tits, even better.' He paused. 'No, I have an insider in the Frimwell family business, involved with the trust fund. And there's stacks of cash there. So stay on my good side, my friendly cop, and you too will be in clover.'

'I'll need to think about it,' came the reply.

'Okay, but don't take too long. And you'd better make the right decision when you've done your thinking. Savvy?'

The man turned on his heels and walked away, his tall form quickly disappearing into the mist and gloom.

'Prick,' Woodruff said. 'It's different days for him now. He either sings to my tune or not at all.'

Gordon and Woodruff turned back towards their car. 'What can you do if he doesn't play along?' Gordon asked.

'Plenty. And if Blythe starts playing up as well, I've got enough to link the two together and bring them both down. The finer detail will be up to you, Gordy, you're our legal man. But it won't be too tough.'

'How's Griffy taking the change? He wasn't happy when I told him about my new role last night at your barbecue.'

'He'll come round. He knows which way his bread is buttered. It'll all be fine, Gordy. The whole thing is sitting there like a big, juicy plum, ripe for the picking. I've been thinking about this for years, ever since I married Sue. And working on it since Frimwell was locked up. I could see what it would mean even then.'

'How can you be so confident?' Gordon asked. 'Don't get me wrong, it's a good plan and I can't see any problems, but you seem so sure.'

'Don't you know? Haven't you twigged? Sue is Ricky Frimwell's sister. She's the brains behind the family trust. That's why I was laughing all the time Tony was up to his shenanigans. He didn't know that my wife is Ricky's sister, and he didn't know anything about their trust. And you, my good friend, with your brains and your legal know-how, are ideally placed to exploit it. Sue is on our side, so we're nearly home and dry. She thinks she runs things, but I know better.' He paused. 'God, I feel on top of the world. How about a couple of beers before we split? I've got a bit of a thirst.'

* * *

Back at the Mitchells' house, Marilyn was pouring nibbles into a couple of dishes when the doorbell rang. She glanced at her watch. That would be Sue Woodruff, a few minutes later than planned. Sue had phoned Marilyn soon after Gordon had left, asking if she could pop round for a chat. Marilyn had been looking forward to an evening with her feet up, watching the television, but she didn't feel able to turn down a request from the wife of Gordon's new boss.

Marilyn walked slowly to the door. Sue was on the doorstep, already slipping out of her coat, ready to hang it up. She was wearing an expensive-looking dress and high heels. She leant forward to give Marilyn a quick hug and a kiss.

'You're looking great, Marilyn. I don't know how you're feeling, but I thought last night how well you were looking.'

Marilyn smiled, trying to appear cheerful. 'Shall we go through to the sitting room? I've got some wine chilling in the fridge if you'd like some.'

Again the warm smile. 'Actually, Marilyn, could I just have a cup of tea? I'm not a great one for the booze, and I suffered a bit this morning after all that bubbly last night.'

'Of course. It will suit me better too.'

Sue followed her through to the kitchen and chatted amiably while the kettle boiled. 'I hope you don't mind me popping round. I wanted a chat out of earshot of the men. They can be such a bloody pain at times.' She laughed. Marilyn began to thaw.

'Not at all. The two boys are in bed, so I haven't got much to do. I must warn you that I'm not great company at the moment, particularly come evening. I've got to that stage where I feel listless.'

'I've never had children, Marilyn. In fact I can't. I had a hurried abortion back when I was a student, and something went wrong. So no kids for us.'

Marilyn didn't quite know what to say. 'Sorry to hear it. Have you thought of adopting?'

'We've thought of it, but decided no. To be honest, I'm not really the maternal type, though please don't take that as a criticism of you. We're all different.'

Marilyn made the tea. She was about to pick up the tray but Sue took it from her.

'I'll carry, you lead.'

Marilyn wondered if she'd misjudged Sue. She spoke well and seemed considerate. 'So you were a student?' she asked, sitting down and propping her feet up on the couch. 'At university?'

'Yes. I did a degree in business economics. I'm not as stupid as I look.' She gave a slightly throaty laugh. 'People underestimate me, and I like it that way. It gives me the upper hand. Keep this to yourself but I make a lot of the decisions, Marilyn, not Wayne. It's me that decides the future course of the company. I used to make quiet suggestions to Phil about good property investments, and he always listened to me. It's a bit harder with Wayne, even though he's my husband. It was me that decided to offer the job to Gordon. I've always thought he was a decent guy who worked hard. It was me that decided to ditch Sorrento. I never liked him after he made a pass at me a couple of years ago at a party. And his recent plans were half-baked. I expected to see him there last night, though. I don't know where he's got to.'

'He gave me the shudders,' Marilyn admitted. 'He never tried it on with me, but I could feel his eyes all over me whenever we met.'

'Exactly. So we women need to stick together. Which is why I've come round for this chat, since Wayne and Gordon are both out. Men are just far too competitive and extreme, Marilyn. Everything seems to come down to willy-waggling and unnecessary violence. I just don't like it.' She paused. 'You have a background in property development, don't you?'

Marilyn nodded. 'And sales. That was before I had the children, though I've worked part time in recent years.' She poured the tea and waited. Was there a proposition coming?

* * *

In their Wareham home, Sophie Allen's husband, Martin, was in the sitting room fiddling with the stereo.

'It's still not my favourite though.' Tracy Daunt, Matt Silver's wife, was in a deep discussion with Martin Allen about the merits of different Jacqui Dankworth albums. 'I saw her at the Harrogate music festival some years ago. It was great jazz, and then she did an encore — Sitting On Top of the World. It's an old blues classic, apparently. It was stunning. Someone told me that she took it a lot faster than most blues groups do. Just perfect. I was on my feet, jigging around, and nearly spilt my glass of wine.'

'I like blues. It goes down well with a pint of decent beer,' Sophie said. 'I keep meaning to pop down to Swanage for one of the blues festival weekends, but I've never made it. The one time I did go it was because there'd been a murder, so I was otherwise engaged. We did have to visit a couple of the pubs, and some of the bands sounded pretty good. Very "sixties" though. Right up your street, Tracy.' She laughed.

'Oh, that hurts. I was just about to offer to clear the dishes away, but I think I'll have a sulk instead.'

'I couldn't sulk, not after that food.' Laura McGreedie had managed to eat more than she'd expected to. 'I don't know where you found that husband of yours, Sophie, but if you ever want to trade him in, I'd be interested. He cooks like a dream.'

Sophie nodded. 'He does, doesn't he? That's why I stick with him through thick and thin. Love may come and go, but good food lasts forever. Jade does the food shopping, Martin cooks it and I enjoy it. Seems a fair division of labour to me.' She reached across and squeezed Martin's hand.

Martin had really come up trumps with the food this evening, particularly the venison en croute with a stilton topping. Laura looked pale and drawn, clearly worried about her forthcoming course of chemotherapy, but she'd obviously enjoyed having an evening out among friends and had more than held her own in the conversation. She was looking more tired now, though.

'Sulk over,' Tracy said. 'Let's get busy clearing the debris. Come on you two. These three coppers clearly need to chat. Alternatively, we three spouses could sit here and enjoy our liqueurs, and they can clear the table and chat in the kitchen. Doesn't that seem fairer to you? Of course it does. Get cracking, you three.' She pushed her husband to his feet, jabbed Kevin McGreedie in the ribs with her elbow and glared at Sophie. 'We can put our feet up, swap cooking tips and gossip about you behind your backs.'

Sophie dutifully led her colleagues into the kitchen, each carrying a load of dishes and cutlery.

'Do we need to talk?' Matt asked her while they stacked the dishwasher.

'If you want. At the moment we're still trying to find out more about this Sorrento character who was found dead yesterday.' Sophie gave a short summary of their progress.

'Are you sure it's linked to the other deaths?' Matt said. 'Could have been coincidence, surely?'

'Last weekend I saw him looking at the first crime scene through binoculars. Why would he be doing that?'

Matt shrugged. 'I'm not questioning you, Sophie, I'm just making suggestions. If you're convinced, then that's fine. Do you have another connection?'

'We're working on it.'

He looked at her. 'Why do I get the impression you're holding something back? That's not like you.'

She was saved by a call on her mobile phone. It was Rae Gregson.

'Ma'am, you were right. We followed him to the central gardens. He met a couple of other men. One was the guy in the photo you had. Mitchell, I think you said? The other was the Woodruff guy, from what you described. The problem is, the photos don't show much. It was too misty and drizzly, and our guy kept his collar up and his umbrella down. They talked for about ten minutes, then he got back in his car and drove off. We followed the other two back towards Poole. Woodruff dropped Mitchell off first, presumably at his house, then drove home. Nice house with a big garden. Very posh area. And I got more information about a certain councillor into the bargain.'

'Thanks, Rae. Get yourself home now. And tell Rose thanks from me for giving up one of her free evenings.'

'She's a real laugh, ma'am, and a totally mad driver as well. We might go for a couple of drinks before we split up. Apparently she knows a pub where they serve chilli and rice until late on a Saturday night. Sounds good to me.'

Sophie was smiling as she replaced her phone.

'Good news?' Kevin McGreedie asked.

'Oh, yes. But that's all I'm saying at the moment.'

CHAPTER 27: PROPOSAL

Sunday, Week 2

The following day was a Sunday, but Barry Marsh was in the incident room early that morning. He wanted peace and quiet in order to analyse the photographic evidence from Friday's murder scene, now the details were all in. The trouble was, he couldn't assemble a picture in his mind. All at once, he shoved the papers into a folder and made his way out to his car. He would have to visit Morden Bog, there was nothing else for it.

Twenty minutes later, he was turning into the gravel parking area on the southern side of the reserve. He spoke briefly to the uniformed officer on duty there, then walked along the rough track into the scrubby woodland. The track petered out after about fifty yards, ending in a shadowy cul-de-sac wide enough to accommodate two vehicles, side by side. This was where they had seen two sets of faint tyre tracks, along with blood scatter on some of the nearby foliage.

Barry stood to one side, photos in hand, trying to visualise the scene. If a vehicle had already been parked on the left side of the small clearing, it would have forced Sorrento to pull in on the right, with his door very close to where the assault seemed to have occurred. Someone could have been hiding just behind that bush, only a yard or two away from where Sorrento would have been getting out of his car. If he'd had a rock in his hand ready, he could have moved forward quickly and hit Sorrento on the side of the head when he was at a disadvantage, off balance as he started to straighten up. The spot was gloomy even in daylight. At dusk it would have been difficult to spot a second person, particularly if Sorrento's attention was being distracted by whoever had lured him to the scene. It all seemed to fit. The forensic team's vehicle expert was fairly sure that the tyre tracks on the right were that of a four-by-four, possibly a Range Rover. That would tally with the boss's sighting of Sorrento's vehicle the previous weekend. The blood spatter on the nearby foliage suggested a hard blow and the trail of disturbed undergrowth matched the image of Sorrento's body being dragged the twenty yards or so to its resting place in the densest clump of shrubs. The areas of flattened undergrowth beside the edges of the clearing indicated that the vehicles had turned before leaving. The drivers would not have wanted to reverse down that narrow track at night.

So, two people, probably arriving in a single vehicle, waiting for Sorrento to arrive. Sorrento would have known at least one of them. Or maybe someone he knew and trusted drove him to this secluded spot under some pretext or other. Whichever it was, he was hit on the head with a rock on arrival, and his body dragged away and hidden. The two vehicles were then driven away, one man in each. Or maybe there were more than two assailants? One good thing, something the assailants presumably hadn't thought of, was that if one of the vehicles had been Sorrento's Range Rover, then it was traceable. The registration was on record, thanks to the boss's observations the previous weekend.

The rock used in the fatal assault hadn't just been carelessly tossed aside, so what would they have done with it? Taken it with them for a couple of miles, then disposed of it somewhere else on the heath, maybe hurling it out of the car window? It hardly mattered. There were so many lumps of rock around the place that it would never be found, particularly if they'd taken the time to drop it in one of the dozens of small, boggy pools.

Marsh now felt that he understood the sequence of events surrounding Sorrento's murder. But why would he have been killed? The DCI was fairly confident. She felt that internal tensions within the gang had erupted into violence following the death of the old leader, Phil Woodruff. Maybe Sorrento had made a move for the top job and had underestimated the opposition he'd encounter. She'd been puzzled by the prison visit to Frimwell. That alone could explain the descent into extreme violence. Had Sorrento upset Frimwell in some way? Had Frimwell got a message to the outside world, instructions to deal with the over-confident Sorrento?

Marsh walked to his car and drove back to the incident room. Too many imponderables. He arrived to find his boss staring out of the window, seemingly deep in thought. She looked up as he approached.

'Morning, ma'am. I've been back to the nature reserve to check over the tyre track patterns. I think I see how it fits.' He went on to explain his ideas.

'Sounds right,' she replied. 'Good work. We need to start tying it all together. We have so many loose ends it's like a tangled ball of wool at the moment. Can you start tomorrow on this councillor, Blythe? He could be the link between the Armitage murders and Sorrento's.'

'Of course.' Marsh looked at the clock. 'I need to be going soon. I'll get a quick sandwich in the canteen, then I'll be off. Gwen's coming over this afternoon. We'll probably go for a walk along the front, then we're heading out for a meal this evening.'

'Well, give her my best wishes. I'll be here for an hour or two yet, then I'm off for the rest of the day. We all need a few hours to unwind, Barry. By the way, I need to find something to keep Blackman and McCluskie occupied. But whatever it is, it can't be anything sensitive. I can't have them blundering about putting things at risk. Any ideas would be very welcome.'

* * *

Marsh made his way to the jewellers, as he'd arranged the previous week, then drove back to his flat in Swanage. It was about time he moved somewhere closer to his work, but it would have been premature to do so with his relationship becoming more serious by the week.

The afternoon stroll was very relaxing and enjoyable. The sun glinted on the rippling wave-tops as he and Gwen strolled along the promenade at Swanage, and then out to Peveril Point before returning to the town for a cup of tea. They returned to his flat to change before heading out for the evening. Barry had booked a corner table at the local Italian restaurant, and by mid-evening the couple were enjoying their food.

'Wow, fantastic wine, Barry. It's not like you to splash out on one this expensive. Is it a special occasion? Have I missed something?'

He answered quietly, 'Yes it is.' He reached into his jacket pocket and extracted a small, velvet-covered box, placing it on the table in front of Gwen. He flipped it open, revealing a glinting diamond ring. 'Gwen, will you marry me?'

She was silent for what seemed like hours, looking alternatively at the ring and her boyfriend. Tears began to glisten in the corners of her eyes. 'Oh, yes,' she finally said. 'Yes, yes, yes.' She reached across the table and put her arms around him, and the couple half-stood, hugging each other. Then Gwen pulled away, allowing Barry to slide the ring onto her finger, to a ripple of applause from the nearby diners, who'd all been watching in smiling silence.

'Barry! You fantastic, lovely, thoughtful person. You've totally surprised me, and I didn't think that was possible.'

'I do love you, Gwen,' he whispered.

'I know.' She took a gulp of wine. 'And I've known for ages that you're the one for me.'

They continued to look at each other, smiling, over dessert.

CHAPTER 28: DARK HORSE

Monday morning, Week 3

Detectives Stu Blackman and Phil McCluskie made their way apprehensively towards Sophie Allen's office. She was reading the preliminary autopsy report on Tony Sorrento, and set it aside as the two men knocked on the open door.

'Come in, guys.' She pointed towards the two chairs in front of her desk. 'You did a good job on crosschecking all the forensic data, so thanks for that.'

The two men visibly relaxed.

'I have another job for you. It's a good bit trickier, but I'm sure you'll cope. There's a company operating out of Bournemouth that owns a string of bars, pubs and clubs. Maybe even a couple of massage parlours. They're all spread out across the Bournemouth and Poole area. They're involved in these murders, but we don't know how or why. Sorrento was one of their directors. We need to gain a good bit more intelligence on them, and that's your job. Find out everything there is to know about them, but without raising any suspicions on their part. Keep it completely low profile. The company's called Woodruff Holdings. Barry and I have already visited their registered office a couple of times, so they know we're interested in them. Don't go near that place or approach any of their senior staff. You can visit a few of the places they run, but keep it very low key and don't let on that you're cops. Don't approach any other CID units about this. It's got to be completely internal to us for the time being. Clear so far?'

'Yes, ma'am.' Blackman sat up, straight and businesslike, as if trying to impress. Shame about the ketchup stain on his tie, thought Sophie.

'Fine. So I want a detailed dossier on them as soon as possible. You have a couple of days. You can move back to your own base now, by the way. This incident room is getting a bit too crowded, and we need your desk space. But don't talk about this, not even to your CID buddies. Barry's created a skeleton framework for your report with headings for what we want to know. You'll find it in our group folder on the server. Here's a hard copy. It has the network address on it. A word of warning. If you find anything unexpected, like links to other businesses or individuals, don't follow them up without talking to me first. Any questions?'

They shook their heads in unison.

'Phil, this is an opportunity for you to redeem yourself. Show me the good detective that I know you can be. Okay?'

'Yes, ma'am,' he replied.

They left the office and went to their desks to clear their few belongings and take them back to the CID office. Marsh watched them leave, then went into Sophie's office.

'How did they take it, ma'am?'

'Don't know and don't really care. Hopefully we'll get something useful from them. Blackman looked as though he was all fired up, but it's impossible to read McCluskie. He's too hard-nosed.'

'I see they've moved out. I didn't know you were planning that.'

'A safety precaution. If word gets out about what they're doing, it'll be taken as a routine CID investigation, not linked to us. And I expect word will get out. It'll be hard for them not to blab to someone, particularly once McCluskie has had a few drinks. I don't want our mole to have his suspicions aroused more than necessary.'

'Won't you tell me who it is, ma'am? If you know?'

'No. And I do know. At least I think I do. But don't try to find out, Barry. If you do, you might raise the alarm. He'll be looking for signs of someone doing some digging.'

* * *

'Well, what do you think of that?' Blackman dropped into his chair and sat back, his chest swelling. 'We've impressed the powers that be. We're back in business. She's seen the light at last.'

'Fuck that. She's up to something,' McCluskie said, wearily. 'I just wish I knew what it was.'

'Don't be such a cynic, Phil. Why can't you take it at face value?'

'Because I know her. All that crap about me redeeming myself. It was all for show. She may have impressed you, but she sure didn't impress me. So the question is, what is she really up to?'

'Listen, we do what she asked, okay? I'm fed up with the reputation I seem to have got since we started working together. I want to get back into mainstream work, and this might be my chance. So we do exactly what she asked. We find out everything there is to know about this shady outfit and we don't blab. Let's do this right.'

McCluskie curled his lip. Blackman started searching through the network for the skeleton report they were to flesh out. For once he felt enthusiastic.

'Here it is.' He scanned through the document. 'Okay, I can see what they want. Let's go for the first couple of sections just now. I'll do the top half of the list, you do the bottom half. Then we can review midday and decide on the next step. Okay?'

McCluskie scowled, but started work.

* * *

Sophie, Marsh and Rae had coffee together mid-morning. Marsh decided to tell the two women his news. He knew he'd not be easily forgiven if he kept them in the dark about his engagement.

'Just to let you know, Gwen and I got engaged yesterday evening.' His heart was beating rapidly. Why was this almost as nerve-wracking as the proposal itself? He wasn't prepared for the resulting onslaught. Sophie threw her arms around him and hugged him tightly.

'Barry! You're a real dark horse. I had no idea.'

He was puzzled by this. Why would she expect to have an idea? Was it that big a deal to anyone other than himself and Gwen? Clearly it was, judging from the reaction of these two women. Rae could barely keep still for excitement. He had only just managed to extricate himself from Sophie's embrace, when Rae threw herself at him and nearly knocked the wind out of him.

'Congratulations, boss! It couldn't happen to a nicer bloke. Trust me, I know, I was one myself once.'

'Celebration lunch!' Sophie cried. 'Oh no, we can't. We're in the middle of a triple murder inquiry. How about when we finish this evening? Fancy a quick drink? I know, let's have a meal out at the weekend instead. What do you think, Barry? We could get Jimmy across, and ask some of the old Swanage team along.'

It fitted in with his own thoughts exactly. Barry had already decided on Saturday as an ideal day to celebrate. He nodded. 'The Black Swan on Saturday. I'll book now, and if anyone needs to spend the night in my flat, I have a spare room and the couch in the lounge.'

'Sounds great,' Rae replied.

'Ideal,' Sophie said. 'But I won't stay over. I'll get Martin to come and chuck me in the car and take me home. My days of sleeping rough on makeshift beds are long gone. We were in need of a pick-me-up, Barry, and you've supplied it. And you and Gwen suit each other so well. I'm thrilled for you both.'

* * *

As requested, Pete Armitage called into the police station later that morning. Sophie and Marsh interviewed him.

'You do lot of decorating jobs for Woodruff properties, Mr Armitage,' Sophie said. 'None of their properties are local to Blandford, so why did you land the contracts?'

Pete narrowed his eyes. 'I thought you asked me in to talk about Ted and Sylvie's deaths? What have the Woodruff jobs got to do with that?'

'There's a strong possibility of a link, so can you answer the question, please?'

'They notify me when they've got a job due. I put in a bid, and sometimes I land the work, sometimes I don't. There's nothing shady about it. What's the problem?'

Marsh picked up a list that he'd brought in with him. 'All the other decorating firms they have on their books are based in Bournemouth or Poole. You're the furthest away by far. It seems a bit odd.'

'Well, it isn't. I always do a good job, and they know it.'

'How did you first make contact with them? How did you get on their list in the first place?' Marsh continued.

'I think it was through Rod. It was when I first took him on, years ago. He told me about a club in Poole that had been bought by new owners who planned to spruce it up. He talked me into putting in a quote and I landed the job.'

'Did you think you were in with a chance?' Sophie asked. 'Were you surprised at all when you got it?'

Pete paused for a few moments. 'I s'pose I was. A bit, anyway. I probably wasn't the cheapest estimate, I never am. But I've got a good reputation for quality work, and they saw that after the first job. It's stupid for a company like theirs to go for the cheapest. Those bars and pubs need to bring in the public and they only do that if they look attractive. It's a speciality of mine, pubs and the like. I know what works, and I tell the owners. Most of them listen to what I say.'

'So was it just by chance that you landed that first job for them?'

'Rod knew the manager of the place at the time and swung it. It was only a year after I took him on. Once I did one, the rest of the jobs followed.'

'Did Rod say how he knew them?' Sophie asked.

'It was a late night club in Poole with a casino. I think he was a punter there. Look, I don't like talking about my family, and with the kind of stress they're under it doesn't seem right.'

'But you've just sacked Rod, haven't you? Hasn't that put him under far more stress than we ever could?'

Pete didn't answer immediately. 'He was taking money from me. From the business, I mean.'

Sophie raised her eyebrows. 'How much? And how did he do it?'

'It worked out at a couple of thousand. He had a bank card for small purchases. It was meant for small-scale stuff that he needed quick like, to get a job done. He's been taking out cash as well and wasn't telling me.'

Marsh looked puzzled. 'How did it get to that amount? Surely you'd spot it in your monthly bank statements?'

There was no response.

'Mr Armitage,' said Sophie, 'This is a murder inquiry. The next step is for us to get your statements from the bank and go through them with a fine toothcomb. We'll be doing that anyway, but we can save time here. You know we'll get to the bottom of it, so why not tell us now?'

Pete cleared his throat and scratched his head nervously. 'Sylvia did my accounts. I never looked through my statements, not until a couple of weeks ago, after she died. I didn't know what was going on.'

'Was it really just a couple of thousand?'

He shook his head. 'That was the amount each year. Probably more like twelve grand over five years.'

Marsh sank back into his chair. 'So Rod was stealing money from you, with Sylvia's knowledge?'

'Yeah, but I had nothing to do with her death. If I'd have killed anyone, it would have been Rod, not her. It explains why she was so nervy in the last few years. I think she must have been terrified of me finding out.'

'Do you know what Rod was doing with the money?'

Pete shrugged. 'Drugs? Gambling? Women? Probably all three.'

'Do you think Ted knew?'

'I didn't even know myself until after they died. So how could I tell?'

'But you must have wondered in the days since then. He was your brother, after all.'

'Yes, but we weren't that close. I got on much better with Sylvia. Or I thought I did. I'm not sure of anything now.'

'I'll ask again, Mr Armitage. Do you think Ted knew what was going on?'

'Possibly,' he whispered. 'I wonder if it may have caused all the friction between them. But it's only a guess. And how can I tell now?'

'Who was your contact in the Woodruff business?' asked Marsh. 'Who issued the job descriptions when they needed decorating done?'

'Justin Griffiths. But that very first one came from Toffee Barber. He's the manager and seems really pally with Rod.'

Sophie shifted in her seat. 'I think we should call it a day now, Mr Armitage. We'll get the bank statements right now to check what you've alleged, though there's no reason to doubt what you've told us. It makes a whole lot of things clearer. Please keep all this to yourself at present while we check further. And stay away from Rod. Leave it all to us to handle. There's a lot more work for us to do. How's Sharon bearing up, by the way?'

Pete rose from his seat. 'I'm a bit worried about her. I thought she'd have been looking a bit better by now but, if anything, she seems worse.'

The two detectives showed Pete out of the building, then walked back to their office. 'Do you know, Barry, his story has a ring of truth in it. I think he might be a decent guy underneath and is genuinely perplexed by what he's discovered.

Maybe you could pop round and see Rod but don't question him on any of this, not yet. Keep it low key. Just to keep an eye on him. We'll let Rose and George know, so they can do the same, but don't share any details with them, not yet. It solves one of the main problems, doesn't it? Ted and Sylvia's murder had to have some kind of family involvement, what with the chosen site being Morden Bog. It would have been fine if we'd fallen for the suicide line, what with it having such good memories for them when Sharon and Rod were small. But once suicide was ruled out, it pointed only one way. And now we know Rod has a link to the Woodruffs.'

'It's going to be hard to pin it all down, ma'am. It's like trying to nail jelly to the wall.'

'Which is why we take it carefully. It goes a lot wider than this, particularly with Rae's discoveries of last week. Frimwell? That name still makes me shudder.'

* * *

Sophie walked into the medical centre and asked to speak to Sharon Giroux. It was after midday, and morning surgery had finished, so Sophie was asked to go directly to Sharon's consulting room. Pete had been accurate in his description of his niece. She looked even more tired and drawn than the previous week.

'You can relax, Sharon. Everything you told me on Thursday checks out.'

'But I knew it would. I was telling you the truth, Chief Inspector. I just can't believe I was being so stupid as to try and rekindle a romance that ended over a decade ago. What was I thinking? Most people would give an arm and a leg for the kind of marriage I have with Pierre. It's shaken me almost as much as Mum and Dad's deaths. What kind of person am I?'

'An absolutely decent one, I expect. So many of us think we should aim for perfection all the time and it just isn't possible. We're human beings, not some kind of divine incarnation. We all make the occasional mistake. Try not to let it get to you, particularly if no harm was done, which was true in your case.' Sophie sipped a glass of water that Sharon had poured for her. 'I've come about something else. You said early on that Morden Bog had a special significance for you as a family, because of your picnics there when you were small. Apart from the four of you, who else knew?'

'Uncle Pete. He came with us once or twice. I think Mum used to feel sorry for him because he was a bachelor and didn't have a family of his own, so she'd sometimes involve him in our trips out. Mum's sister, my Aunt Phyllis, knew. She liked looking at the photos we sometimes took. She died about ten years ago. I don't think anyone else was aware of how often we went there.'

'That's helpful.'

Sharon picked up a pen and started tapping it against the desktop, then suddenly put it down. 'I read that the body of a man was found in Wareham Forest at the weekend, near the nature reserve. Is it connected?'

'I can't comment in any detail, Sharon. If it is, it's opened up a whole new angle. If it isn't, it's really muddied the water. That's why no one's dropped in to see you over the last few days. As you can imagine, we're working like stink.'

'You look tired too.'

'It goes with the job. When we're in the middle of something like this, I grab a few hours of relaxation when I can. And there are occasional moments that cheer us up and make us realise that there is a life outside of the case. Barry, my sergeant, got engaged yesterday and told us this morning. That provided us with quite a boost. Those are the moments to treasure, Sharon. You'll get some good times back, trust me.' She smiled. 'Maybe I should have been a doctor.'

Sharon seemed amused by this.

Sophie had a brainwave. 'My daughter, Jade, is in the sixth form at school and plans to study medicine. She's wanted to be a doctor for some time. Would you be able to give her a little bit of time and talk things through with her?'

'Of course. It's the least I can do.'

CHAPTER 29: SNUBBED

Monday afternoon & evening, Week 3

Rae had finished looking through the internal information on the person they suspected of being the police mole. Sophie had managed to negotiate temporary access for her to parts of the personnel database, and this had helped with some aspects of her investigation. But she needed more personal information, to flesh out his character and personality. But how to do that without alerting him? Every method she thought of would set alarm bells ringing. Was it worth trying social media again, in more depth? All serving members of the county police force were warned about the dangers of using online forums, but Rae knew that a few did so using false identities, creating additional accounts in an attempt to keep some of their activities hidden. Rae spent hour after hour googling and networking, and every attempt led her down cul-de-sacs and blind alleys. Then, finally, she spotted his photo on a forum for pub pool-playing enthusiasts from Hampshire. He was masquerading under the name "Hampshire Wolfman." Clever. He lived and worked in Dorset, but he'd found a way around the police guidelines by pretending he was a Hampshire man. Once she had a name, even though it was a mere fictional handle, she was up and running. And, slowly, a picture of the man began to emerge. He had more than a little vanity, and clearly imagined that his own opinions counted for a great deal. A bit of a self-indulgent narcissist, he offered boastful accounts of his sexual exploits and conquests. He was a misogynist to boot. Unfortunately there was nothing that could be counted as evidence of criminal intent, but Rae hadn't expected that. Most importantly of all, she discovered where she might find him that evening.

* * *

Rae walked into the pub and took a long look around, fixing the layout in her head. Not bad. A fairly upmarket place with a comfortable feel to it. Clean. Small vases of flowers on the larger tables. She walked to the bar and ordered a small glass of lager, needing a clear head. It was a Monday, not a night for raucous merrymaking. She took her drink to a small table and sat down, choosing a corner seat that gave her a good view of both the room and the pool table, which was set in an alcove to her left. She took a sip of her drink, extracted her Kindle from her bag and settled back, moving her eyes between her book and the room in front of her.

Rae had taken a taxi from the station to get to the bar, had tipped the driver generously and booked him to collect her in good time to catch the last train back to Wool from Bournemouth. She didn't want to find herself stranded, particularly in an area that she didn't know well. She'd taken a lot of trouble over her makeup, with good results. Smoky eyeliner, dark plum shadow and matching mascara. Her blusher blended well with the foundation, and the mulberry lipstick looked lovely. She'd curled her hair for the very first time, and it really altered her appearance. She liked the new look. Maybe she should consider making it permanent. She stretched out her slim, denim-clad legs and checked her high-heeled ankle boots. No scuffs yet.

After twenty minutes, a young man who'd been playing pool came across for a chat. She spoke amiably for a while about the pub (very nice), her reason for being here (new to the area) and her interests (music and reading). Then the conversation turned to the young man (Craig), his interests (darts and pool), his job (warehouse manager for a local electrical store) and his upcoming holiday plans (camping in Wales). Even if Mole failed to appear, the evening wouldn't have been wasted. When he did turn up, Rae couldn't help feeling mildly disappointed — she'd been enjoying her chat. Craig was obviously a friend of her quarry, even though he was a good few years younger. Rae wondered if the friendship was just down to spending time at the pub playing darts and pool. She noticed that Craig's attitude seemed to change once Mole joined them. He'd been amiable and open, but now he was more macho. Typical bloke, she thought.

She reached across to shake Mole's hand. 'Hi! I'm Rachel.' She noticed the wariness in his eyes. It was common to many of her fellow cops in social situations.

Craig invited her to join them for a game of pool, and she saw a look of irritation flash across Mole's face. She ignored it and followed them to the table.

'I've only played a little before,' she said, truthfully. What she didn't say was that she'd spent much of her teenage free time playing snooker. She waited until she'd won the first game before telling them that.

Craig laughed. 'That's unfair. Come on, the way you said it we took it at face value. I wasn't even trying and now you've humiliated me!'

She smiled. 'No I haven't. True humiliation would have been if we'd played for money. Anyway, what's humiliating about losing to me? Is it because I'm a woman? Are you stuck in the middle ages or something?'

Craig grinned back, but Rae noticed that Mole remained silent. She waited until he'd gone up to the bar and asked about him.

‘Your friend is a bit moody. Is it just tonight or is he always like it?’

‘He’s normally okay, but he’s been like this since last week. Something’s bugging him. We don’t talk much. I don’t even know what his job is. We just talk football, darts and booze. Oh, and women.’

‘What about women? Go on, tell me.’

He shrugged. ‘The usual. Who’s really hot. Who’s got good legs. What they might be like in bed.’

‘Well, thank you for being honest with me. And how do I do on the Craig rankings? For looks, I mean. Don’t even try to guess the last one.’

He grinned again. ‘Pretty good, I’d say. But you’re not his type. He’s into slim blondes. I’ve never seen him with a brunette.’

Mole returned with the beers, one each for himself and Craig, but nothing for Rae. She would have felt humiliated if her reason for being there had been purely social. Was this some kind of test? She decided to act that way. She stood up and glared.

‘Obviously I have to buy my own drink. While I’m at the bar, would you two gentlemen like anything? Nuts, perhaps?’

Craig came to the bar with her. ‘I don’t know what’s got into him. That was way out of line. He was like it on Saturday night too. Sorry. Let me get this.’

‘No, it’s fine. He’s got a huge attitude problem, though. That was quite deliberate.’

As they turned away from the bar, she saw Mole leaving by a side door, with a mobile phone clamped to his ear. She turned to Craig.

‘I need the loo. Can you take my drink? I’ll be back in a tick.’

Rae hurried out past the toilets. A path led around the building to the rear garden, and here she spotted Mole. He was deep in conversation with another person. No one else was around. Rae crept closer, keeping behind a line of shrubs. She switched her phone into record mode and held it out towards the two men.

'Are you fucking mad? This is my place and you shouldn't be here. I told you, don't bother me. I'm out of it. Can't I make it any clearer?' Mole hissed.

'I need to know what your lot are up to. Find out for me. I need to know we're in the clear before I sign on the dotted line for Frimwell's places. That's all I want. But it needs to be quick.'

'Jesus. You're unbelievable. You fucking come here without warning and expect me to jump through hoops for you? Listen. I won't do it. It's too risky. This is way beyond the few favours I did for your dad.'

'Ten grand. Just for this. Then it ends and you won't hear from me again.'

The ensuing silence seemed endless. Rae could feel her heart beating hard in her chest.

'Okay. Then I never want to see you again. If I do, I'll fucking slam you in the clink. Understood?'

The other figure moved off towards the car park. Rae slid silently back around the building and made her way to the toilets. She washed her hands, patted them dry with a paper towel and checked her makeup. Still passable. She thought she looked quite sultry. She made a face at herself in the mirror and returned to the bar. Craig and Mole were arguing. Craig was making it clear that he was annoyed by the earlier snub to Rae.

'Oh, fuck off you wanker.' Mole finished his pint of beer in one swallow, pushed Rae aside and walked out.

Craig shook his head. 'I've never seen him this bad. Maybe I've never seen the real him before. Or maybe something's really worrying him. Whatever it is, there's no excuse. I'm really sorry.'

Rae smiled at him. 'Don't worry, I've got the hide of a rhino. It all just bounces off me. How about another game of pool? I've got another couple of hours till my taxi comes. How about playing for a fiver? I might manage to pay the fare back to the station then.'

CHAPTER 30: TAKING THE BAIT

Tuesday morning, Week 3

Sophie Allen and Barry Marsh walked up the steps of Bournemouth's ornate town hall and entered the lobby. They were both in business attire, Marsh wearing a blue suit and Sophie in powder grey. The receptionist looked up from her desk and smiled.

'We'd like to see Councillor Blythe, please,' Sophie said.

'Do you have an appointment?'

Sophie held out her warrant card. 'Detective Chief Inspector Allen. No, I don't have an appointment, but I know he's in this morning. No need to let him know we're here. Just point us in the right direction.'

'Ah. Second floor, turn left and look for the third door. I'll have to log your visit.'

The door opened into a small secretarial area, where a member of staff was working behind a desk. She didn't look up. Sophie waited a few seconds then said, 'Councillor Blythe, please.'

With her eyes on the screen in front of her, the secretary held up her hand, as if stopping traffic. Sophie pushed her warrant card wallet into the outstretched fingers and the woman looked up. 'Oh,' she said, then, 'He has someone with him. I'll phone through that the police need to see him.'

Sophie shook her head. 'Phone, but don't tell him we're police. Just say he has very urgent visitors who can't wait more than two minutes.' She smiled coolly at the receptionist.

'Would you like to take a seat?'

'No, we'll wait right here.'

Looking perplexed, the receptionist phoned, using Sophie's precise words. The two detectives waited at the desk for exactly two minutes, walked to the door bearing Blythe's nameplate, opened it and walked in.

A fleshy man in his late forties was talking to a young couple. All three looked up in surprise. 'I'm sorry, but you can't just barge in here like this,' said Blythe. He had probably been handsome a decade or so earlier, but now the years were beginning to take their toll. Sophie would have bet that his red face was due to more than annoyance, and the heavy jowls and bulbous nose indicated years of rich living.

'Oh, but I can. I'm Detective Chief Inspector Sophie Allen from Dorset police and it's very important that we talk. Right now. So if these two people wouldn't mind waiting outside for a few minutes, please?' She smiled brightly at the couple, who stood up in some confusion. 'The receptionist outside will make another appointment for you if you need one. I really do apologise.' She waited until the couple had left and sat down opposite the scarlet-cheeked councillor. He looked as if he wanted to explode in anger, but there was wariness too.

'I'd better explain,' Sophie began, smoothing out her skirt. Marsh sat down in the other chair and took out his notebook.

'Yes, you'd better,' Blythe hissed. 'This is unacceptable. Why didn't you let me know in advance?'

'It's a murder inquiry. A triple murder inquiry, in fact. I see people when I'm good and ready, and I don't give them warning.' She paused. 'Phil and Wayne Woodruff, Councillor Blythe. Tell me about them.'

'But Phil Woodruff's death wasn't murder, not as far as I know. I thought his death was down to a stroke.'

Sophie nodded. 'Yes, it was. Left hemisphere. Fatal. But it isn't his death we're investigating.'

'So whose is it?'

'My question first, please. Tell me about your relationship with the Woodruffs.'

'I'm not sure I know what you mean.'

'You were at Phil's committal at the crematorium. A committal usually involves family and close friends only, unlike the main funeral service, which is often open to anybody who wants to come.'

Blythe visibly relaxed and sat back. 'I couldn't make the main service because of an important council meeting here. I told the family and they suggested I go to the committal instead. That's all there was to it.'

Sophie nodded. 'Why were you there at all? They don't live in the ward you represent. No other councillors attended either service.'

Blythe leaned forward again, stabbing the air with his finger. 'Why is this of any importance? I can go to funerals if I want to. We don't yet live in a police state, despite what you may wish. What's it got to do with you? Why are you here? All I have to do is lift my phone, call the Chief Constable's office and complain about your heavy-handed approach to whatever it is you're investigating, and you'll wish you'd been a bit more careful.'

'Go ahead. I'll wait.' The air almost crackled with tension.

Blythe sat poised, then relaxed back into his seat. 'Never let it be said that I refused to help the police go about their work.'

'Good. Now tell me how you come to know the Woodruffs.'

'They own leisure properties in the area. Leisure and tourism is this region's lifeblood. As a councillor, it's my job to keep a finger on the pulse.'

Bloody timewaster, thought Sophie. 'Well now, Councillor. We could sit here all morning playing silly games, but it will just end up wasting time for both of us, so let's just get down to the nitty gritty, shall we? Two elderly people were found dead nearly two weeks ago. They'd died in extremely suspicious circumstances. Their bodies were found in their abandoned car, hidden deep in a nature reserve in Wareham Forest. You'll know all this from the press coverage. What interests me is the fact that they were at Poole Crematorium to attend a funeral directly after Phil Woodruff's committal. You bumped into them when you came out in rather a hurry and, apparently, in a bit of a temper. You scowled at them. A few days ago the body of a senior employee of the Woodruff organisation was found only a mile or so away from where we found the bodies of the couple a week earlier. He too had been at that same committal. Coincidence? It's possible but unlikely.'

'I thought the couple's death was down to suicide. That was the press line.'

'We always wait for detailed forensic evidence before drawing conclusions, Councillor. We get facts from the post mortem, from searching the immediate scene, from sifting through anything we find. It's only then that we make a judgement.'

She waited.

Blythe took the bait. 'I heard the search was rushed.'

'What do you mean?'

'A whisper that the search team missed something.'

'Who told you that?'

Blythe hesitated, then said, 'I can't remember. Does it matter?'

'No, not at all, particularly since I have total faith in the forensic search team. Do you have contact with an insider?'

'No, no. Of course not. Maybe I misheard.'

He's just realised that he's let the cat out of the bag, thought Sophie. Time to move on. 'So you sit on the planning committee for big leisure developments?'

'Yes,' he replied guardedly.

'So Woodruff's application for the conversion of one of his clubs into a casino complex would have come forward for scrutiny?'

'Yes, I believe there was one a month or two ago.'

'And was it ratified?'

Blythe nodded, his eyes narrowing. His ruddy complexion had faded somewhat, and he looked ill at ease.

'I understand you spoke quite eloquently in support of the application. You must have been pleased when it was approved by the committee. By a slim majority vote, wasn't it?'

Blythe nodded again. It was as if he didn't trust himself to speak, in case he gave something else away.

'I'd like to return to my first question, Councillor Blythe. The one that you haven't yet answered. How do you come to know the Woodruffs so well? Would you care to answer it now?'

'As I said, we were bound to meet. Our interests in the leisure industry overlap.'

Sophie stared at him. 'So the fact that your wife and Wayne Woodruff's wife are twin sisters doesn't come into it?'

The ensuing silence seemed to last for minutes. Eventually Blythe said, 'They don't get on. They hate the sight of each other.'

Sophie stood up. 'This has been very useful, Councillor. I may want to speak to you again.' She moved towards the door with Marsh following, but then turned to face Blythe. 'You never made that call to the Chief Constable's office complaining about my heavy-handed approach. Feel free to do it now.'

The two detectives left the councillor's office, passing the puzzled-looking couple, still waiting outside.

'That was interesting, ma'am,' Marsh said. 'He blundered right into it, didn't he?'

'Give a fool enough rope. He'll be on the phone right now, warning the whole lot of them. But it's too bloody late for them to cover it up now. I think we've had all our suspicions confirmed, so it's just a question of getting the evidence. It'll have to be completely watertight. We'd better hang around here for a while. There's a good chance that Blythe will head off somewhere interesting once he calms down and gathers his thoughts. Maybe a bit of tailing is called for.'

'That could be a problem, ma'am. As well as this entrance, there's a staff-only one that leads from the office area to an internal car park. Shall I take that one? I'll try to find somewhere to wait that isn't too obvious.'

'Okay,' Sophie replied. 'I'll wait here in the main parking area, but you can tail him if he does leave. I'll need to pay a visit to the ACC at headquarters later this morning and time is ticking by. If he does come out, it's more likely to be by car, so you'll catch him. I'll wait about twenty minutes.'

* * *

Marsh only had to wait fifteen minutes before a car appeared from the tunnel and slowed to a crawl as it approached the junction with the road. There was no mistaking Blythe's angry face as his vehicle was forced to wait for a line of slow moving traffic. Marsh started his engine and pulled out behind the councillor's car, keeping his distance along straight sections of road, but moving closer as the traffic approached junctions and roundabouts. They were heading north towards Winton, one of Bournemouth's main residential areas. The traffic thinned for a while, so Marsh could afford to drop back further, but then it began to get busier as they approached the commercial centre of Winton. Blythe slowed and pulled into a parking bay. Marsh took a left into a quiet side street, parked his car and walked quickly to the corner. He watched as Blythe left his car, crossed the road and entered a coffee shop — the Priory Cafe. Wasn't that one of the properties on the Woodruff list? Marsh bought a newspaper from a vendor and walked to a low wall that surrounded a nearby playground. It provided a near-perfect vantage point. Who could Blythe be meeting? One thing was for certain. This was no coincidence. His and Sophie's visit had caused the councillor to panic, exactly what they had hoped for.

Blythe left the cafe some fifteen minutes later, still looking angry. Marsh wondered whether to follow him further or make an attempt to identify the person he'd met. Clearly the councillor hadn't got his own way, so it would be useful to find out who he'd talked to. Marsh made his way across the road to the cafe. It was clean and a welcoming aroma of hot food emanated from the warming cabinet of pasties and pies. He sat at a table near the door and waited for the waitress to take his order for coffee. He resumed his study of the newspaper, taking out his pen and making a start on the crossword. Several other tables were occupied, but he doubted that it was any of these people that Blythe had met. They all looked to be shoppers having a welcome rest.

The waitress arrived to take his order and he complimented her on the cafe's welcoming atmosphere. She recommended the flapjack and he took a slice with his coffee. When she returned with his order, she began telling him about the business side of the cafe chain. While they were talking, a middle-aged man emerged from the back of the premises and headed out into the street, looking preoccupied. He was one of the three men who'd been at the Rising Moon pub the previous week, having lunch with Sorrento and Woodruff.

The waitress told him what he wanted to know. 'That's Mr Griffiths, one of the company owners. He's really nice.'

Barry thought back to the list of senior personnel in the Woodruff business. Following the death of Sorrento, Justin Griffiths was now second-in-command, according to DS Stu Blackman's findings the previous day. Pete Armitage had also mentioned the name as the originator of the decorating contracts. Presumably he'd been here to meet Blythe. Things were falling into place nicely. The problem was, although they now had the links between most of the major players in the business and some idea of the factors that had led to the Armitages' murders, there wasn't enough evidence to make any arrests yet. And Marsh had no idea where that evidence would come from. They really needed help from an insider, and how likely was that?

* * *

Sophie Allen was lost in thought as she made her way out of county police headquarters at Winfrith. The meeting with Jim Metcalfe, the ACC, had provided her with some unexpected information. She'd reported her suspicions about the police mole, the insider who'd been leaking information to the Woodruffs, and played him Rae's recording from the pub garden. There had always been a possibility that the bent cop wasn't really bent, but was working undercover. Sophie didn't know whether to feel relieved or disappointed when Jim Metcalfe had denied it.

'I'd have known,' he'd said. 'No, we have a rotten apple. There's no one working undercover inside this Woodruff lot. How could there be? We didn't even know about them till this case.'

It was his second piece of information that had caused her to worry. 'He was a firearms officer some years ago,' the ACC had reported. 'So you need to tread carefully, and keep me fully in the picture. No action without full backup from an armed unit. I'll get Greg Buller's squad primed, so contact him as soon as you're ready. What you don't know, and we've kept under wraps for a couple of years, is that one of our handguns went missing four years ago. It's never been found. He was one of the suspects at the time. Be extra careful, Sophie. We don't want anything to go wrong when he's lifted.'

Sophie looked up as a familiar vehicle pulled into the parking space beside hers. She gave Matt Silver, her boss, a wave and walked to his car.

'Well, surprise, surprise. You didn't tell me you'd be here this morning. I'd have rescheduled if I'd known,' he said.

'It was just a quick visit to see the ACC,' she replied. 'A few developments over the weekend.'

He waited but Sophie did not elaborate.

'Am I out of the loop for this one?' he asked eventually.

'Sorry, Matt.' She paused. 'You were in the firearms unit here some years ago, weren't you? How easily could a gun have gone missing?'

'Oh, that old story. I've never been sure how reliable that was. The booking-out procedures are watertight and always have been. It could be that the number of handguns was entered wrongly when we changed the recording system in the armoury. The data from the old system had to be entered again by hand when we started the new system. It was easy for something to be entered twice.'

'But with different serial numbers? How likely is that?'

'As far as I know, it was all a bit manic at the time.'

'Okay. But if it was, it provided an ideal opportunity for one to be filched.'

'Why the worry now?'

'If one did go missing, I'm wondering where it might have ended up. And what it might be used for.' She looked at her watch. 'I've got to go. I'll catch up with you soon, okay?'

CHAPTER 31: SKATE PARK

Late Tuesday morning, Week 3

Why was the whole world against him?

Phil McCluskie felt isolated and aggrieved. Even Stu, his partner of the last two years, was starting to give him the cold shoulder. He'd obviously fallen for everything that witch had said. It was transparently obvious that she was just manipulating them. Those pathetic little jobs she'd asked them to do! Stupid Stu had fallen for it, lock, stock and barrel. Sucker. One look from those big green eyes and Blackman rolled onto his back, like a spaniel asking to be tickled. Well, fuck that for a game of soldiers. He, Phil, wasn't so easily impressed.

He yawned and stretched. What was she up to? The more he thought about it, the more certain he became that there was something bubbling away below the surface. He'd seen those little *chats* with that amorphous cow with size nine feet, Rae Gregson. He'd also spotted that the DS, Marsh, had been deliberately excluded from these conversations, and that whatever Gregson was doing, it was hush hush. Something was going on separate to the murder cases. It had to be a leak, or some kind of cover-up. Nothing else made sense. But who or what? Maybe he should visit a few mates from the old days and pick their brains. Someone might know.

Blackman was nowhere to be seen. He'd gone out to chase up a couple of documents. McCluskie pulled his aging leather jacket from the back of his chair and made for the door. On Tuesday lunchtimes a group of ex-cops met for lunch and a chinwag at a pub in Poole. He might learn a thing or two there if he played his cards right.

* * *

'Well, would you believe it! It's that well-known teetotaller from Blandford. How are you, Phil?'

'Good. I had a couple of hours spare, so I thought I'd pop down to see you lot.' He looked down at the four men seated round a table. 'Drink, anyone?'

He took the order to the bar and added a pint for himself. Better leave out his usual whisky chaser, he needed to keep a clear head. He returned to the table with the tray of drinks and sat down.

'We really pity you, Phil. We pity anyone still working.' The speaker, who'd issued the earlier greeting, was a retired traffic cop, thick-set with short, grizzled hair. 'I mean, a woman chief constable? What's the fucking world coming to?'

McCluskie sipped his lager. 'They're all over the place, Mickey, in every nook and cranny. And they're all so serious. Targets, clear-up rates, interfacing with the public. What has all that got to do with nabbing low-lifes? That's what I ask myself.'

'University degrees. What's that all about?' Mickey went on. 'How's that gonna help? Is being able to quote Hamlet or do some fancy maths any use when you're chasing a skanky drug dealer? Where will eye-of-fucking-newt get you then?'

'That's from Macbeth, Mickey. If you're going to quote Shakespeare, you could at least get the right play,' chipped in Charlie, a former custody officer. 'You're a couple of misogynists you are, always complaining about women. I mean, what planet are you from? I've got three daughters, all grown up now. They worked really hard at school and college, and they're all in good jobs. Debbie, my youngest, is a cop in Brighton and she's aiming for promotion. She'll probably get further up the scale than I ever did, and good for her. She deserves it.' He bent his head to his drink, and the other two men nodded. Mickey scowled.

Phil changed the subject. 'Listen, did any of you ever come across the Woodruff family? Owns a chain of pubs, hotels and cafes across the area? Been going for well over ten years?'

'They own a pub down the road here,' Charlie said. 'They're legit, aren't they? They never came up on my radar.'

'Was anyone keeping an eye on them? From inside our lot, I mean.'

Everyone looked blank. McCluskie sighed. Maybe this hadn't been such a good idea after all. 'I'm getting a sandwich. Anyone else for grub? Not that I'm paying, mind.'

An hour later, just as McCluskie was about to leave, his phone signalled an incoming text message. He looked at the screen but didn't recognise the number. 'Woodruff. Be at the Quayside in half an hour. At the skate park.'

* * *

A crowd had gathered, drawn by the flashing blue lights of the ambulance and the police cars. The victim was a middle-aged man, now being loaded into the ambulance on a stretcher. He had an oxygen mask over his face, but there were bloodstains on his sallow skin. The police were talking to a teenage boy holding a skateboard. He wasn't proving to be very helpful, judging by his shrugs and vague hand gestures.

'What's happened?' an elderly lady asked, as she joined the watchers.

'Don't really know,' replied her neighbour. 'He was lying by that car. No one saw nowt. The only person around was that lad, but we don't know whether he arrived later. Maybe he got out of his car and fainted or sommat. Someone said they smelt booze on his breath. We don't think he's dead.'

Sophie Allen arrived with Rae Gregson, quickly followed by Stu Blackman in a second car. They looked up at a train passing close by the scene. It was a well-chosen spot for an assault, only a few hundred yards from the busy Poole Quay, but hidden from view by a railway embankment and clumps of bushy shrubs. It could be seen from a skate park off to one side, but it was a school day and this would have been quiet.

They walked to the ambulance, which was closed and ready to leave. The paramedics reported that McCluskie had serious head injuries. They watched as the vehicle accelerated away from the car park.

'He'll be in A and E in five minutes,' Rae said.

Sophie turned to Blackman. 'What was he doing here? Why was he in Poole?'

Blackman looked stricken. 'No idea. I went out of our office for ten minutes to collect some more information about the Woodruffs. He was gone when I got back. No message.'

'Could it have been a lead of some kind?' Rae asked. Blackman shrugged.

Sophie shook her head. 'He's a maverick, always has been. But he's also pretty shrewd. Why didn't he do what I said and tell us first? I should have guessed he'd go it alone. Jesus. I just hope he pulls through.' She looked at Blackman. 'You stay here. We'll have a chat with that lad.'

She and Rae walked across to where the teenager stood with a uniformed officer. Sophie introduced herself and led him to the skate park, where they sat on a low bench. He must only be about fourteen, she thought. No wonder he's scared.

'I know you've already talked to the officers that got here first, but I'm the senior detective and my job is to find out what happened. Let's start with when you arrived. What time do you think it was?'

'About half one, I s'pose.' The teenager, who was called Wayne, looked anxious.

'Shouldn't you be at school?' Sophie asked gently.

'Yeah. I bunked off double French.'

'Okay, I'll explain that you're helping us, then you won't get into trouble. But in exchange, you've got to tell me everything you saw. Is that a deal?'

He nodded. 'But I didn't see everything. I was on the ramps and didn't take much notice at first. There were a few cars there, then that guy drove in, the one that got hurt. He came in kind of slow. I didn't see what happened next but I heard a bump. When I got up to the top of the ramp the other guy looked over and saw me. He got into a car and drove away, fast like.'

'Did you see what he looked like?'

'Nah, not really. Too far. He was bigger than the guy that was hit, but that was all.'

'What car was he in? The one who drove away?'

'Blue Audi. He went out quick. His tyres skidded.' The boy looked pale and scared. 'Am I in danger? He could've seen me. Me mum'll kill me.'

'Is your school local?' Sophie asked.

He nodded.

'In that case, we'll go there first. Then I'll take you home if there's someone there.'

He shook his head. 'Mum won't be back till six.'

'Do you have someone else? Grandparents? Aunts or uncles?'

He nodded. 'Me gran lives close.'

She walked back to the other two detectives. 'Rae, can you stay here and deal with forensics when they arrive? I'll pick you up when I've finished with young Wayne here. Stu, you get to the hospital and see how Phil is. If he can talk, see what he has to say but don't push it. If he's got serious head injuries it may be hours or days before we can expect anything from him. Keep me posted, will you? We'll join you later.'

She took Rae aside. 'I think it was our rotten apple, Rae. The boy's description of the car matches. Barry's probably still in Bournemouth. Phone him and get him to come across but whatever you do, don't tell him what we think. The real question is, what was McCluskie doing here? Could he have been involved somehow?' She shook her head. 'What a bloody can of worms.'

* * *

It was mid-afternoon before Sophie had a chance to phone Jim Metcalfe, the ACC, and tell him what had happened. McCluskie was in a bad way, but stable.

'He's assaulted a fellow officer, sir. We need to move quickly.'

They discussed their next course of action. The best option would have been to apprehend the mole at work, but their suspect seemed to have vanished. No one had seen him since midday. Jim Metcalfe was using all of the resources at his disposal but, so far, with little result. Sophie hoped that their quarry would be traced soon. The last thing they could afford was a rogue cop on the loose with a gun, if it had been him who'd taken it years before.

CHAPTER 32: DEATH AT THE WATERSIDE

Tuesday evening, Week 3

Barry Marsh let himself into his small flat in Swanage and dropped his keys onto a shelf. He looked around the apartment that had been his home for the past six years and experienced a pang of nostalgia. It probably wouldn't be his home for much longer. He and Gwen had already started talking about finding somewhere half way between their two workplaces in Dorset and Hampshire so they could move in together. A different future was looming and Marsh wasn't sure how he felt about it.

He had just put the kettle on when the doorbell rang. He went to the hall and peered through the spy-hole in the door. Ah! An old friend. He opened the door. 'Hello, Bob. Long time, no see. What are you doing here?' He stood aside to admit his colleague from Bournemouth.

Bob Thompson seemed to be disoriented. He shrugged. 'I just felt like things were getting on top of me, so I went out for a drive. I thought of you, so I came here on the off-chance.'

'Okay. Do you want a drink? The kettle's just boiled, but I've got beer in the fridge if you want one.'

Thompson stood looking around, as if unsure of where he was. 'Not sure what I want.'

Marsh had an idea. 'How about going out for a curry? It's years since we went out together. It'll be like the old days in Bournemouth when we flat-shared.'

Thompson smiled at last. 'Okay. That'd be good.'

* * *

Half an hour later the two detectives were making their way to the local Indian restaurant. It had started raining and the wind was beginning to pick up. Tourists who had been happy to saunter slowly along the seafront were now beginning to hurry to shelter.

They arrived at the restaurant and Marsh pushed open the door. 'It's okay in here. The Madras is probably the best choice.'

They sipped at their lagers as they waited for the food to arrive. Marsh was becoming concerned about Thompson. He was jittery and seemed unable to concentrate on anything. 'Listen, Bob,' he said. 'If you're worried about something, tell me. You ought to be celebrating, after passing your inspector exam. You'll be in with a chance for the next DI job to come up. You're a good copper and you'll do well.'

Underneath, Barry wasn't so sure about this. He'd been friendly enough with Thompson during their years as rookie cops in Bournemouth, but he'd never been able to get close to his friend. He'd been hurt when, after they'd moved to different parts of the county, Thompson hadn't bothered to keep in touch. It had begun to look as if, for Thompson, the friendship had just been one of convenience. Ah well, thought Marsh, all water under the bridge. Clearly something was upsetting Thompson just now. The problem was, Thompson was being very uncommunicative, even for him. He answered every one of Marsh's questions with a single word, or a shrug.

Marsh tried again. 'C'mon, Bob. You can do better than that. Matt Silver's taken you round every possible place in the county. You must have some idea of where you'd like to go.'

The food arrived, but Thompson merely picked at it. Marsh had had enough. 'Okay, Bob. Out with it. What's bothering you?'

There was a long pause and then Thompson said, 'I've fucked it all up. All of it. It's all gone down the pan and I don't know what to do.'

At this, Marsh's brain began to whir. He started to process the events, clues and hints that he had picked up in recent days. But before he could think how to react, the restaurant door opened. A familiar figure entered and looked him in the eye.

She shook her head gently.

* * *

Sophie was at home in Wareham, waiting restlessly. Bent police officers were her worst nightmare. Her role-models in the force, Harry Turner and Archie Campbell, had both told her that a single rotten police officer could do more damage than a whole gang of crooks. That one person could destroy trust and working relationships that had been built over years, causing people to question the value of upholding the law.

She wondered if Martin, her husband, had noticed how edgy she was. Probably, but he knew her too well to make any comment. He just refilled her coffee cup when required.

Her mobile phone rang shortly before eight o'clock. It was Jim Metcalfe. When the call ended, she picked up her keys and was almost out of the door when she stopped in her tracks. She turned, went back to her husband, and hugged him tightly.

'Martin, I love you so much. I may not say it often, but you are the very best thing in my life. I just wanted you to know that.'

She turned and left, leaving Martin with his mouth open.

Sophie drove to Swanage, and pulled up in the lower end of the High Street, close to an unmarked police car. She spoke to the occupants, and waited. Within ten minutes Greg

Buller's snatch squad arrived in their van, closely followed by Jim Metcalfe. Sophie was determined to try and resolve the situation without resorting to violence, and argued her case forcefully. The area was full of visitors, tourists and locals out for a relaxing evening. Sophie pulled off her fashionable green and gold zipper jacket and put on a bullet-proof vest. She tried to put the jacket back on but couldn't get the zip all the way up. No matter. It hid most of her protective layer. Then she walked, head held high, to the restaurant door, accompanied by Buller's reassuring bulk.

'Where are they sitting?' she asked.

'At a table halfway along the back wall. We've had someone go inside for a moment, to collect a takeaway menu. He's just described the layout. Take care, won't you? We could wait till they come out, like I said just now.'

'I don't think it will pan out that way. I think he's come down here to see Barry for a reason, and it won't take Barry long to guess what's been going on. I'm worried that he'll make some kind of move himself, and I really don't want to chance losing him. They were friends years ago, Greg. Barry will feel betrayed.'

She turned and opened the restaurant door. Inside, the two detectives were sitting exactly as Buller had described, with Marsh facing her. He looked up in surprise as she entered, and Sophie put a finger to her lips and moved over to their table. Thompson glanced up as she slid into the seat next to his. He had been holding his fork in his right hand, and he lowered it. Sophie grabbed hold of his wrist, keeping it clamped against the top of the table.

'Let's be sensible about this, Bob. There are too many people here. Look around you.'

At the table beside theirs sat a family with three children, two chattering away and the third working on a colouring book. On the other side an elderly couple were sitting, about to order dessert.

She felt Thompson's arm muscles tauten, and then relax. 'How long have you known?'

'Known? For a few days. Suspected? Since the middle of last week. But today was something else, Bob. McCluskie's been working for me, so what you did made it personal. And do you know what the worst part was? I had to keep it all from Barry, something I've never had to do before. And you forced that on me.' While she was speaking, her left hand was feeling in the pockets of his jacket, which hung from the back of his chair. Nothing. She breathed a sigh of relief.

'Stupid of me,' Thompson said. 'I can guess what you're looking for. It's out in the car back at Barry's place, in the glove box, neatly wrapped in a cloth, all ready for you like a present.' He laughed. 'I mean, what would be the point of bringing it out with me when all I was doing was going for a curry with an old mate?' He turned to face her. 'I bet Buller's outside with the heavy mob.'

She nodded and looked across at Marsh. 'It wasn't meant to be like this, with Barry here. I knew that he still valued the friendship you had. McCluskie went out on a limb, and what you did to him forced the issue. And you still haven't asked how he is, by the way.'

'That's what the job does to you. Removes all trace of human feeling. I've turned into a bloody robot.'

'So why did you end up nearly killing him?'

'One of the guys in the pub called me,' he said. 'He knew that I used to keep an eye on old Phil Woodruff, so he let me know that McCluskie was poking his nose around. That's why I messaged him about meeting up. I wanted to warn him to steer clear. But when we met he went at it like a bull in a china shop. He wanted to get even with you and use any information about the Woodruffs he could get his hands on to spike your guns. He wouldn't take no for an answer and I was running out of patience. I just lost it all of a sudden, and socked him one. He fell heavily. I looked up and saw that kid watching, so I left.'

'So you were involved with the Woodruffs?' Sophie asked.

'I'm saying nothing more, not now.'

Sophie looked around her. 'Enough of this. Let's go, and let these people get on with their meals.'

She kept her arm on his as they got up. Could she breathe a sigh of relief? She wasn't sure. She could still feel the tension in Thompson's body. Should she have tried to cuff him? Surely he'd realise there was no escape?

A fraction of a second before Thompson acted, she knew she'd misjudged. But she had no time to make a move. He suddenly lunged sideways to break her grip, twisted around and crashed through the doorway to the kitchen, colliding with a waiter carrying a tray of food. Sophie and Marsh hurried after him, treading broken crockery, as Thompson made for the delivery door at the rear. The door slammed back against the wall and Thompson tussled briefly with the cop stationed at the entrance, who lost his footing on the wet, cobbled surface. Thompson disappeared along a narrow alley, with Sophie and Marsh in hot pursuit. More booted feet followed behind them. She and Marsh heard other unit members hurrying along the High Street, parallel to the alleyway.

'He can't get anywhere,' Marsh gasped. 'He's cut off, but he doesn't know it.'

They took a left turn, following Thompson's shadowy form as he burst across the High Street, just in front of Buller. Thompson slowed as he approached the seafront, hesitated then turned left. He was trapped. He ran onto a nearby boating jetty and then stopped, looking around him. He moved slowly to the edge of the timber platform.

'Don't be stupid, Bob!' Marsh shouted. He and Sophie had stopped a few yards short of their quarry. 'The water's bloody freezing at this time of year and it's only three feet deep. You'll get cold and wet, and I'll have to get cold and wet coming in after you. What good would that do anyone?'

They watched in horror as Thompson shrugged his jacket aside, pulled a handgun from his waistband and held it to his head.

'Fooled you though, didn't I? Fuck the lot of you!'

He pulled the trigger, and the explosive crack echoed across the water. Thompson toppled sideways into the dark sea.

* * *

The local police premises had been temporarily taken over for the debriefing. The atmosphere was subdued. Barry Marsh was silent and pale, shaking his head occasionally as if the whole event had been a bad dream.

Jim Metcalfe, the ACC, listened to their accounts. 'I think he had some kind of plan for this evening. I don't know what it was, but it probably involved you, Barry. He had the gun with him and to me, that suggests he was up to something serious. We'll never know what it was. What I will say is this. We brought things to a conclusion that may not have been satisfactory from our point of view, but the important thing is that public safety was not threatened. It could have developed into a hostage situation, but it didn't. We must be grateful for that. I'll speak to the chief and tell her what's happened. Let's all go home and try to get some sleep, then we'll work on it tomorrow. We have to think where we go from here.'

The group dispersed and made their way out of the building.

'I still can't get my head round it,' Marsh said to Sophie. 'I keep thinking it can't be true. How did it come to this? Why would he do it? Why would he ruin his career by getting involved with an outfit like the Woodruffs? It just doesn't make sense.'

'It didn't start just in the past couple of years, Barry. My guess is that it had its origins all those years ago when you were both young cops and came into contact with the old guy, Phil Woodruff.'

'But why didn't I know? No one ever came near me.'

'They spotted a weakness in him, that's why. He's always been a bit full of his own importance — in my opinion anyway. The way they work is as old as the hills. Start small, then work up. They'd have slipped him a tenner, or done him a favour. Anything to get a young, inexperienced cop hooked. And then, slowly, it gets more serious. And before you know it, you can't escape. I've seen it before. By the time he realised what was really going on, it was too late. You weren't approached because they didn't see that same weakness in you. And, let's face it, he hasn't been the most loyal of friends from what you've said. There was a superficiality about him, a self-obsession. Why else would he take that gun and hide it unused for four years? What does that tell you?'

'I don't want to hear this,' Marsh said.

'Of course you don't. What you need is some company. I'm going to phone Gwen. You need her with you tonight.' She sighed. 'And then I've got to phone Kevin McGreedie. He'll be devastated. He was Thompson's boss for the last three years.'

CHAPTER 33: POACHING PLANS

Wednesday morning, Week 3

Sophie sipped at her coffee. She was sitting in the Assistant Chief Constable's office at police headquarters, discussing the latest developments with Jim Metcalfe. He asked for her thoughts.

'I think Blythe's been oiling some cogs in the casino licensing process, and he gets cash in return. He went to Phil Woodruff's funeral for a purpose, maybe to collect the money. After all, it should have been totally safe, with only close family and friends there. But the Armitage couple wandered in by mistake. My guess is that that they didn't see anything suspicious, but Blythe and Woodruff didn't know that. So the old couple were tracked down and killed.'

'Seems extreme, doesn't it?'

'Woodruff has applications in for several casino developments with a total value of ten million. If it got out that bribes were involved, the whole scheme would be scuppered. They wouldn't want to chance that.'

'Where's the money coming from?' Metcalfe asked.

'It's Frimwell cash. Blythe's wife and Woodruff's wife are twin sisters. Ricky Frimwell is their half-brother.'

The ACC looked shocked. 'Are you the right person to be dealing with this? With the Frimwell connection, I mean?'

'I don't have a problem with Frimwell,' Sophie replied. 'It's his uncle, Charlie Duff. Him, I never want to see again or even think about. I wonder if Frimwell has been running all this from his prison cell in Long Lartin. His sister Carol, Blythe's wife, has been visiting him regularly. Sorrento, whose body we found last week, also went to see him. You know what Frimwell's like. He doesn't pussyfoot around. Anyone who crosses him gets chopped. We know that. It explains why we've got these dead bodies on our hands, two of them innocent of anything at all.'

'How did the gang identify the old couple? They couldn't have been there more than a minute or two. Whoever killed them went to a lot of trouble.'

Sophie shrugged. 'If they watched them getting into their car, then they might have used the registration. It's possible that Thompson played a part, using the PNC. If so, we should be able to trace his activity. But there are another couple of issues that are muddying the water for us, so we're not ready to move yet.'

The ACC stroked his chin. 'How's your DS taking last night's events? He was close to Thompson at one time, wasn't he?'

'Barry will be fine, sir. I got his fiancé to come over last night. She's a DS in Southampton. She'll have looked after him.'

'What about the Armitage daughter? The doctor? How's she coping?'

'I'm seeing her now, on my way back to Blandford. She likes to be kept up to date, but I'll give her the abridged version.'

The ACC looked at his watch. 'Time for me to set off for Poole Hospital to check on McCluskie. I phoned earlier and they told me he was in a medically induced coma. They plan to keep him that way for a couple of days. But I need to show my face. What was he up to, Sophie?'

She rose, deciding not to tell him everything she'd gleaned from Thompson the previous night. With McCluskie still critically ill, the right thing to do was give him the benefit of the doubt. 'God knows,' she finally said. 'Some scheme of his own. Blackman is adamant that McCluskie was acting alone. Apparently he was asking his old cronies what they knew about the Woodruffs. We're assuming that someone didn't like it and somehow let Thompson know. But the attack followed so fast. To my mind, that means one of those men McCluskie met for lunch knew about the Thompson-Woodruff deal. Whoever it was called Thompson right away. And they were all ex-cops, which makes it a bit worrying. Well, it's your problem, sir, not mine. Thank goodness.'

* * *

Barry Marsh and Rae Gregson were back at the council chambers. They were scrutinising every commercial planning and licensing decision that had involved Councillor Blythe, and had spotted a sequence that would have benefitted the Woodruffs or the Frimwells. There was little doubt — these two family-based businesses seemed to have received favourable treatment for several of their club and casino developments. The two detectives took away copies of some of the planning application documents and minutes of the planning meetings. Councillor Blythe had played a prominent role in all of them.

'Do we have the expertise for this kind of work?' Rae asked. 'I'm a novice at this type of sleaze. How about you?'

He shook his head. 'Me too. We'll talk it over with the boss.'

They left the council chambers and drove back to the Blandford incident room, where they told Sophie of their concerns.

'It's brainwave time,' she replied. 'I know the very person, and it solves so many problems. Leave it with me. I'll have to get the approval of Matt Silver and the ACC.'

Rae and Marsh left Sophie's office. 'Did she actually look happy just then?' said Rae. 'What's she up to?'

Marsh sighed. 'Don't ask me. I can never tell what's going on in that brain of hers. She'll have thought of some scheme that will be way beyond anything I could have dreamt up. Let's just get back to work on this stuff and see what we can pick out.'

* * *

Sophie was on the phone to her boss, Matt Silver. 'Can we poach her, Matt? It's exactly what she's been specialising in, over in Bath. She did commercial fraud last year and is doing this kind of stuff now. And Barry and I know her so well. It would be fantastic if you could get her on loan from Avon and Somerset. Can't you think up some angle that would get her released for a couple of days? Even offer my services in part exchange? I'm anybody's if the price is right.'

She replaced the handset, feeling more cheerful than she had in days. It would be great if she could get Lydia Pillay back for a short while to help them with these complex council records. But her plans went further than that, though she hadn't mentioned them to Silver. With Thompson dead, there would be a vacancy for a DS to work for Kevin McGreedie in Bournemouth, and Sophie had heard through the grapevine that Lydia had passed her sergeant's exams with flying colours. If only she could be tempted back to this area! Maybe a few days with her and Barry, being reminded of happy times, might cause Lydia to consider the possibility. Along with a few gentle nudges, of course.

CHAPTER 34: BUSINESS PROPOSALS

Wednesday afternoon, Week 3

In Long Lartin high security prison, Ricky Frimwell paced the length of his cell. What the fuck was going on? Why had everyone suddenly stopped answering his questions? Even his half-sister, Carol, the one with a bit of loyalty, had clammed up and was refusing to answer his calls. She'd even cancelled this afternoon's visit, according to the warden. As for her twin, stuck-up Sue, she hardly ever visited anyway. Ricky was becoming increasingly convinced that he'd miscalculated with Sue. Too many principles and too many reservations, that was her trouble. She'd even got to his mum, infecting her with that holier-than-thou attitude. It was fucking upside down, those twins and their lives. Sue was too prim and proper, but was married to a would-be gangster. Carol shared his own outlook on life, grab as much as you can whenever you can, and she was married to a fucking councillor! Where was the logic? Women! He'd never get to the bottom of how their minds worked. Didn't any of them realise he was just trying to help them? He wasn't going to gain anything from all this planning, not stuck in gaol for the rest of his life. It was all for their benefit, not that they appreciated what he was trying to do. Maybe he should just give up on the scheming and settle for an easy life.

The thought of that fucking cop still needled him. Bitch. He remembered when they'd first met, on that derelict farm on the edge of Poole Harbour. That look she'd given him. Even then she'd known. From then on she'd never let go. Like a fucking terrier with its teeth clamped on his leg, dragging him down. He'd desperately wanted a way to get back at her, and it had looked as though this could be it. Maybe he'd been too hopeful. Anyway, what did it matter? She was only a side issue. The main thing was to keep the properties in family hands. Was that plan still on? Had he misjudged things by telling Woodruff that Sorrento needed to be permanently removed from the scene after all his meddling? What had gone wrong? He couldn't tell, not locked in a prison cell with all contact chopped for some reason. Something was going on outside. He could sense it.

* * *

Marilyn Mitchell walked slowly into the lobby of the Merwell Hotel in Poole and looked around for the entrance to the lounge. Very plush, she thought. Nice carpets, wood-panelled walls, smart staff at the reception desk. So this was the type of environment that Sue Woodruff moved in. Well, maybe she could get used to it. If she did agree to work with Sue, it would have to be according to the law. She wasn't going to be persuaded to do what she knew was wrong. She ran a hand over her belly, feeling the bulge. A receptionist in a smart uniform asked if she needed any help.

Marilyn followed the directions to the Rose Lounge, and walked through an archway into a sunlit seating area filled with roses in giant pots. She spotted Sue sitting to one side, sipping from a china cup, and walked over to her.

Sue rose to greet her. 'You look lovely, Marilyn. Pregnancy suits you.'

Marilyn laughed. 'Not sure about that. But at least I know what to expect this time. I've been through it twice before.' She sat down heavily and allowed Sue to pour her a cup of tea and push across a plate of cakes. 'Those look wicked,' she added. 'But hey ho, what's to lose?'

'Have you had a chance to think over my proposal?' Sue asked.

Marilyn nodded. 'I have.' She reached down and took some papers from her bag. 'I have a few minor issues with one or two of the ideas, but the overall plan looks good and I'd be happy to work with you. I need to make clear, though, that I won't tolerate anything illegal, or even slightly shady. Some of the things your Wayne has got involved with are a bit dodgy, and I won't let Gordon get involved if I think things are suspect.'

Sue shook her head. 'No, no. I promise. I've had enough. I don't think anyone realises what it was like, growing up with that half-brother of mine. Ricky always was an out-and-out bastard, even at home. Wayne's very different, but I've had enough of him too.'

Marilyn listened in silence.

'We'll concentrate only on the Woodruff places that we can run legitimately. The cafes, hotels, and maybe a couple of the pubs. The rest we ditch. I think I've got potential buyers for most of them. They pulled Wayne down, those places, with the lowlife that went there. I thought I'd seen the end of that kind of thing when Ricky got put away, but Wayne's started going down the same route. I know what he's up to. I've always kept him up to date regarding my family trust — he's my husband, after all. But now he's muscling in on it for his own ends. The thing is, the Woodruffs didn't have any kind of plan. They just accumulated properties willy nilly. Wayne thinks the merger with Frimwell will be a way out. He thinks I agree, but I don't. I've already started selling off the crappier properties, and I bought old Phil's shares in Woodruff Holdings before he died. Wayne doesn't know yet. I told Phil it would keep the business in the family. Phil didn't know that half of the shares were already in my name. I'm now the majority shareholder, but no one's twigged yet. Same with Midwinter Tide and the Frimwell trust.' She took a long sip of tea. 'I've worked for years to get to this position, Marilyn. And none of them realise it. I have all the power now, but I haven't started flexing my muscles yet. I was waiting till I got the right people behind me. And that's Gordon, you and maybe Justin. I'm finished with Wayne. He's been off again with some floozy for most of the weekend, and I warned him last time that I wouldn't tolerate it any more. He's got what's coming.'

'Revenge may not be the best motive for branching out like this, Sue.'

'I know that. I hated the way Ricky ruined everything for our family, and Wayne seems to be heading in the same direction. That bastard Ricky ruined Mum's life. Can you imagine what it's done to her, being the mother of a murdering psychopath? People don't know he's my brother 'cause I have a different surname. I've told Mum to change her surname by deed poll, but she's not done anything about it yet. No, revenge isn't my main reason for doing this. The time is right to merge the two businesses, but it's me that's going to do it, not Wayne and Ricky. People think I'm just a dumb blonde, but they have no idea how wrong they are.'

'Well, you impress me, Sue. You seem to have covered every angle from the look of your business plan. And this type of work would be right up my street. I think I've got the experience, though this little one will get in the way a bit.' She patted her stomach. 'I've only got about three months of work in me before things get too much.'

'That's not a problem. And I'll include child care in your contract when you come back after the birth. So are you in?'

Marilyn nodded. 'Yes. I'm in. And Gordon will be as well. Though he doesn't know it yet.'

* * *

Gordon Mitchell was feeling increasingly uneasy about Wayne Woodruff. He'd always thought Sorrento had been the crooked one, but he was now beginning to see that he'd seriously misjudged the situation. Sorrento had an unpleasant personality, but Wayne was shifty. Sure, he was easier to work with, but his disregard of all legal constraints was becoming a real worry. And Gordon was beginning to suspect that Wayne had been involved in Sorrento's death. The thought terrified him. He kept thinking back to his conversation with Marilyn the previous week when she'd told him she wanted him to stop working for the Woodruffs and start a new job, one that was clean. How would she react if she got to know his latest suspicions? To cap it all, Wayne had introduced him to that bent cop, and the guy had clearly been unhappy about it. Didn't Wayne understand that he was playing with fire? And now Sorrento was dead. Would Gordon be expected to take his place? And if he crossed his boss too often would he too end up dead and hidden under a bush in some God-forsaken bog? Christ. What had he got himself into?

His mobile phone rang. It was Marilyn, asking him to come to some posh hotel in Poole for a top-secret meeting, and telling him to keep it secret from Woodruff. As it turned out, Wayne was visiting one of the casinos and wasn't expected back until later. Gordon drove to Poole and was astonished to see Marilyn in the hotel lounge talking to Sue Woodruff, of all people. What was going on?

He listened to the two women in amazement. He looked at the business plan that Sue had drawn up, along with the financial figures. He asked questions about the legal position and was astounded to discover that Sue was absolutely right in her claim. She was, without a doubt, the major shareholder in both the Woodruff and Frimwell family businesses and so could dictate any future policy. This proposal would solve his dilemma! Not only that, Marilyn would be back at work, using her experience of commercial property management, and working alongside him. Maybe the gods were smiling down on him at last. Sue handed him a glass of champagne, bubbles sparkling in the sunlight streaming in through the window. He looked out at the view, at the blue sea in the distance.

'I'm with you. What's the first step?' Gordon raised his glass.

CHAPTER 35: STITCHED UP

Thursday morning, Week 3

Justin Griffiths poured himself a coffee. 'So what's this all about, Wayne? A company meeting at nine o'clock in the morning? Phil would have had a fit.'

Woodruff shrugged. 'No idea. It's that wife of mine. She kept going on about it all last night. In the end I agreed just to get a bit of peace. I dunno what's got into her head. Women!'

Griffiths suspected that something was up, but he had no idea what it could be. He looked up as three women came into the room, followed by Gordy. It wasn't often that old Betty Woodruff came to any meetings, especially since the death of her husband, Phil. Sue always attended, but Alison Carter, Wayne's younger sister, had never attended a company meeting before. Justin had only met her a couple of times, most recently at old Phil's funeral. Well, well.

The group took their places at the table, with Wayne at the head. He stretched out his legs in front of him. 'Okay, folks. Sue wanted this meeting to discuss the way forward for the company. I'm not really ready with my plans yet, but I can give you a rundown of how far I've got.'

Sue interrupted. 'That isn't the purpose of this extraordinary meeting. I thought I'd explained that to you last night.' Wayne looked blank. She turned to the others. 'I've called this meeting in my capacity as majority shareholder. I propose a motion of no confidence in the current chairman and business manager.'

'I second that,' said Alison Carter.

Woodruff looked blankly at his wife and sister. 'What? What do you mean, majority shareholder?'

Sue looked across at Gordon, now company secretary and legal adviser. Griffiths could feel the tension.

'A motion has been proposed and seconded. We vote according to shareholding stakes in the company.' Gordon glanced down at the paper in front of him. 'Wayne holds twenty per cent. Betty has ten per cent, Alison and Justin each have five. Tony Sorrento also held five, which will pass to his next of kin, so obviously his shares can't be used at present. Sue holds fifty-five percent.'

In the stunned silence that followed, Wayne looked around him. 'What?' he said again.

Sue's face was expressionless. 'Phil sold his shares to me before he died. Thirty-five per cent. Added to my own, that makes fifty-five. That means I own the company. Can we continue with the vote, Gordon?'

Gordon nodded. 'All those in favour of the no confidence vote, raise your hand, please.'

Griffiths looked around, and almost laughed. So this was it. The great, all-powerful Wayne Woodruff, outmanoeuvred by little Sue. Stitched up, zipped up and set up. Griffiths watched as Sue raised her hand. No one else need do anything, if those figures were correct, but someone did anyway. Wayne's sister, Alison, raised hers. Change was on the way. Maybe it was for the good. Griffiths swallowed hard and lifted his hand.

'All those against.'

Wayne raised his hand, and looked around him. Betty, his mother, kept her hand on the table. 'I abstain.'

'Motion carried,' Gordon said. 'I think we have a new chairman.'

Sue stood up and walked to Woodruff's chair at the head of the table. 'We need to swap places, Wayne. I run the company now.'

Woodruff stood up. 'How did you fucking do that? How did you get your greedy hands on Phil's shares?'

Sue sat down. 'He didn't trust your judgement, Wayne. He told me so. He knew there was a good chance you'd ruin us all if you got total control, so we partly planned this together. It was all above board. I bought those shares fair and square. The money is in a trust account in the names of your mum, Alison and you. You've lost control but you've gained a lot of cash. You should be happy. Your share will pay for any number of weekends away with those prostitutes you seem to like so much.'

Woodruff scowled at her, turned and stalked out of the room, slamming the door behind him. Sue looked around her at the intent, silent faces. 'Gordon, I'd like you to continue as company secretary. You have my full confidence. Justin, would you like to keep the role of vice-chair and assistant manager?'

Griffiths felt a weight lift from his shoulders. Maybe at last the company could put its past behind it and move towards a better future. Maybe they'd become totally legitimate for the first time. 'Yeah,' he said. 'Of course.'

He started slightly at Sue's next words. 'Our first priority is to help the police get to the bottom of Tony Sorrento's murder. We give them absolute co-operation, is that clear? If there is a link to anyone in this company, then that person gets no help from us. Now let's get on with the other business.'

As she continued, Griffiths looked at Gordy and smiled. Gordon nodded.

* * *

At about the same time, in his cell at Long Lartin prison, Ricky Frimwell was reading a letter from the Frimwell family lawyer. Then he read it again. No, he hadn't misread it. Sue Woodruff had taken over the running of the Frimwell family business and trust, and his mother agreed.

He recognised Sue's writing on the second envelope. He looked at it for a long while before opening it and taking out the letter.

Dear Ricky,

You should receive this on the same day as a letter from our solicitors about a change in the running of all our family concerns. With Mum and Carol's agreement, I managed to find buyers for a couple of our more rundown properties. With our share of the money, Carol and I bought out Mum's stake, so we now own the business. Well, I do, with Carol as a minor shareholder who's agreed to let me run things as I see fit. It means Mum's comfortably off for the rest of her life without having to scrimp and save. She's finally agreed to change her name by deed poll and move to somewhere a bit more comfortable, so at long last she can escape from your evil influence and its disastrous effect on her life.

I'm going ahead with the merger plans with Woodruff Holdings, but on my terms. I'll then get rid of the crappier properties. Don't bother trying to influence Wayne or hope that he can salvage any of your schemes. I've ousted him as well. I've had enough of all his floozies and his half-baked business plans that would only spell disaster for us.

I won't come to visit. I never have before, so why would I start now? I can't stand the sight of you. It was your influence that set Wayne on the slippery slope. Thank God he's never quite sunk to your level. Whether Carol comes to see you is up to her.

I might wish you well for the rest of your life, but that would be a lie because I don't. You wrecked Mum's life and nearly ruined mine. I hate you for it.

From your sister, Sue

Ricky flung the letter aside. He got up and kicked at the wall. Then he began to wreck the contents of his cell, item by item, flinging the objects to the floor, turning over the furniture. The noise alerted the wardens, but Ricky had already begun to calm down before the sedative kicked in. He'd been completely outmanoeuvred and he knew it.

CHAPTER 36: FOOT IN THE DOOR

Thursday morning, Week 3

Sophie watched Woodruff stalk out of the building, kicking at a large planter filled with spring-flowering blooms.

'He doesn't look happy, does he?' She, Marsh and Rae watched their quarry take out his mobile phone and make a short call. He then got into a shiny, black Mercedes and reversed it out of its parking place, engine revving.

'Shall I follow, ma'am?' Marsh asked from the driving seat.

'Why not? We're in no hurry, and he looks as though he's off to meet someone. I may alert some of the mobile squads that we're on the move.'

They followed the big black limousine towards the centre of Bournemouth, where it pulled up in a side street in the commercial district. Marsh drove Sophie's car close in behind it.

'Follow him, Rae. He hasn't met you. I want to see what he's up to.'

Rae got out of the car and hurried after the striding figure of Woodruff. He walked down the hill and into a bank. Rae followed, pulling her purse out of her shoulder bag as if she was just about to withdraw some cash. Woodruff spoke to a receptionist. Clearly he was demanding to see a manager. A few seconds later, a smartly dressed man appeared and ushered Woodruff into an office. Rae lingered near the door, leafing through some investment brochures. She didn't have long to wait. The door crashed open and Woodruff stormed out, his face red. He turned to the bank manager, who held his hands out.

'There's nothing I can do, Mr Woodruff. The accounts have all been frozen by the new board. Your wife phoned in the instruction just ten minutes ago.'

'It's my fucking money! Mine. Not hers! Christ. What do I have to do to get some cash here?'

The manager glanced over to a bank security guard who'd started to walk towards them. He stood waiting, a few yards away. Woodruff looked around him at the people queuing for the cashier. They were all staring.

'Ah, fuck the lot of you!' Wayne marched towards the door, where he hesitated before flinging the door open.

Rae followed Woodruff out of the building, and returned to Sophie's car.

'My guess is that he made an attempt to clean out the accounts,' she reported. 'But he got nothing. His wife's blocked him. At least that's what I think's happened. He was still arguing with the manager when they came out of his office.'

Sophie was watching Woodruff. 'He's making a phone call. Let's wait and see what he does next.'

The Mercedes turned and headed a short distance back along the road before taking a left turn.

'I think we need to update the control centre. He may be up to something. Keep talking about where we are, Barry, while I make the call.'

'This road takes us down past the council chambers,' Marsh said. 'Could he have been phoning Blythe?'

The Mercedes pulled up close to the council offices and waited with its engine still running. Within a few minutes, Councillor Blythe hurried out of a side door and crossed the road. He leaned in the passenger window, seeming to argue with the man in the driving seat. Finally, Blythe got in the car and they drove away. Marsh followed, keeping a safe distance, as Woodruff's car skirted the town centre and made its way west. Sophie asked the mobile units to remain on alert until needed. They trailed the Mercedes towards Poole, and into the entertainment district. Their quarry finally turned into the car park of a casino club, closed at this time of day. Marsh drew up in the street nearby, and they watched as the two men left their vehicle and walked to a side door which opened to Woodruff's knock.

Marsh checked his notes. 'The Boulevard Casino Club, one of the Woodruff places. The licensee and manager is Terence Barber, nickname Toffee. He has a record for theft and petty crime plus one conviction for intimidation, none of it recent. He's kept out of trouble for a long time now.'

'Or so it seems,' Sophie added. 'I know this is difficult for you Barry, but we don't know how much Bob Thompson was protecting them.'

'What could they be here for?' wondered Marsh.

'A panic meeting, I expect. They're probably talking through their options,' Sophie replied. 'From what Rae overheard at the bank, Woodruff's wife has just frozen all the accounts. What's her name, Rae?'

'Sue. And Blythe's married to her sister, Carol.'

'So the locked accounts might have affected both of these two. I've been trying to remember their wives from the Frimwell court case two years ago. I think I might have spoken to Sue once. She was with the mother, and they both looked totally devastated. I wonder what's been going on?'

'Maybe the rest of the family have discovered what those two have been up to,' Marsh said. 'Maybe they were happy to go along with a bit of sleaze and bribery, but once they realised that people were getting murdered, they backed off. They are our prime suspects, aren't they? For the murders, I mean?'

'Woodruff and Blythe? It's looked that way for some time. This guy Barber is new, though. We haven't looked at him, have we?'

Rae shook her head. 'No. And this is the nearest of their places to Wareham Forest. It's easy to get to from here, twenty minutes tops.' 'Anything else we need to know?'

Marsh scanned his notes again. 'You remember the decorating jobs that Pete Armitage did at some of the Woodruff places? Well, this was the first one. From what he told us, I'd guess it was about ten years ago.'

A mobile phone trilled, making them jump.

'I've got Thompson's mobile in my bag,' Sophie hissed. 'Answer it for me, Barry. Keep it to a minimum and try to sound like him.' She handed the phone over.

'Yeah?' grunted Marsh. It was Woodruff.

'We've got a problem. We need to meet. Just you, me and Toffee.'

Sophie shook her head.

'No,' Marsh replied.

'Waddya mean, no? Don't try to fuck around with me, you creep. You do as I say, or a big, fat dossier lands on your boss's desk and you're up shit creek. We're at the Boulevard club. Get yourself across here now.' The call ended.

Marsh shook his head. 'So Bob was being blackmailed. Now we know.'

'We'd guessed that, Barry. That's why he seemed so depressed and withdrawn. He couldn't see a way out. The problem for us is what do we do now? Any ideas?'

'They know both of you, ma'am. They don't know me,' said Rae. 'Can we use that?'

'These men are probably killers, Rae. I'm not sending you in there on some kind of scouting mission.'

'But isn't there a standby unit waiting just round the corner? I could be wired up.'

'What for? No, absolutely not. I've been prevaricating far too long. It's time to confront them, so let's do it. You stay here, Rae, and keep an eye on the place. I'll check that the support units are ready, then Barry and I will go in for a chat.'

'I'm with you, ma'am,' Marsh said. 'Let's stir them up a bit. It's about time.'

Sophie's phone rang with an unknown number, and a woman spoke.

'Is that DCI Allen? It's Sue Woodruff here. I've taken over the business, and I don't like some of the things that have been happening. Can we talk? Off the record, I mean?'

* * *

The two detectives rapped on the door and waited. It was opened by the same man who'd let Woodruff and Blythe in, ten minutes earlier.

Sophie held out her warrant card. 'Mr Barber? I'm DCI Allen and this is DS Marsh. We're responding to a call for police attendance made from this building to a local CID officer a few minutes ago. We have a backup unit just around the corner. May we come in?'

The man looked puzzled. 'But there was no . . .'

Sophie put her foot in the door. 'The caller was clearly distressed and seemed to know the CID officer personally. We have a duty to check that everyone is safe. Please let us in. I don't want to have to force an entry, but I am prepared to do so as a result of the call, which gave us significant cause for concern.'

Barber stood with his mouth open, and the two detectives pushed past him into a clean, well-lit lobby area.

'Thank you for allowing us entry, Mr Barber,' Sophie said. 'We'd like to check on the safety of the caller, so if you could point us in his direction please?'

They walked in. Nice colours, thought Sophie, looking around her. Pete Armitage had been right to praise his own work. They could hear voices coming from an open door to their left, obviously the manager's office. Woodruff made a lunge for the doorway as Sophie and Marsh entered, but Marsh grabbed his arm and twisted it behind his back. Sophie slipped her taser from its holster and turned to Barber. 'Don't try anything. It really wouldn't be in your best interests.' She radioed the backup unit, then turned back to the man at the desk.

'Good morning, Councillor. And to you, Mr Woodruff. We met briefly last week at your pub over in Pokesdown, if you remember.'

'What the hell are you doing here?' Woodruff spluttered, his face contorted with anger and his arm still held in a lock by Marsh.

'Responding to the call you made for a CID officer. I explained this to Mr Barber at the door. I know you requested a specific officer — DS Thompson — but he's unable to make it.' She waited.

'It wasn't a 999 call. I called his mobile.'

'Yes, I know. Why did you need him here? It sounded extremely urgent. I've brought a five-man snatch squad with me because the phone message sounded so desperate. They're parked just around the corner, kitted out in all the gear. Raring to go. Ready to tear limb from limb, as it were. Do you mean there isn't an emergency?'

Blythe looked at Woodruff blankly.

'In that case why did you make that call to DS Thompson's phone? How did you get his number? Why was he known to you? It was you, wasn't it, Mr Woodruff? Can you answer me, please?'

Woodruff was silent. She walked across to the desk and glanced at the documents spread across its surface. A shredding machine sat beside the desk, unplugged.

'Mr Woodruff, you are aware that we are investigating the suspicious death of your business manager, Tony Sorrento. I expressly forbade the shredding of any of your organisation's documentation. We assumed that everything of importance would be at your head office in Pokesdown, but clearly that isn't the case. I can see some planning documents here, with council stamps on them.' She pulled them towards her. 'And the signing-off initials are TB. Would they be yours, Councillor, by any chance?' She looked at the three men, her face expressionless. 'Let me explain the situation. We've had three murders. The elderly couple found at Morden Bog and Tony Sorrento a mile away, in Wareham Forest. These places are only twenty minutes' drive from here. In both cases there's a link to you, Mr Woodruff, and to you, Councillor Blythe. This stuff,' she waved her hand across the spread documents, 'Reinforces that connection.'

They heard the sound of a van drawing up outside the window. Marsh looked at Barber. 'Better be quick and let them in, otherwise your door will be flattened. They love using the ram, those guys.'

Barber hurried out of the room and they heard the sound of heavy footfalls approaching.

Sophie looked at Woodruff. 'I am arresting you for the murders of Edward Armitage, Sylvia Armitage and Tony Sorrento. You do not have to say anything. But it may harm your defence if you do not mention when questioned something which you later rely on in court. Anything you do say may be given in evidence.' She then turned to Blythe and repeated the words, just as the uniformed police officers entered the room.

She turned to Barber. 'Is that your vehicle? The green Land Rover in the manager's slot?'

'Yes,' Barber said.

'The one with several weeks' worth of accumulated mud in the wheel arches?'

He glared at Sophie.

'Wonderful stuff, dried gunk. Forensic analysis can pinpoint its origins down to the exact mud patch it came from. Barry, over to you this time.'

Marsh read Barber his rights and he, too, was led out.

'I think we got here just in time, ma'am. Another hour and all this stuff would have been shredded.'

CHAPTER 37: BALACLAVA AND BASEBALL BATS

Thursday afternoon, Week 3

A young Asian woman rapped on the glass door of Sophie's office. She waved and started to rise from her seat. Lydia! 'Hello, ma'am, I'm a bit confused. My boss only spoke to me late yesterday about coming on loan to you for a day or two. It's great to be with you again, but what's it all about?'

Sophie gave her a hug. 'First, I hear congratulations are due. You've passed your sergeant exams. That's great news! And I love the new hairstyle. That short, spiky look really suits you. Listen, would you like to stay until the weekend? Our spare room's always ready, and Jade would love to have you around for a few evenings.'

'That's very thoughtful, ma'am, but I'm not sure . . .'

Sophie elaborated. 'Barry's got engaged to Gwen. He proposed last weekend. We're having a celebration on Saturday night.'

Lydia laughed. 'Well, that changes everything! Count me in, though I haven't bought any party clothes with me.'

'Not a problem. We'll go out on a celebration shopathon with Jade on Saturday morning. She's always telling me I need new clothes.' She paused. 'That's if we can get this all wrapped up before then. That's why you're here. We need an expert in licensing and planning fraud, and also someone who can spot discrepancies in accounts. And then there's the other thing.'

Lydia waited. 'I'm not a mind reader, ma'am.'

Sophie told her about Bob Thompson.

Lydia shook her head. 'I can't believe it! How's Barry coping?'

'He's okay. It's hit him hard, though, I can tell. But he'll get over it. The two of them hadn't been close for years, apparently.'

'So . . . what you're saying is, there'll be a vacancy for a DS in Kevin McGreedie's unit?'

Sophie nodded.

'And you want me to apply?'

'Yes. You've done two years in the financial unit, and it's been good experience for you. But don't you think it's time for a change? Anyway, I've missed having you around, Lydia. Not that you'd be working for me, because I've got Rae. You'd be Kevin's second, and that means you'll be Jimmy Melsom's boss.'

Lydia laughed. 'I don't know whether that would be a good or bad thing. But the idea is very tempting. I'll definitely consider it. And thanks for thinking of me.'

'We don't have anyone in the force with your specialist auditing skills, Lydia. You could train up Rae, she's got the right mindset.' Sophie looked at her. 'And I hope you've got over your doubts about me.'

Lydia was silent for a few moments. 'Rae's your transgender person, isn't she? Things must be hard for her. I can sympathise, being from a minority myself. You can see people's response, even if they don't say anything, but in her case it'll be worse.'

Sophie saw that she wasn't going to get a response. 'She's a really good detective and she works hard. She's out on a search at the moment, but you can have a chat with her at Barry's do at the weekend.'

'Okay. Well I'd better start looking at these accounts, hadn't I?'

They went through to the main incident room, where Barry Marsh was sorting through the pile of folders retrieved from the Rising Moon and the Boulevard club. Sophie left them working, and made her way to the interview room to confront Toffee Barber, the club manager. They needed more information about Rod Armitage's connection with the club. But Barber refused to speak. Sophie looked out of the window at the pouring rain. I must be losing my touch, she thought wearily.

* * *

Barry Marsh felt as though his emotions had been squeezed through a mangle. The events of Tuesday evening, when his erstwhile friend Bob Thompson had been revealed as crooked and had then taken his own life, were still resonating in his brain. Some of the tension had dissipated, but Marsh couldn't relax. Aspects of the case just didn't ring true. Exactly how had they murdered the Armitage couple? Okay, it was meant to remove two people who'd witnessed the handing of a large backhander to Blythe, but what of the actual sequence of events? Marsh was having trouble concentrating on the files in front of him, whereas Lydia seemed to relish the task. Well, he could leave her to it now she was here. Maybe some fresh air was the answer.

He left the police station and walked south, soon reaching the green waters of the River Stour. He looked about him, seeing swans and ducks. Parents with toddlers were throwing bread to the birds. He shaded his eyes from the sun's glare and looked along the course of the flowing river. There would be a long-distance footpath along the riverbank as it meandered towards the coast. Dorset had countless miles of footpaths, heading in all directions, crossing farmland, moors, woodland, coastal cliffs, and bogs.

Of course! You could walk from here to Morden Bog. You'd need to go about three miles south-west by the river, then turn due south for five miles. Eight miles in total. Someone without a vehicle, someone fit, healthy and used to walking would be able to complete the journey both ways in less than six hours. There would have been no need for a car. That's why no tyre tracks had been found.

Who knew about Morden Bog? Who stood to gain from the deaths? Who would know the footpath network? Who was fit and healthy enough to manage a sixteen mile walk overnight? Who'd known all about the Woodruff setup? And finally, who owned surprisingly high-quality walking boots and waterproofs? Marsh punched the air, then looked around, embarrassed. Nobody had seen him, thank goodness. Suddenly he was feeling a whole lot better.

* * *

Sophie picked at an errant strand of her short, blonde hair. 'The problem is, Barry, his flat's been searched, thoroughly. Blackman and McCluskie did a really good job on it, and found nothing. If he did gain something for his trouble, where would he have hidden it?'

'But what if it wasn't money at all? What if he owed them a lot? Maybe a gambling debt? Remember it was him that suggested Pete put in a bid for decorating the Boulevard club. He was already a regular there. Maybe the relationship goes deeper than we've assumed.'

'In that case, we need to go through their stuff really carefully. It won't be in any official accounts, not if it's a longstanding gambling debt. It'll be in a notebook somewhere, probably in that mass of material we lifted this morning. Let's get started. I want to interview Woodruff and the others in a couple of hours. It would be good if we had something concrete by then.'

They joined Lydia at the pile of folders and files, and started sorting through them. Any notebooks they found were put to one side. In less than twenty minutes they'd finished, creating a small pile of eight notebooks containing handwritten notes and jottings. Sophie and Marsh scanned through these, while Lydia returned to the financial statements. It didn't take long to find the notebook they were looking for. It was old, stained and torn at one corner, but the notes inside were gold dust. Names, dates and sums of money, all recorded in detail. They saw clearly that Rod Armitage had somehow managed to accumulate a gambling debt amounting to several thousand pounds. That debt had been cancelled four weeks previously.

'Bring him in,' Sophie said. 'Meanwhile I'll have a little chat with our man, Toffee Barber. I'm sure he won't feel particularly loyal to an outsider. Maybe he'll be willing to drop our young Rod in the deep stuff right away.'

Marsh tilted his head. 'He might look for a deal, ma'am. Wouldn't you in his situation?'

Her lip curled. 'I have no intention of ever being in his situation.'

With a squad car behind him, Marsh drove to Rod's flat but the supposedly disorganised young man was nowhere to be found.

* * *

Marsh phoned Sharon Giroux at her surgery but she claimed to know nothing of her brother's whereabouts. She sounded upset and angry, so Marsh asked what was bothering her. Sharon told him that she'd paid Rod's overdue rent bill before leaving for her family holiday, but had just discovered about the large sum that their mother had given to Rod, supposedly for the same purpose.

Marsh went to see his boss in her office. 'Rod gave us a pretty convincing story, ma'am. But he's devious, and he's tricked his family into paying off his debts. He's always projected this image of being just self-centred and dozy. But he's been very clever at wheedling money out of them when he needs it.'

'He did have that assault complaint made against him as a teenager, Barry. I know it was dropped, but we need to bear it in mind.' Sophie sighed. 'Okay, we need to step up the search for him. He obviously knows more than he's been letting on. I just wish we could find out who else was told that Sylvia might have been planning to make a large charity donation. They've all denied it, apart from Sharon. I'm just about to interview our sweet man, Toffee. I think he knows more about this whole business than he's been telling, and he might be the weak link in the chain. I'll probe a bit.'

'Why would he know?'

'It's possible he was directly involved in at least one of the murders. Maybe all of them. He got a bit jumpy at times. It just made me wonder. He would have seen Rod fairly regularly, and Pete, when there was a decorating job on. We've got the evidence to nail Woodruff and Blythe, particularly with the help we got from Sue Woodruff, but maybe it's more complex than that. I need to ask him about the storerooms at the back of his club. Rae radioed in about them, but she can't find any keys.'

Sophie and Marsh made their way to the second interview room, where Barber was talking to his lawyer.

'You have a couple of outhouses at the back of your club, Mr Barber. Could you tell me what's in them?'

'Spare furniture. You know, tables, chairs, that kind of thing.'

'What about the smaller shed?'

'We don't use it,' he replied.

'But it's kept locked. Why's that?'

He shrugged. 'It's used by the builders and decorators who do work on the place.'

'Like Pete Armitage?'

Barber looked wary. 'Yeah. He has the key at the mo. They do loads of work at our place, so they use that shed to store their stuff.'

Evidently Barber was now more willing to talk about Armitage. Maybe his lawyer had made him see sense.

'Rod or Pete?'

'Either, depending on who's doing most of the work at the time.'

'I've got officers still there, Mr Barber, and they need to get into those storage rooms. Where can they find a key? Either that or we break the doors down. Which would you prefer?'

Barber hesitated. 'No comment.'

Sophie and Marsh went out to pass on the news to Rae, but the doors had already been forced. 'The locks were rotten, ma'am, and fell apart easily. There's a mix of stuff here. The bigger shed was okay, just old bits of furniture and fittings. This one didn't have a key anywhere I could see, so we had to force the lock. I've just spotted a load of decorating stuff. Wait a mo.'

They heard thumps and bangs, and then Rae's voice again. 'Paint thinner, brushes, cleaning rags. Hang on. There's a pile of stuff here at the back, half hidden, and it looks suspicious. Some boxes with what look like antiques in them, and other valuable-looking stuff. We may need to get forensics to take a look.'

Sophie was about to answer when Rae spoke again. 'Whoa. There's a couple of baseball bats in the corner. And a balaclava.'

'Back off, Rae. We'll get the local CID in to start fingerprinting. Stay there for the time being and don't let anyone else in. Okay?'

'Should we visit Pete Armitage?' Marsh asked.

Sophie looked at the clock. 'I think we have to, but I need to phone Kevin McGreedie first. He can deal with the stuff that Rae's found. I wonder what those two supposed decorators have been up to?'

CHAPTER 38: DIRTY HARRY

Thursday evening, Week 3

It was now mid-evening and Pete Armitage was nowhere to be found. He lived in a small semi-detached bungalow on the south side of Blandford but there was no answer at the door. According to his neighbour, a bright-eyed pensioner who had answered her door suspiciously quickly, he hadn't been back all day. She told Sophie and Marsh that he usually came home at the same time each evening but she hadn't seen him since he'd left that morning. Armitage's driveway passed close to her sitting room window and her chair was positioned so that she could watch the comings and goings in the neighbourhood.

'Is he alright? He keeps himself to himself and doesn't chat very much. He does put my bins out for me, though, and that's really helpful.'

Sophie and Marsh walked slowly back to their car.

'We need someone to keep an eye on this place. I don't know what this means,' she said. 'He might come back once it gets dark, to gather a few things together before making a run for it. Maybe Blackman could do it. He's due a late shift, and he seems a bit lost without his mate Phil McCluskie to keep him company.'

* * *

Stu Blackman had been sitting with Rae Gregson for several hours in their car, keeping an eye on the row of neat properties. Each house had a small front garden, most with a low hedge and a few shrubs. CID officers hated these surveillance jobs, including the young woman officer beside him, but he didn't mind them. Maybe they suited his temperament, he thought. Easygoing and easily amused. She was fidgeting restlessly in her seat.

'Go for a wander for a couple of minutes,' he said. 'As long as you stay in sight, you'll be alright.'

Rae climbed out of the car and walked to the end of the road, turned and came back towards the car. Blackman saw her suddenly stop and move towards the front wall of the house they were watching. She ran back to the car.

'I think someone's moving around inside, Sarge. I heard a door bang. Maybe he's climbed over the back fence and got in that way. Should we radio in?'

'Could it just be the wind or something?'

'I don't see how. The boss said all the windows and doors were shut when she visited earlier.'

Blackman made a call to the control room and relayed the information to Sophie.

'Stay where you are,' she said. 'We'll get support to you directly. I'll be there as soon as I can.'

Blackman got out of the car. 'If it's someone who's come in at the back, they'll leave that way and we won't see them. I'm going round there. You stay here.'

The young detective looked worried. 'But we're meant to stay here . . .'

But Blackman was already gone, crossing the road towards Armitage's driveway. His solid bulk quickly disappeared in the shadows cast by the bungalow. He moved surprisingly quietly for someone his size. He crept to the side of the house and took a peek around the corner before tiptoeing into the rear garden. It consisted mainly of lawn, with what Blackman guessed were soft-fruit bushes beneath the high fence. He went up to the back door and found it was ajar.

What to do? He hesitated, debating with himself about the wisdom of entering a silent house with an unknown intruder inside. Did he feel brave enough? Maybe not. Maybe he'd come far enough. But the decision was made for him. The door suddenly swung open, taking him by surprise and pushing him back down the single step where he lost his footing on the damp surface and went down. Blackman stuck his leg out, causing the shadowy figure to stumble as it ran by. It kicked him in the ribs, and in his stomach. Then he heard Rae calling as she came around the house. The assailant ran towards the fence and clambered over.

'I'm alright,' Blackman gasped. 'Get after him. I'll call in and get some help.'

* * *

Rae scaled the fence, and dropped to the ground on the other side, landing in what felt like a bed of rhubarb, judging by the texture of the leaves that enveloped her. The house was partly illuminated by a well-lit rear window, but Rae could see nothing moving. She straightened up and made her way along a path that ran alongside what she guessed to be a lawn. It was difficult to make out any detail in the near darkness. She could hear no sound. Did that mean that the assailant had already left the garden or was he still lurking somewhere, watching her? She extracted a torch from her jacket pocket and swept the beam around the garden. It was largely devoid of shrubs or bushes, so there was nowhere for the man to hide. He must have fled. Rae moved along the side wall of the house to the front driveway. From here the road looped away in front of her, curving towards the river, with a path leading down to a bank covered in trees. Someone could easily hide there. Time to call in for reinforcements.

Rae went back and climbed the fence into Pete Armitage's garden. Blackman was moving towards the open back door, and Rae joined him.

'Backup will be here in a mo. Let's just have a look inside.' They moved slowly through the house, seeing no one, until they reached the spare bedroom upstairs.

Pete Armitage lay on the floor, breathing in shallow gasps. Blood oozed slowly from a deep gash at the side of his head. Rae knelt down beside him and felt for his pulse. Weak but steady. She radioed for an ambulance, then looked around her. A cash-box lay on its side a few feet from Pete's body with several bank notes on the floor beside it. Jagged chunks from a broken vase were scattered across the carpet, the largest stained with blood.

* * *

Across the rain-spattered town the police were out in force, searching for Rod Armitage who was nowhere to be found. In one of the squad cars Rose Simons and George Warrander were exploring the area around the river on the south side of town. They parked their car in the last of the riverside car parks and Rose got out for a look around.

'Can't see anything further than about twenty yards,' she said. 'Not in this darkness and drizzle. Tell you what, young George, we need to stretch our legs, especially a fit young feller like you. Let's walk along the river bank for a bit. We'll leave the jalopy here, stroll to the next bridge then come back. Torches at the ready and, whatever you do, don't fall in. It would ruin my evening if I had to jump in to rescue you. I put clean undies on before I started this shift, so I'd be bloody annoyed. Okay?'

Warrander looked up at the night sky and grimaced. 'Right, boss. I promise to be careful.'

'Keep your walkie-talkie on. Mine's on the blink again.'

George suspected that this was untrue. She used her walkie-talkie's supposed unpredictability as a cover for bending the operational rules whenever it was convenient. He pulled his collar up and they set off along the path. They were on the final leg of the walk, and had not yet seen anything remotely suspicious, when a tall figure appeared in the distance. He was walking slowly down a footpath towards the river, and keeping to the shadows.

'Torches off,' Rose hissed. They waited quietly. Warrander could just make out the shape of the next bridge. The flashing blue light of a squad car appeared and stopped beside it. Whoever it was shrank back into the shadows.

Rose whispered to Warrander. 'Cut across the grass and get behind him. I'll stay here. Let him know you're there.'

George moved silently across the open grassy area, getting behind their quarry on the footpath. He switched his torch back on and didn't try to hide the sound of his footfalls. He spotted the tall figure ahead of him leave the shadowy path, and move towards the riverside, then turn towards the place where Rose Simons was waiting. George followed. He could now see the riverside with its dark bushes lining the path and the hurrying figure approaching the spot occupied by his boss. Rose moved out to block his path but the man shoved her aside. George started running but he was still some yards away when their quarry swung a punch at the sergeant. Big mistake, thought George. Rose dodged aside so that the blow glanced off her shoulder, and then she grabbed her assailant by the arm, swung him around and forced him to the ground, held in an arm lock. When George arrived the man was face down on the ground and Rose was stooping over him, her knee firmly lodged in the small of his back. It was Rod Armitage.

'This isn't some Wild West town, young sonny-boy. We aren't in Dodge City and I'm not some John Wayne type of sheriff who you can shove aside if you feel like it.' She paused and stepped back. 'Anyway, I'm more of a Clint Eastwood fan.' Her voice deepened to a growl. 'Feeling lucky, punk? Go on, make my day.' She held out her right hand, fingers shaped like a pistol.

CHAPTER 39: GREENHOUSE FRUIT

Friday morning, Week 3

Lydia Pillay was on her second full day on loan to the unit. 'I think I've found something, ma'am. I've just spotted an anomaly in the accounts, but I don't know how significant it is. And there could be others. I've only just started this particular check.'

Lydia had sections of the Woodruff Holdings and Boulevard club accounts open on one side of her desk, and the Armitage Decorating bank statements on the other. Her finger rested on the Woodruff figures. 'Look. There's a withdrawal of exactly four thousand pounds cash from the Boulevard, but there's no record of where it went.'

'Sure it's cash?'

Lydia nodded. 'And how many legitimate bills are ever conveniently rounded off like that? Exact, to a thousand? It's a payment for something, but something that they maybe didn't want recorded.'

Sophie looked at the figures, thinking through the possible explanations. 'When was this?'

'Four years ago. Up until then, everything balances. All the payments for decorating jobs come from Woodruff

Holdings' accounts, not direct from the Boulevard, and they seem to correspond to legitimate decorating jobs. But look here.' She pointed to data from early the following year. 'Same again. A payment of three thousand going out direct from the Boulevard. Let's check the account details.' She ran her eyes down the columns of figures in the second set of papers. 'No entry again. All the other sums coming in from Woodruff look legitimate, and about what you'd expect for commercial decorating jobs.' She paused. 'There's one more, later that year, for the same amount, look. Then nothing until five weeks and three weeks ago. Two cash withdrawals, each five thousand, but this time from Woodruff Holdings. Well, would you believe it? Just around the time that the old couple were murdered. In fact, one probably just before and the other just after.'

Sophie peered. 'Suspicious? Could we check the serial numbers of the notes? I mean, if Woodruff got them as cash direct from the bank, they may still have a record. And Rae found that empty cash box last night at Pete's house. Which means that Rod may have hidden the contents somewhere. He only had an hour or two before he was picked up and he doesn't drive. It would be somewhere local. Maybe I'll get Rose Simons up from her beauty sleep and pick her brains. She's local and might have an idea where he could have gone after leaving Pete's house.' Sophie started to move away, then stopped. 'Those other payments, the ones of three and four thousand. Can you give me the dates again? I might give Kevin McGreedie a ring. It's just occurred to me that they might connect to the things Rae found in that shed. Stuff from house break-ins. He can check the dates against burglaries that occurred. Those sums came from the Boulevard rather than the Woodruff parent company. I wonder if our friend Toffee Barber is running a fencing operation for goods that Rod and Pete have been stealing.'

'There's something else a bit worrying about these decorating accounts, ma'am. When you look at them in detail, the business isn't really profitable. So where's his money coming from?' Lydia laid a hand on the records involving Blythe. 'I've only had a quick look so far, but there are a couple of suspicious planning decisions here. Leave it with me for a few more hours.'

'Lydia, you're a star.'

* * *

It was Barry Marsh who came up with another breakthrough. When he heard about the money that Rod might have hidden, he guessed immediately.

'Let Rae and me have a look, ma'am, before you disturb the locals. The way he approached the river last night means he could have come from his parents' house. There's something else that's been at the back of my mind for days. Every time we see Rod he goes on about how much he hated gardening and his dad's obsession with it, particularly the greenhouse. I want to have a look. It's only a mile or so from Pete's house, so the timing fits with what happened last night.'

And so it was. On the far corner of the greenhouse shelving, behind a row of seed packets, was an innocuous-looking plastic bag. Inside were bundles of banknotes, most of them still with wrappers around them. And tucked in behind them at the very back? A roll of grey sticky tape, partly used. Marsh thought back to George Warrander's discovery of the tape roll at the murder scene and the boss's observation that it looked too new to have been used. It was all coming together.

* * *

Pete Armitage was still in hospital, suffering from concussion. The doctor treating him was fairly sure that his injuries weren't serious, but he wanted to keep Pete in hospital for another day or two for observation. The china vase used to assault him had Rod's fingerprints all over it and that, together with the money found in Ted's greenhouse, gave them a starting point for their questions. A lawyer arrived, and they were finally ready to interview Rod.

Marsh took the lead. 'What happened at your uncle's house last night, Rod?'

Rod shrugged.

'We have your fingerprints on a vase found on the floor beside Pete. He was unconscious from a head wound, caused by that vase. Those are the facts, Rod. We need an explanation.'

'He owed me some dosh and wouldn't hand it over. It was bugging me. That cash was mine.'

'What money?'

'Toffee had given him some cash to pass onto me. Pete was holding onto it.'

'What was it for?'

'A job I done recently at the club. I needed some ready dough. I was skint.'

'How much?'

'About five hundred.'

'So where is it, Rod? You didn't have that much on you when we brought you in last night. Where's the rest?'

Rod shrugged. 'Probably at home. Maybe I dropped some when you lot *assaulted* me in Pete's garden.'

Marsh looked at him. 'Are you alleging assault against us?'

Rod didn't reply immediately. He was obviously thinking hard. 'No, I s'pose it was dark and your guy couldn't see who it was. But that's where I could've lost some of the cash.'

'So you didn't take it away and deliberately hide it somewhere? And it was only a few hundred? Think carefully before replying, Rod. Lies have a habit of coming back to haunt you.'

Rod reverted to his habitual bemused expression. 'Why would I do that?'

'I don't know, Rod. That's why I'm asking you.'

Rod shook his head. 'No. I ain't hid nothink. I lost it, like I said.'

'It's just that your fingerprints are all over the greenhouse in your parents' garden, and they weren't there last week when we dusted. There were bits of mud on the floor this morning, still damp. And their shape fits the sole-pattern on your boots exactly, our forensic team have checked. There was a reel of sticky tape hidden inside the greenhouse, with your prints on. It wasn't there when it was searched after your parents' bodies were first found. There was a package of money tucked away, hidden at the back. It had your prints on the outside. You were there last night, weren't you? Hiding incriminating evidence. And it was a huge amount of cash, not just the few hundred you've claimed it to be. Where did that cash come from, Rod? How did you earn it?' There was no reply. 'We know where the money came from, which bank handed it over, and who to. So the really important question, Rod, is what did you have to do for Wayne Woodruff to earn you that much? It's probably more money than you've ever had before. Can you explain that to us?'

There was no answer.

* * *

Sophie and Marsh called on Sharon Giroux late in the afternoon, and told her the news.

'We'll be charging Rod, Sharon. It might well be that he was only an onlooker when your parents were murdered, but he knew about it and helped to plan it, we're convinced of that. Their deaths eased the pressures on several people who knew each other, but they stood to gain for different reasons. Your mum and dad were at the funeral when Woodruff slipped a bribe to Councillor Blythe, and he became paranoid about it. For Rod it was different. He got wind of your mother's idea of cutting him out of the will, possibly Pete knew as well. Pete was involved in the burglaries without a doubt, but we don't think he was in on your parents' deaths. His business wasn't paying well and the break-ins gave him some easy money. The link between them all was Toffee Barber. He and the other murdered man, Tony Sorrento.'

Sharon was in tears. 'Mum was starting to talk about giving a lot of her money away, like you said. I told her it was hers to do as she liked with, but wouldn't Rod need something to help him pull himself together? She said it would just get wasted, like all the rest she'd given him. She said that maybe he needed a hard lesson, just like Dad kept saying. She swore me to silence. Rod wasn't to find out. I wonder if she somehow found out what they were up to with these burglaries. Maybe that's the real reason she was thinking of rewriting the will.'

'Why didn't you tell us?'

'I couldn't. I was trying to get on better with Rod. I could see that he'd need me when Mum and Dad finally passed away, and I was trying to keep some kind of a relationship going. I decided that even if they did change the will, I'd still give half of my inheritance to him. But I didn't tell them that, and I didn't mention it to him.' She gave Sophie a long look. 'He's my brother. Despite everything, I still loved him and I really didn't believe for a moment that he was involved with killing them. But now? After what he's done? He can rot in hell. And Uncle Pete?' She shook her head. 'I don't know what my life is about any more. Every time I think it can't get any worse, it does. And those burglaries! They've been going on for some time, you say?'

'Five years, we think,' said Marsh. 'Rod, Pete and Toffee Barber together. Barber had contacts all over the area and he got rid of the stuff they stole. They were being helped by a bent police officer.'

'What will happen to him?' Sharon asked.

'He's dead. He killed himself a few days ago.' Marsh paused. 'He was a friend of mine.'

CHAPTER 40: CATSUIT

Saturday evening, Week 3

The Black Swan Inn is an old, stone-floored pub, situated on Swanage High Street, a few minutes' walk from the town centre. Barry Marsh's engagement party was now in full swing in the function room. Buffet food was laid out on a couple of side tables alongside a large bowl of punch. He'd suggested an informal party, but had been overruled by Gwen, who'd surprised herself lately by discovering a taste for exotic fancy dress costumes. She'd come as Nell Gwyn, complete with a basket of oranges. Marsh wore a swashbuckler's outfit, and felt decidedly self-conscious during the early part of the evening. Most of his friends, though, had put real thought into their costumes and, as they turned up in Spiderman, zombie and Ghostbuster outfits, he began to relax. The captain of his amateur football team came as a very attractive Wonder Woman and his wife was a surprisingly realistic Batman.

An hour or so into the party, Marsh looked around him. There was Rae, recognisable despite her Marilyn Monroe dress and blonde wig, chatting to her new boyfriend, Craig, dressed as a gunslinger. And Lydia, only just arrived and resplendent in regal attire. Even Jimmy Melsom had made an effort, although he was undoubtedly in danger of suffering from heatstroke inside his gorilla suit. But where was the boss?

He sidled across to Lydia, who'd been staying with the Allens for the last two nights. 'Why hasn't the boss arrived yet? I thought she was coming with you.'

Lydia laughed. 'Haven't you spotted her? Not surprised. Back at their house it took all my will-power not to gape when she appeared downstairs. I think Martin was having a fit and I wouldn't be surprised if we saw him sooner rather than later. He was on the phone making hurried changes to his evening plans when we left. She was a bit shy and crept in behind me.'

Marsh looked around. 'So she's here? Where?'

Lydia nodded towards a corner, trying hard not to giggle. 'Over there, trying to hide behind the people at the punch table. Jade spotted the outfit in a charity shop and wore it to a New Year party, apparently. She talked the boss into it. Well, bullied her to be more accurate.'

Barry looked over and his jaw dropped. 'Not . . .?'

'Oh, yes.'

'Christ. I wondered who had dared to wear that. I thought it was one of my teammates' girlfriends, doing it for a prank. She looks, well, stunning. But very extreme.'

'I think we need to go over and calm her nerves, Barry. She'll be fine once she gets a drink or two inside her.'

Sophie was wearing a skin-tight, stretchy cat suit in a leopard-print pattern, complete with mask, whiskers and tail, along with stiletto-heeled knee boots. She was sipping at a small glass of punch as Marsh approached. 'That bloody daughter of mine! She talked me into this, Barry. I need a pint.'

'Of milk?' he replied with a straight face. 'Shall I fetch a saucer?'

His boss aimed at him with her glass. Luckily it was empty.

Lydia laughed. 'Miaow.'

THE END

AUTHOR'S NOTE

This book is a work of fiction and any resemblance to actual persons, living or dead, is purely coincidental. Dorset County Council and Bournemouth District Council operate with absolute probity and I wish to make it clear that the corrupt councillor thread of this novel is entirely a product of my imagination. In fact I admire councillors for the work they do, often in very difficult circumstances and with little thanks for their efforts.

CHARACTER LIST

Detective Chief Inspector Sophie Allen is Dorset's acknowledged expert on murder and violent crime, newly appointed to run the county's Serious and Violent Crime Unit. She is 42 years old as the series starts, and lives with her family in Wareham. Sophie has a law degree and a master's in criminal psychology. Sophie may appear at first to be somewhat of a 'cold fish,' over-intellectual and too clever by half, but conceals a dark past.

Detective Sergeant Barry Marsh is in his early thirties and in Dark Crimes, the first novel, is based at Swanage police station. He's quiet, methodical and dedicated, the perfect foil for Sophie's hidden fragility.

Detective Constable Rae (Rachel) Gregson joined the team in book 3, to replace Lydia Pillay. She is astute and hard-working. Rae is transgender with a troubled past.

Detective Constable Jimmy Melsom worked with Barry Marsh in Swanage but transferred to Bournemouth CID at the end of book3. He is a little gung-ho in his attitude to crime investigation.

Detective Constable Lydia Pillay is a talented young officer based who worked with DCI Allen at Dorset County police HQ but transferred to Somerset Police at the end of book 2. Sophie wants to get her back

Detective Inspector Kevin McGreedie is attached to the Bournemouth and Poole division of Dorset police. His assistant is DS Bob Thomson.

Detective Chief Superintendent Matt Silver is Sophie's immediate boss. He helped to appoint her to lead the Violent Crime Unit but, to his regret, has a largely administrative role in the county police hierarchy.

Martin Allen is Sophie's husband. He is head of the mathematics department at a large secondary school in Dorchester. Martin has a minor, but very supportive, role in the novels. He and Sophie met while at university. He has a more prominent role in later novels in the series.

Sophie and Martin have two daughters. **Jade** is fifteen in the first novel, and appears in all the subsequent stories. She has a lively and very quirky personality. **Hannah**, the elder daughter, is a drama student in London. She is quieter in her approach to life. She appears as a minor character in the first novel, but has a more important role in later books.

Sergeant Rose Simons is a uniformed officer based at Blandford Forum. Rose is rather cynical about her work but is a reliable, hard-working and scrupulously honest officer. She lives alone with her young son and has a wacky sense of humour.

Constable George Warrander is a rookie officer in his first year with the police, working under Rose Simons. George appeared in novel 1, interviewed by Sophie Allen and Barry Marsh when they were investigating the death of Donna Goodenough. During that interview he indicated his wish to join the police.

THE JOFFE BOOKS STORY

We began in 2014 when Jasper agreed to publish his mum's much-rejected romance novel and it became a bestseller.

Since then we've grown into the largest independent publisher in the UK. We're extremely proud to publish some of the very best writers in the world, including Joy Ellis, Faith Martin, Caro Ramsay, Helen Forrester, Simon Brett and Robert Goddard. Everyone at Joffe Books loves reading and we never forget that it all begins with the magic of an author telling a story.

We are proud to publish talented first-time authors, as well as established writers whose books we love introducing to a new generation of readers.

We won Trade Publisher of the Year at the Independent Publishing Awards in 2023 and Best Publisher Award in 2024 at the People's Book Prize. We have been shortlisted for Independent Publisher of the Year at the British Book Awards for the last five years, and were shortlisted for the Diversity and Inclusivity Award at the 2022 Independent Publishing Awards. In 2023 we were shortlisted for Publisher of the Year at the RNA Industry Awards, and in 2024 we were shortlisted at the CWA Daggers for the Best Crime and Mystery Publisher.

We built this company with your help, and we love to hear from you, so please email us about absolutely anything bookish at feedback@joffebooks.com.

If you want to receive free books every Friday and hear about all our new releases, join our mailing list: www.joffebooks.com/free-books

And when you tell your friends about us, just remember: it's pronounced Joffe as in coffee or toffee!

Printed in Great Britain
by Amazon

55207104R00152